A Very Good Life

A NOVEL

Lynn Steward

A Very Good Life

© 2014 by Lynn Steward. All rights reserved.

A Very Good Life is a work of fiction. Names, characters, with the exception of some well-known real-life persons and public figures, places, and incidents in the novel are either the product of the author's imagination or used fictitiously. Where real-life persons appear, the incidents and dialogues are entirely fictional and have been included to provide historical context. Any resemblance to actual events, locales, or persons, living or dead, is entirely coincidental. No part of this publication can be reproduced or transmitted in any form or by any means, electronic or mechanical, without permission in writing from the author or publisher.

For my parents

Acknowledgments

I am grateful to Ezra Doner, my attorney, who advised me to keep writing; to Wendy Cowles Husser, my editor, for her cheerful willingness to embark on this journey, and for her guidance throughout; to my friend, Carol McGarry, for the tedious task of proofreading the manuscript; to Jane Wesman and Felicia Sinusas, my publicists, for their invaluable advice; to my creative team for their talent and patience: Greg Bennett, Jason Frelich Design, McKnight–Kurland Design, and Kathy Pilch; and to Amy Siders, Jen Dunsmore and Rob Reid, the helpful and professional staff at 52Novels. With gratitude and appreciation, I thank my dear family and friends for their unwavering confidence and encouragement.

A Very Good Life

Chapter One

Dana McGarry, her short blond hair stirred by a light gust of wind, stood on Fifth Avenue in front of the display windows of the B Altman department store on the day after Thanksgiving, November, 1974. Dana, public relations and special events coordinator for the store, pulled her Brooks Brothers camel hair polo coat tighter around her slim, shapely frame. Shoppers hurried past her, huddled in overcoats as mild snow flurries coated the streets with a fine white powder. It was now officially Christmas season, and Dana sensed a pleasant urgency in the air as people rushed to find the perfect gift or simply meet a friend for lunch. The frenetic pace of life in Manhattan continued to swell the sidewalks, but pedestrians were more inclined to tender a smile instead of a grimace if they bumped into one another. Dana often told her friends that Christmas was a time when there was a temporary truce between true believers and grinches. As far as business was concerned, she was pleased to hear the cash registers of B Altman singing their secular carols inside the store, but she also still believed that the holidays brought magic and balance, however briefly, into a world of routine and ten-hour workdays.

Balance? Dana smiled wistfully, for balance was becoming harder to achieve. She was only twenty-nine, but the pressures of life were already assaulting her mind and spirit in numerous ways. She tried to please multiple people in B Altman's corporate offices on a daily basis, not an easy task given that the seasoned professionals who were grooming her had various agendas, not all of which tallied with each other. And then there was her marriage to Brett McGarry, a litigator at a Wall Street law firm. Brett was as busy as she, and simultaneously attending to her career and the needs of her husband was sometimes difficult, if not downright burdensome. His needs? Well, "demands" would be a more accurate description of what Dana had to contend with. Although Brett didn't overtly order Dana around, he informed her of what he would or would not be able to do with her on any given day. His growing air of superiority was extremely subtle and couched in affable smiles that most of Dana's friends could not accurately read.

Dana's eyes had become unfocused as she stared past the display window, but she quickly snapped her attention back to the present moment. People, coated with a dusting of light snow, continued to stream through the portico outside B Altman's. Magic and balance still held the better claim on Friday, November 29. She'd worry about Brett later.

"I think they like it," commented Andrew Ricci, display director for the store, as he stood to Dana's left, referring to the happy, animated shoppers. "Good idea, Mark. Christmas was the right time to bring in live mannequins." Andrew, slender and dressed in a gray suit with sweater vest, wiped snowflakes from his salt and pepper hair, wavy and combed straight back. Even as Andrew said this, a little girl waved both hands, trying to get the attention of one of the Sugar Plum Fairies behind the window, saying over and over, "I saw her blink! I did! I saw her blink!"

Mark Tepper was the president of the Tepper Display Company, and B Altman had been a good account for ten years.

"You're welcome. I want you guys to look good. Bloomie's is just twenty-five blocks away," said the suave president, dressed in a blue pinstripe suit. He stood to Dana's right. His light brown hair was parted neatly above a broad forehead, and he had intense blue eyes that could capture the slightest nuance. He was of average height, in good physical shape, and his ideas seemed to emanate from a bottomless reservoir of energy. "You can't go wrong with a Nutcracker theme." Mark stepped back and surveyed the scene. "Now if I could only figure out a way to make the live mannequins stop blinking," he said with a grin.

Dana and Andrew laughed at Mark's quick wit, the result of keen intelligence combined with a sophisticated playfulness. He could be highly focused without taking himself too seriously.

Andrew rubbed his hands together and exhaled, his breath drifting away in a small cloud of vapor. "Say, would you two mind coming inside to look at the blueprints for the cosmetic department? I have to make one change."

Dana, like all B Altman employees, was energized by the transformation of her beloved store, and being a close friend of Andrew's, she knew of changes starting with the planning stage. More than a year ago, when Dana first learned that the cosmetic department would be renovated, she thought it might bode well for her idea to add a teen makeup section.

Inside, the store was glowing from Christmas decorations, chandeliers, and red-capped mercury lamps illuminating counters that curved and zigzagged across the main floor in every direction. A decorated tree in the center of the main floor rose fifteen feet into the air, a grand focal point for the holiday atmosphere. Andrew led the group to one of the counters in the existing cosmetic department and unrolled a set of blueprints he'd stored beneath the glass counter. The trio would be undisturbed since holiday shoppers were buzzing past them on their way to the gift departments, many to see the new million-dollar menswear section that opened the previous month and extended the entire block along 34th Street.

"We're aiming for the new department to open the first week of May," Andrew said, "followed by a black tie gala." He poked his index finger onto the center of the blueprints for emphasis. He then looked up proudly and pointed to a section of the floor where the new cosmetic department would be installed.

"Good placement," Mark said. "And nice layout, too." Mark usually spoke rapidly and in short sentences. Insightful, he sized things up quickly and didn't waste time. It was another aspect of his confidence that allowed him to act professionally without losing his innate charm. He also had a knack for including everyone around him in any discussion.

"So what does the public relations and special events coordinator think?" he asked, pivoting to face Dana, sensing she had something to say.

Dana cocked her head slightly while mischievously narrowing her eyes. "I think we shouldn't forget that a teen makeup section is just as important as an updated cosmetic department. Otherwise, why are we bothering to update it in the first place? Our demographic is getting younger. Girls today are wearing makeup by the time they're fourteen."

Dana turned to Andrew. "What do you think, Mr. Ricci?"

Andrew chuckled at Dana's use of his surname, which she occasionally did when talking business with her friend and confidante. Andrew was the quintessential Renaissance man—artist, craftsman, and cook. He and Dana attended art lectures at the Met, and he had personally taken Dana under his wing to give her what he called "a gay man's culinary expertise" when her husband announced they were hosting a dinner party for a few of the firm's partners. Andrew was not only Dana's close friend, but he was also a consummate professional in his capacity as display director. He was a passionate man, at times almost compulsive, but he commanded respect from the refined corporate culture at B Altman.

Andrew rolled up the blueprints and sighed. "Good luck trying to persuade Helen. She's done a great job with her department, but she's from the old school—if it ain't broke, don't fix it." Andrew paused. "But the fact that Helen isn't on board isn't going to stop you, is it?"

Helen Kavanagh was the junior buyer at B Altman.

Dana shook her head and winked. "Not for a minute. I'm an optimist, Andrew. Besides, it's Christmas. I've been a good girl, and Santa owes me."

Mark was clearly enjoying the good-natured exchange. "Santa naturally wasn't big at Temple when I was growing up. No stockings hung by the chimney with care—although I remain an ardent fan of stockings. That having been said," Mark continued, "I think—"

The conversation was interrupted by a no-nonsense twenty-something secretary, dark brown hair falling to her shoulder. "Ms. Savino would like to see you in her office as soon as possible, Ms. McGarry," she said. The secretary turned on her heels and promptly disappeared into the busy throng of shoppers without waiting for a response from Dana.

Bea Savino was Dana's boss and the vice president of sales promotion and marketing.

"She's new," Dana commented. "Poor girl—she's scared to death. We *all* were when we started."

"I still am," Andrew laughed, "and I don't even report to her. Bea can kill you with that look. You know, when her eyes tighten and she peers over her reading glasses—ouch! But give her a martini, and it's party time. Bea's a moveable feast."

Dana nodded. "True enough. I better see what the indomitable Ms. Savino wants. Gentlemen, it's always a pleasure."

Dana headed to the bank of elevators on the far side of the store, passing a dozen lively conversations that blended into what she regarded as a delightful holiday symphony. People were spending money—and *happy* to be spending it. She envisioned a teen makeup section facilitating that same enthusiastic banter at some point in the future.

"Dana!"

Dana wheeled around to see Mark hurrying past shoppers, his outstretched arm indicating that he wanted her to pause until he could catch up.

"People just can't get enough of my infectious optimism," Dana proclaimed.

"You're cursed with good genes," Mark said, stopping a foot from Dana. "Seriously, the teen makeup section is a smart move. I think you should ask Helen if she's been following the incredible success of Biba."

"I think *everybody's* eyes are on London."

"If not, they should be. Biba just moved to a seven-story building in Kensington, and the store is attracting a million customers a week. Teen makeup sure seems to be working for the Brits. The birds, as the English call young girls, are flocking to the store in droves." He paused. "I'm mixing my metaphors—birds, cattle—but you get the gist."

Dana put her hands on her hips and burst into laughter.

"When was the last time you used the word droves, Mark?"

"Hey, I've watched cowboys on TV like anybody else," he replied with mock defensiveness. "Head 'em up and move 'em out. And that's what Biba is doing. The customers are in and out, and most of their wallets are quite a bit lighter when they leave. That's the idea, right?"

"Absolutely!"

"Go get 'em, tiger," Mark said, touching the side of Dana's arm right below her shoulder. He walked away, turned back with a big smile and a thumbs-up, then disappeared.

Mark's energy and enthusiasm, as well as his one-minute pep talk, were just what Dana needed to boost her confidence and keep her idea alive.

As Dana neared the far side of the store, she and Helen Kavanagh simultaneously approached the same elevator.

As always, Helen was impeccably dressed, and her carriage bespoke an elegant, stylish demeanor. She was in the later years of middle age, but she advanced towards the elevator briskly, her blond hair pulled severely back from her face and secured with an ever-present black velvet ribbon. Her face expressionless, she glanced at Dana, her pace unchanged. A signal had clearly been given. In point of fact, Helen truly admired Dana, but the young events coordinator was in her twenties, and there was a protocol in Helen's universe that she didn't believe needed to be articulated. Respect carried the day, with camaraderie offered in moderation, preferably outside of the workplace. Dana therefore halted just long enough to allow Helen to slip into the elevator before she followed, the doors closing behind her. The two women were alone as the elevator ascended to the executive suite of offices on the fifth floor.

Nothing ventured, nothing gained, Dana thought. Besides, Mark had literally gone out of his way to suggest that she approach Helen. Mark, of course, could be aggressive and disarming at the same time, so such a feat would naturally be far easier for *him* to accomplish. Still, she was quite aware that Mark had her best interests at heart. It was worth a try.

"Good morning, Helen."

Helen nodded and smiled thinly. "Dana."

"Helen, I was wondering if you shopped Biba when you were in London last month. They're pulling in a million customers a week. A *million*!" Dana raised her eyebrows, her clear blue eyes sparkling even in the dim light of the elevator.

Helen tapped a silver ballpoint pen against the brown leather case holding her yellow legal pad. "Biba," she said with frustration. "Biba is filled with non-paying customers who rush in before work to try on free makeup. Free, Dana. Are they running a business or having a party? Try it before you buy it? I don't think so. They're crazy. Excuse me—as the British say, they're quite mad. They'll be out of business in a year."

Dana's heart skipped a beat, but she wasn't going to show any nervousness. Instead, she laughed. "Well, I'm sure you're right. Shows what I know!"

It was a self-effacing remark, but Dana knew when to back down.

Helen, who had been facing forward, turned and looked at Dana squarely. "And don't even think of taking this to Bea."

Dana smiled as the elevator door opened, but she said nothing.

The two women stepped onto the fifth floor, the rooms of which were a facsimile of the 1916 interiors of Benjamin Altman's Fifth Avenue home. Dana and Helen walked through the reception area, which was a replica of Altman's well-known Renaissance room. Fine art adorned the wood-paneled walls beyond the anteroom, with elaborately carved woodwork accenting the hallways. The President's Room was a reproduction of Altman's personal library, while the Board Room was a faithful rendering of his dining room. Oriental carpets lay on the polished parquet floor, and Dana never ceased to marvel at the rich interior of the executive suite and its expensive art collection no matter how many times she entered the area. It had the ambience of a corporate cathedral, and the first time she stepped onto the floor years earlier, she had unconsciously lifted her right hand for a split second, as if to dip her fingers in a holy water font.

Dana and Helen walked in the same direction for fifteen paces until it became obvious that they were both heading for Bea Savino's office.

"I was told Bea wanted to see me," Dana stated.

"I'm sure you were," Helen said flatly. "But I need to see her first. That isn't a problem, is it?"

"No. Of course not."

It was another elevator moment. Dana gave Helen a politically correct smile and stepped back, allowing her to open Bea's door and slip into the office.

Dana walked up and down the hall, admiring the landscapes hanging on the dark paneling. Miniature marble sculptures stood on pedestals and library tables with inlaid mother-of-pearl. She hoped Helen wouldn't be long since she wanted to get back home, walk her dog, and double-check arrangements for the annual McGarry Christmas party, now only six days away. It was one o'clock, but if Bea called a special events meeting, Dana's afternoon would be lost. She was overseeing the expansion of the adult programs, known as "department-store culture," and she and Bea were still working out the details for the rollout in January. B Altman was a pioneer for such a program, and Dana would be programming three events a week in the Charleston Garden restaurant that seated two hundred. A smaller third-floor community room was newly renovated for the expanded sessions that included mini-courses in art appreciation, cooking demonstrations, book signings, self-improvement, and current events.

She reversed direction and walked past Bea's office, noticing that the door was slightly ajar. She turned around and decided to wait outside Bea's inner sanctum to make sure Helen wouldn't slip out unnoticed. Heart pounding, she stood near the open door and heard Helen expressing dismay.

"You know how I feel about having shoes in my department, Bea. Can't you help me convince them to find somewhere else to put this Pappagallo shop? Shoes belong with shoes. It just doesn't work for me. I don't want to see them. Period."

There was clear exasperation in the junior buyer's voice.

"But it works for Ira and Dawn," Bea responded calmly, "and they firmly believe in the merchandising potential for this young market. "Don't quote me, but I heard Ira's daughter will be working in the shop this summer. You gotta get on board, Helen. Think young. Think upbeat." Her voice rose with sudden enthusiasm. "Think Biba!"

"Bea, if I hear that name Biba one more time!" Helen interrupted.

Bea ignored her. "The kids are all drinking espresso, and I'll probably go down for a cup in the afternoon."

"What are you talking about?" Helen asked. "You're going to—"

"Helen," Bea slowly responded, "Pappagallo stores have love seats and espresso machines. It's that Southern hospitality. They were introduced in Atlanta. Anyway, we have no choice. Remember, Pappagallo is leasing the space."

There was a noticeable silence inside Bea's office.

"Breathe deeply, Helen," Bea advised with a laugh. "You're going to hyperventilate. It's not the end of the world."

"Espresso machine?" Helen repeated. "Love seats? Taking up selling space. I'm not putting up with this. Fine. Then they'll just have to give me a larger department. I'm not giving up without getting something in return."

Dana smiled. If Ira Neimark, the executive vice president and general merchandise manager of B Altman, together with his hand-picked vice president and fashion director, Dawn

Mello—Helen's boss—were looking for ways to bring young people into the store, maybe the teen makeup department wasn't a lost cause after all.

Helen came flying out the office, brushing past Dana by mere inches as she talked to herself under her breath. "B Altman will be out of business before Biba. It's all totally absurd." She took no notice of the young events coordinator.

Dana moved forward and stood in the doorway. "You wanted to see me?" she asked.

"Yes, Dana. Come in."

Bea Savino was a tiny but feisty Italian woman with snow white hair, a chain-smoker with a no-nonsense approach to life and business. Bea had married five years ago, at the age of forty, and had no children, but she felt compelled to give her adopted young staff reality therapy every chance she could, believing they were too influenced by the soft dress-for-success career articles in fashion magazines. With Dana, Bea's mantra was "Toughen up, for God's sake!" When Dana had been passed over for an assignment and complained to her boss, Bea merely said, "It's the squeaky wheel that gets the grease, kiddo. I didn't even know you were interested. Carol was in here every day, begging. Speak up, Dana."

Bea lit a cigarette, exhaled a plume of smoke, and laughed. "I think poor Helen is headed for a stroke. I saw you standing outside, so I know you heard our exchange. Ah well. She'll get over it. She's a tough old broad, God love her." Bea shuffled some papers around her desk before finding the folder she was looking for. Her office was not a model of perfection and order, as were Helen's and Dana's.

Dana cringed at the term "broad." The expression seemed out of place on the sacrosanct fifth floor, but she merely took a deep breath and remembered that Bea didn't mince words. She decided to pitch her idea despite Helen's warning.

"Bea, since Mr. Neimark and Ms. Mello are interested in the youth market, why can't we go one step further than the Shop for Pappagallo and add a teen makeup section too? As I told Helen, Biba is pulling in a million customers a week."

Bea leaned back in her chair and took another puff of her cigarette.

"You always tell me to speak up," Dana said, her voice rising slightly as she shrugged her shoulders. "So . . . ?"

"It's not a bad idea," Bea conceded as she surveyed her cluttered desk, "but it's not going to happen, at least not now. One step at a time. Let Helen adjust to the intrusion of Pappagallo first. It's too much at once."

"But—"

"Go whine to Bob. I know you two are thick as thieves. I asked you here to discuss something else."

Bob Campbell was the store's vice president and general manager. He was Dana's unofficial mentor, a fact that often irritated Bea to no end. It was she, not Bob, who was the young woman's immediate boss.

Dana clasped her hands behind her back, squeezing her right fist in frustration. Was she supposed to toughen up and be vocal or remain silent? Bea's mixed messages could be infuriating. Dana was advocating the same teen strategy that the general merchandise manager and fashion director of the store apparently believed in, and she couldn't help but think that she was being penalized for her youth. Or maybe it was because Helen might pitch a fit. Either way, Andrew had been right: Bea was a moveable feast.

"Bob has chosen the winner for this year's teen contest. You'll announce the results next week at the Sugar Plum Ball. It's a favor for a friend of Mr. Campbell. His friend's daughter, Kim Sullivan, will be this year's winner." Bea sighed deeply and crushed her cigarette in a large glass ashtray on her desk. "Have a good weekend, Dana," Bea said, summarily dismissing the figure standing before her.

Dana was speechless. The contest involved getting the best and brightest teens to write essays, make brief speeches, and model clothes, and they were down to the five finalists. She'd run the contest for three years, but the idea that the contest was rigged this year—and by Bob Campbell of all people—left Dana dazed and temporarily unable to move. The Sugar Plum Ball was the annual December benefit for the Children's Aid Society. The idea of committing fraud was bad enough, but she would also have to disappoint the girls who would be competing in good faith. Did such a prestigious charity event have to be marred by dishonesty?

Bea looked up, glasses perched on the end of her nose. "Is anything the matter, Dana? You look positively pale."

"No. Everything's fine."

Everything was most decidedly *not* fine. Dana had the ear of Bob Campbell, and she would use her access to the general manager to express how odious the idea seemed. One way or another, she'd find a way to avoid making the contest into a sham.

Feeling manipulated, Dana turned and left Bea's office. Her normally fair complexion was red with anger, and her breath came in quick, short bursts. She marched down to the Writing and Rest Room for Women, a beautifully carpeted room with chairs upholstered in blue velvet. The mahogany walls and soft lighting made this one of the most elaborate rest areas in any store, and Dana sometimes came here because of the quiet and repose it offered. Today the room was, not surprisingly, filled with shoppers taking a moment to compose themselves. She hurried to her office in the General Offices section of the fifth floor, retrieved her purse, and tried to calm down.

Regaining her composure proved impossible, however. She took a deep breath and decided that she would have no peace for the rest of the day until she spoke with Bob Campbell. Bea must have been mistaken. Bob would never rig the yearly teen contest.

Dana got up from her desk, hoping to get a few minutes with the general manager. She walked back to the executive suite, ready to make her case.

Chapter Two

Brett McGarry walked confidently into the offices of Davis, Konen and Wright on the thirty-seventh floor of 80 Broad Street. The address was in the heart of New York's financial district, a suitable home for the powerhouse corporate law firm where Brett hoped to soon make partner. The imposing limestone edifice of the Art Deco building, with its many tiers of set-back facades, was near Battery Park, the Staten Island Ferry, the New York Stock Exchange, and other famous landmarks in lower Manhattan. Brett felt at ease in the financial district, and whenever he entered the area, he felt a spring in his step. This was where he belonged, and when it was time to have a drink with colleagues, he could walk to Fraunces Tavern, the Georgian-style building on nearby Pearl Street where General George Washington had bid the officers of the Continental Army a fond farewell at a dinner in his honor. On any given evening, one could find newsworthy faces at the tavern, and for Brett, scotch neat went down that much easier when at Fraunces.

He turned the corner of one of the quiet corridors of the firm, hitting his stride. He had every reason to believe he was on the fast track to partnership, so the light snow and gray skies outside hadn't dampened his spirit. On the contrary, he felt invigorated by the cold air, with gray skies matching the venerable gray buildings on Wall Street.

It was Friday morning, and the offices were almost deserted on this day after Thanksgiving. He intended to pick up some files that he'd need the following day for a meeting with a client and then return to his home in Murray Hill. He could easily have gotten the folders on Saturday morning, but Brett loved being in his element. He'd therefore brought his beloved *New York Times*, as well as honey buns from Mary Elizabeth's tea room—the combination was a ritual he was not going to forfeit on *any* day—in order to breathe in the odor of the corporate offices and take in their ambience. He would soon be a more integral part of the firm, and it gave him pleasure to walk through the halls and reflect on his accomplishments.

At thirty, Brett was in decent shape, working out at least twice a week at the New York Athletic Club, although lately he'd doubled his workouts in order to keep excess pounds off and tone his muscles a bit more. At six feet tall, he felt that he had a commanding presence in the court room. Square shoulders, dark brown eyes, a powerful voice—he thought that he was not only a great lawyer, but looked the part as well. When it came to possible partnership status in this old-line firm, image mattered, and no one had understood the power of image better than his wife. Dana's preference for fine tailored clothing and English fabrics served Brett well on a daily basis. Even as a first-year associate, he'd exhibited the understated, successful look of a senior partner.

He was, therefore, always conscious of his appearance, and he frequently glanced sideways when passing a mirrored surface to make sure every hair was in place and that his tie had the perfect four-in-hand knot. Today, however, he was dressed casually in tan cords and a gray Shetland crewneck sweater. His brown hair was parted perfectly, and he couldn't resist a quick look to his right as he passed an antique mirror hanging in the hallway that led to his office.

"Good morning, Brett," came a female voice from behind a secretary's desk in the center of an office suite occupied by the firm's litigators.

Startled, Brett jerked his head forward. He had expected to find only the cleaning staff shuffling through the hallowed offices on this Friday morning. The voice belonged to Janice Conlon, the firm's new junior litigator. Brett stopped in his tracks and surveyed the five-foot-ten leggy blond dressed in tight jeans and an even tighter turtleneck covered by a brown distressed suede jacket. Long straight hair splashed across her shoulders, and her deep blue eyes gazed at Brett above high angular cheekbones.

"Good morning, Janice," he said, recovering quickly from his vain sideways glance. "What brings *you* in this morning? I would expect you to be out Christmas shopping today."

"Shopping? My salary barely covers the rent, so my family and friends aren't expecting gifts," Janice replied glibly. "Besides, I can't stand the crowds. Say, what's all the fuss with these display windows?"

Brett smiled at the question, common to residents who were not native to the city or not yet attuned to the sights and sounds of its many concrete arteries. "They're a big New York attraction. Department stores spend the whole year working on them. They're mini productions, complete with set designers." Brett tilted his head while extending the thumb of his left hand, motioning to the city below that was now in full holiday mode. "You should get in the spirit of the season and take a look."

"What makes *you* such an expert?" Janice asked. "Next you'll be telling me that you're a department store Santa in your spare time."

Brett threw his head back and laughed. "My wife works for B Altman."

"Who in the world is B Altman?" asked Janice. "Should I recognize the name?"

"It's a store, not a person, although Benjamin Altman was indeed the founder," Brett answered with a smile. "It's one of the oldest and finest department stores in the city." He was amused at Janice's confusion over one of the city's more well-known landmarks.

Janice's curiosity had been piqued. As a litigator, her natural inclination was to ask follow-up questions in order to garner information. "Then what fine thing does your wife do for this exemplary department store? If you don't mind my asking, that is." The last remark had been tendered as an innocent afterthought to offset her direct, prodding manner.

"Something with special events," Brett said. He'd come to expect Janice's aggressive style, which had also been duly noted by others in the firm.

"Something? Now *that's* a rather vague job description."

"Public relations, too," Brett said. "I believe she's making sure that one of B Altman's windows has enough snow this morning." In reality, he wasn't at all sure what his wife was currently doing. "I guess you could say she wears many hats."

"Oh, I'm sure she wears quite a few," Janice said.

Brett's smile faded as he looked at Janice. Her remark had been delivered with a lack of emotion, and he wasn't quite sure whether it was a simple observation or an outright criticism.

"Well, it all sounds very interesting," Janice said with a plastic smile. "As long as she's happy inside her window."

Janice was quite aware that Brett took notice of her barbed remarks, and yet he never outright objected to them, a fact that made her all the more curious about his relationship with Dana. She rather enjoyed pressing for information about the happy little couple. In fact, were they truly happy, or did they live in their own little professional worlds? Was it a marriage of social convenience? Janice was an astute observer, and she knew that Brett was hyper-focused on making partner. It would be the height of irony, she thought, if the appropriate Mrs. McGarry were mere window dressing for her ambitious husband.

Brett had already dismissed Janice's inquiries.

"I just need to grab some papers," he said, walking to the other side of the reception area. He was in high spirits, and Janice's penchant for directness was not something he dwelled on. He entered his well-appointed office, sitting behind his desk in order to select the folders he needed from the corner inbox. Janice had held the bag of honey buns while Brett found his key, and she followed him inside, placing the pastry on his desk.

Brett always disliked it when someone had a height advantage over him. He motioned for her to be seated, offering to share his honey buns, but she remained standing.

"Anyway, why are you here?" he asked.

"Same as you, I suppose," she replied. "To pick up some papers for our meeting tomorrow with Jacob Heller over at 30 Rock. I'm always prepared, aren't I?"

Brett leaned back in his brown leather chair, took a deep breath, and surveyed the new litigator. He had to admit that, although she was a bit rough around the edges, she was proving to be an asset to the firm. Janice Conlon was from Akron, Ohio, later transplanted to the free-spirited, liberal culture of the West Coast. Now twenty-seven, she'd earned her bachelor's degree in California before attending the Berkeley School of Law. She'd briefly worked for the firm of Drexel and Combs, where she proved herself to be an unflappable litigator, never intimidated by older and more experienced opposing counsel. Richard Patterson, the managing partner of Davis, Konen and Wright, had met her on a business trip to Los Angeles, where an old friend from law school had assured him that Conlon was the quintessential shark despite her youth. She could be ruthless on cross-examination, and Patterson had reasoned that Janice was young enough to be groomed for his own firm's purposes without sacrificing her formidable skills and cool demeanor under fire. Thus far, she had taken second chair in cases handled by Brett.

"And this must be Dana," Janice commented, picking up a framed picture of Brett's wife from a library table in a sitting area on the opposite side of the office. She had, of course, seen Dana's picture before, but always during business hours. "Matching coats," she said as she eyed Dana's camel hair polo coat in the picture and then the one Brett had dropped on his couch. "Cute."

In reality, Janice didn't think Dana was anything but bland, boring, and all too perfect, just like Dana's spoiled little life inside her window. Little Miss Priss would probably give birth to spoiled kids—2.5, of course—and they, too, would surely wear matching camel hair polo coats one day.

Dana's window? More like her snow globe, Janice thought. She pictured Dana standing in a tiny glass-enclosed world, snow gently falling around her. Her world could be shaken but never broken. She was far too insulated.

"Yes, that's Mrs. McGarry," Brett replied as he rubbed his palms together to clear away crumbs after finishing a honey bun.

"Vassar?"

"No. Cabrini. It's a Catholic college in Radnor, Pennsylvania."

"Ah, a good convent girl. Taught by the nuns, I suspect."

"No convent. Maybe nuns, though. I forget. I take it you're not Catholic."

"Lapsed, as they say. I don't believe in all that superstition and ritual."

She returned the picture to the table as she tossed her head to the side and faced Brett, her hair fanning out before again settling on her shoulders.

Brett leaned forward and clasped his hands. "As for our meeting tomorrow—"

"I hear you've been chosen by Mr. Patterson to give me a makeover," Janice interrupted.

"Does that bother you?"

Brett had indeed been given such an assignment by the managing partner, who hadn't seen Janice's navy suit since her interview. The partners were complaining, and her short skirts had embarrassed Brett on more than one occasion in court.

Janice shook her head and smiled. "Me bothered? Not at all. I clean up well. And I know how to take directions . . . from the right person, that is."

To Brett, the halls now seemed especially quiet. He and Janice had never had such an intimate, isolated conversation before.

"You're not concerned that we might be cramping your style?" he asked.

Janice smiled broadly and approached the desk. "So you think I have style?"

Brett knew he'd been trapped. This was exactly how Janice handled individuals on the witness stand. She asked leading questions, and Brett had taken the bait.

"I've really got to be going," Janice said abruptly, preventing Brett from giving a reply. She had, in a manner of speaking, withdrawn her question for the witness. She stretched out her arms and yawned, forcing her chest forward.

"It's cold out there," Brett remarked, trying to avert his gaze from Janice's tight sweater. "You should be wearing a coat."

Janice winked and turned to leave. "I'll be fine for now, counselor. Maybe you can pick out a coat when you do my makeover. I assume the firm is picking up the tab."

And then she was gone.

Brett picked up a second honey bun, furrowed his brows, and then dropped the pastry into the bag. He knew when he was being flirted with, although he didn't think Janice was seriously interested in him. For her, it was just sport—so very California. He wasn't overly concerned, but he made a mental note to handle Janice a bit more firmly the following day if need be. He knew he was being closely watched, and even a suspicion of impropriety by one of the firm's partners could blow his career out of the water. And wouldn't Janice like that turn of events?

Still, it was nice to receive the attention of a rather stunning blond. In fact, he secretly liked her blasé shoot-from-the-hip attitude, although he would never confess that to anyone he knew. She was a refreshing change from his politically correct world. He stood, and his reflection in the window overlooking the skyline of lower Manhattan stared back at him with a grin. Yep, he was in damn fine shape. He could understand why women were attracted to him.

And that included Dana. He looked down at the picture of his wife that Janice had examined in such a cavalier manner. Yes, he'd picked the perfect wife— pretty but not threatening. She was discreet, and the partners loved her. More importantly, so did their wives. Brett knew he was on the path to partnership when Patterson's wife had sponsored Dana for membership at the Colony Club.

"Good move, Dana," he said aloud. "You're a lucky girl. Your husband is about to be the next partner of Davis, Konen and Wright!"

He was on top of his game.

Chapter Three

*D*ana entered the executive suite with determination while trying her best to avoid being seen by Bea. If Bob Campbell indeed reversed his position on Kim Sullivan winning the teen contest, Bea would be furious, but she'd worry about her boss' notoriously short fuse when and if it became necessary. But did she really stand any chance at all of changing the mind of the store's vice president and general manager? Dana thought a well-placed word might convince him she was right because she'd known Bob for many years outside the store, meeting him at summer events at the Garden City Country Club on Long Island. Dana and her parents, Phil and Virginia Martignetti, were frequently invited to the club by their good friend, John Cirone, owner and president of the House of Cirone, a manufacturer of ladies eveningwear and a B Altman vendor. When John entertained Bob and his family at the club, the Martignettis were often invited, and it was during one of his dinner parties—the summer before Dana's senior year at Cabrini—that Bob offered her a job at B Altman during the holiday season.

Bob and Dana had therefore been on a first-name basis for years, and when Dana had begun working at B Altman, Bob spread a protective wing over someone he regarded as his third daughter. He knew she was bright, energetic, and ambitious, and he'd been eager to help a good friend of John Cirone get a leg up in an industry for which she clearly had both passion and talent.

After making discreet inquiries, Dana learned that Helen had left for the day, while Bea was in a closed-door meeting with other executives. Bob Campbell, she was told, was alone in the board room, having just finished an impromptu meeting. Dana tapped lightly on the door, and entered.

"Dana!" Bob exclaimed, rising from one of the fourteen hand-carved chairs. "A belated Happy Thanksgiving! How is your family?"

Dana smiled as she summoned her courage. "They're fine. Thanks, Bob. I was wondering if I might have a word with you."

In his late fifties, Bob Campbell was dressed in a gray suit, although his coat was draped over the back of a chair, white shirt sleeves rolled up to the middle of his forearms. His wavy gray hair looked very stylish and mature, and he had a warm, paternal smile. He walked around the ten-foot-long mahogany table and put his arm on Dana's shoulder. "Come have a seat and tell me what's on your mind," Bob said, sensing a note of concern in Dana's voice.

The regal board room had dark wood paneling, with a Waterford crystal chandelier hanging over the center of the table. Dana slumped into a chair near Bob, who sat at the table's head. He shuffled some papers around and closed a manila folder, his attention focused solely on Dana.

"Bob," Dana began, "I feel like my voice just isn't being heard. I've been working here for seven years—I'm not just some kid out of college. Mr. Neimark and Ms. Mello are both behind the Shop for Pappagallo in order to pull in the youth market. It's a terrific concept, so I urged Helen and Bea to consider a teen makeup section as well, and Helen thought it was the most ridiculous idea she'd ever heard. She also thinks Biba is going to go under because the kids, as she terms them, are taking over the store. Bea's more open to the suggestion but thinks Helen needs to be given a wide berth. If that's the case, I'd gladly shoulder the burden personally." Dana paused. "And then, out of the blue, Bea hits me with an order to announce Kim Sullivan as the winner for this year's teen contest. She claims that it's coming straight from you." Dana sighed heavily and rubbed her eyes, feeling emotionally drained.

Bob nodded patiently and ran the fingers of his right hand through his hair. "Dana, trust me when I say that I know how you're feeling. It's not easy to work with powerhouse women like Helen and Bea. I'm sure they can be intimidating—even overbearing—at times. But they're smart as hell or they wouldn't be here, just like you. The problem is that there are a lot of changes happening at the store right now, and change isn't easy for them. In fact, it's not easy for anyone, especially when the status quo is working. All the buyers are currently dealing with many pressures you're not aware of, and they're all looking over their shoulders. Ira is here to make B Altman more competitive in mainstream retailing, and these changes are happening fast. Everybody wants to get it right, but most are more than a little intimidated.

"But that's my point," Dana continued. "I can handle the pressure, and I want to be part of these new changes. I could make a real difference, but they're shutting me down. That teen makeup section would be great for this store. If Bea would sign on, I'm willing to bet that Mr. Neimark and Ms. Mello would, too."

"I don't dispute that you've got a solid idea," Bob countered, "but I can't do an end run around Bea or Helen. It wouldn't be fair. They're not just good at their jobs—they're good people, period. If I gave a nod to your teen makeup section over their objections, they would have every right to be furious. They need time to adjust to the many changes already occurring store-wide before committing to new ones."

Dana tilted her head back, gazing at the chandelier. "So good ideas—money-making ideas—have to take a back seat to seniority?"

Bob rose from his seat and, hands in his pockets, began to pace slowly around the room. He pursed his lips, a pensive look on his face. "Not necessarily, Dana. Older women at B Altman like Bea and Helen—and many others, for that matter—were all where you are now, and all had great ideas shot down at one time or another. But they didn't give up."

Dana suddenly had the sinking feeling that she was being administered a patronizing pep talk.

"You've got to be creative," Bob advised. "Think outside the box. Be diplomatic, but be persistent. Look for an opening. You know the old saying—there's more than one way to skin a cat."

Dana clasped her hands, sighed deeply, and looked at Bob. "I don't suppose you'd care to be more specific. Creativity—sure—but I don't know what it is you expect me to do."

"There's no formula for getting your ideas off the ground. Every problem is unique and therefore has a unique solution. All I can tell you is that I can't wave a magic wand without causing a firestorm. Tensions are already high, and if I mandated certain changes, they would be regarded as unwelcome interference. I'd come off as a tyrant."

"You're telling me to be a team player while looking for an opportunity to become a maverick who breaks the mold. It sounds contradictory."

Bob raised his eyebrows and smiled. "I wouldn't have put it that way, but yes, I guess, in a manner of speaking, I am. I used to see you down by two sets on the court, but you hung in there and found a way to win the match."

Dana knew that Bob was throwing down the gauntlet. She also knew that she'd been foolish. The general manager wasn't going to ignore the opinions of Bea or Helen about a teen makeup section proposed by a twenty-nine-year-old events coordinator.

"Okay, Bob, but Kim Sullivan is another matter altogether. How can we penalize the other finalists who are working so hard? It just seems so wrong, Bob."

Bob turned his head to the side and stared at a cart holding a silver tea service. "That's a sticky situation, Dana. Believe me when I say that I agonized about the contestants and didn't make the decision lightly."

"But—"

"Hear me out," Bob said. "Kim's going through an especially difficult time. Her parents, both surgeons who weren't around the home very much, are now divorcing, and Kim—an only child, I might add—is caught in the middle. Her father thinks that winning the contest will give her a boost, and I tend to agree. Kids in a divorce can feel like such losers."

"Divorce is a tragedy," Dana retorted, "but is Kim's welfare more important than the other girls? I'm sure they all have their own stories."

"To paraphrase Shakespeare's Polonius, you sometimes have to get your hands a little dirty to set things straight."

Dana's frown indicated that she wasn't following.

"Ever read *Hamlet*? Hamlet sees his father's ghost, who tells him that his uncle murdered him. The answer? Kill the uncle, who is the illegitimate king of Denmark. It's not your everyday solution, but the melancholy Dane does it. The message? Life demands that we make some unpleasant choices. It isn't always fair, Dana."

"Apples and oranges, Bob. You're saying the ends justify the means."

Bob looked at Dana with steady gray eyes. The expression on his face was that of a boss, not a longtime friend who had cheered for her and his daughters when they competed on the tennis court. "I'm saying that my decision is going to have to stand. For what it's worth, the matter rests entirely on my shoulders. No need to feel guilty." He paused. "Now, is there anything else I can do for you today?"

Dana forced a weak smile and rose from her chair. "No. Thanks for listening, though."

Choking back tears, Dana returned to her office, picked up her purse and then took an elevator to the main floor. As she waded through shoppers to get to the doors on the far side of the building, she spied Andrew talking with a fellow employee near the fragrance counters. Normally, Andrew would be the first person she'd seek out in order to release her pent-up emotions. She shared everything with Andrew, from her growing realization that Brett seemed to be totally absent in spirit from their marriage to the frustration she felt when the executives at B Altman ignored her creativity. Andrew always listened patiently, whether he was absorbed in making fresh pasta in his kitchen while Dana sipped chardonnay or whether he was giving the McGarry library a new look with a fresh coat of terra cotta. He could always intuitively sense his friend's saddest moments or when it was time to offer her a hug.

Dana needed one of those hugs right now, but Andrew was absorbed in conversation, and she needed to get home so she could walk Wills, their Cavalier King Charles Spaniel. The magic and balance she'd experienced that morning in front of the display window had disappeared, and the long green garlands festooning the main floor now looked like little more than decorations taken out of storage once a year to boost sales.

Dana exited B Altman on Madison Avenue and began walking the five blocks to her apartment at 77 Park Avenue.

"Hey, lady, look where you're going!" said a gruff voice.

Dana, her eyes not focused on the stream of pedestrians flowing past her, had bumped into a gray-bearded man who scowled at her and then resumed walking.

Dana continued on, her mind absorbed by the conversations she'd had at work. Regardless of Bob Campbell's reasoning, there was no way to rationalize throwing the contest. And yet she was being told to do so. Bob could claim responsibility all he wanted, but Dana was the one who had to do the dirty work. She would have to coordinate the contestants' efforts, knowing that their hard work was in vain. She was the one, not Bob, who would have to look them in the eye every day for the next week, knowing their hope had been misplaced.

As for the teen makeup section, everyone knew it was a good idea—probably even Helen—but it all boiled down to store politics. B Altman would, of course, one day create such a section—it was inevitable—but would she get the credit? Given her youth, it seemed unlikely.

Dana couldn't help but think of her parents, Phil and Virginia Martignetti, as she walked along. Her father would have reminded her that she had a great career ahead of her, a career that would only come to fruition with patience. Things always worked out in the end. *You do a great job, Dana. Go home and clear your head. Go out to dinner with Brett and enjoy the evening.*

Phil was an easygoing man, someone who his wife said was as soft spoken and calm as Mr. C himself, the very relaxed and reassuring Perry Como. An executive with IBM, Phil was always appropriately dressed, politically correct, and at home in a conservative corporate culture. People liked him immediately. He was kind, made everyone feel important, and never rocked the boat. Rarely would he disagree with other employees, let alone argue. Above all, he desired peace and harmony in any situation.

Dana knew that her father was very much a part of her soul. Like him, she'd always tried to be gracious and thoughtful, and most people sensed and appreciated her kind but professional demeanor. It was these attributes that allowed her to succeed in her public relations role at B Altman, and she was very aware that top executives thought that such a deferential style boded well for her future at the store. Why not just go along for the ride? Why blow a promising career over teen cosmetics?

But she also carried her mother's DNA, and Virginia had a streak of independence that made her unflinching when her mind was made up. Like her mother, she was an achiever at heart, although Virginia wasn't shy about letting her drive be known. Attempts to persuade Helen, Bea, and Bob—all on the same day—had definitely mirrored her mother's more aggressive style. She and Virginia loved a good challenge—loved to win, in fact—but at present, Dana was still learning how to balance the different styles of her parents. She knew with some certainty what Virginia would tell her. *Speak up, Dana. They still can't hear you. You won't get ahead being good. It's your great ideas that will succeed.*

Dana continued walking, eyes cast down. Her legs moved with a steady rhythm, one foot in front of the other. That's how the entire day had been: one step at a time in order to hold body and soul together while people had alternately tried to warn or pacify her.

Earlier in the day, she had followed the instincts she'd inherited from Virginia. She'd disobeyed Helen and spoken her mind, first to Bea and then to Bob, but she'd taken it on the chin and stepped back in line. She would have to follow orders as well as stifle all her creative energies.

She'd only gone one block when her thoughts, more melancholy with each successive step, turned to Brett. Where was he? Where was her partner, her friend who shared her dreams? After almost eight years of working and planning for the life they wanted, it was all coming together, and yet at the same time it seemed to be flying apart. They'd done everything right—made all the right moves—and had usually been in agreement about the path of their lives together. But something was different in their relationship. Sometimes she felt as if she were a ghost inside her own home. Was he so self-absorbed that he didn't see or hear her when she walked through a room or offered an opinion? She listened attentively whenever he spoke of the firm, but she wondered how much he knew or cared about her activities at B Altman. Then again, maybe he was very aware of her but no longer liked what he heard or saw.

So what was she going to do? Play the loyal employee and wife and, as her father might say, wait for things to fall into place? Or would she, like Virginia, fight the good fight and try to make things happen? Would she confront Brett or perhaps force him into counseling? Would she risk her job by remaining vocal? Dana wasn't sure how to answer these questions, but she felt as if she'd crossed a threshold of sorts. She was a different person than the Dana McGarry who had arrived at B Altman that morning, brimming with enthusiasm. Was such a radical transformation really possible?

Yes, it was most certainly was. She'd been asked to do more than just sit on a terrific money-making concept and wait for B Altman's corporate gears to align with her way of thinking. She'd been ordered to lie. She sensed that her life was about to change, although she couldn't predict how. The day was almost over, but Dana sensed that a new journey was beginning.

Dana quickened her pace. She didn't quite know who Dana McGarry was any longer or what she was going to become. But she knew that things were going to change. Like her father, she would continue to be the good employee. Like her mother, she felt compelled to stand up for herself and challenge the status quo.

Chapter Four

John Cirone put down his glass of Barolo and rose from the overstuffed chair in the spacious den of Phil and Virginia Martignetti. Their house sat on the edge of Macy Channel in the community of Hewlett Harbor on Long Island.

"I tell you, Phil, I can't accept this, and I won't," he said. "I've never liked this Farnsworth girl, and now she goes and pulls a stunt like this. For God's sake, she's not even Catholic! What is my son thinking! What kind of a life will Johnny have if he's married to a Main Line Philadelphia socialite? A WASP!"

John Cirone, known affectionately to the Martignetti children simply as Uncle John, paced the floor of the den anxiously. The stunt he alluded to was the mailing of wedding invitations ahead of schedule by his son Johnny's fiancée, Suzanne Farnsworth.

"She did it to make sure Johnny doesn't back out at the eleventh hour," John asserted. "She knows I've been against this union from the beginning, and this is her Main Line response."

"John, you need to sit down before you have a stroke," Phil counseled good-naturedly.

Phil was a tall man in his mid-fifties. His warm eyes and close-cut salt and pepper hair gave him a look of sophistication and maturity. Virginia was a tall slender woman with short blond hair and deep-set blue eyes. Although she was Phil's age, she looked younger.

John sank onto the leather couch next to Phil, shaking his head. "If Lena were still around, she would know what to say and Johnny would listen. He *always* listened to her. But no matter what I say, it comes out wrong. I just can't sugarcoat the words 'I don't want you to marry this girl.' Lena Cirone, John's deceased wife, had died two years earlier.

Phil crossed his legs and spoke calmly. "John, Lena would want Johnny to be happy, and that means that you have to let him live his own life." He glanced at his wife, hoping for a little emotional reinforcement to help keep John calm.

Virginia had to bite her tongue. She believed that Phil was probably right, but she also felt strongly that, if Lena were alive, she might have put some considerable pressure on Johnny to go to his local parish priest for a little counseling. Marrying inside the Catholic Church had been as important to Lena as it was to Virginia.

Uncle John took a deep breath and spoke defiantly. "I can't watch my son take his wedding vows in an Episcopalian service. I've decided that I'm not going to the wedding."

"Now John," Phil said, "that's a bit extreme. Not going to your son's wedding is something that you'd regret for the rest of your life, and you might drive a wedge between Johnny and you. Who knows—he might even quit the business."

Uncle John glanced sideways, grunted, and lowered his voice. "And maybe that's why Suzanna—"

"Suzanne, John," Virginia corrected. "Her name is Suzanne."

Growing more restless and agitated, John stood again and walked across the oriental carpet and stood to the right of the fireplace. He gazed through the tall double window set into the den's knotty pine paneling. His stare was vacant, not focused on the fresh snowfall or the frozen waters of Macy Channel beyond.

"Like I was saying, maybe that's what this Farnsworth girl really wants—to take Johnny away from the House of Cirone. Maybe her father is waiting to give him a position with one of his own companies." Uncle John covered his forehead with his right hand. "What can I say? This is a nightmare."

The Martignettis knew all too well that Johnny's heart wasn't in the business, at least not totally, after seven full years with the House of Cirone, the ladies' eveningwear manufacturing company founded by his grandfather. It was always assumed that he would work for the company after graduating from Villanova, and, always the dutiful son, he hadn't disappointed his father. He'd joined the business and done everything Uncle John had asked of him.

Johnny was big and burly, and at twenty-nine, he was an honest, hardworking man—and a bit of a teddy bear despite his muscular build and his love of contact sports.

He was loyal to his family, but after his mother died, Johnny had been completely devastated. A friend introduced him to Suzanne, and, to his father's chagrin, the couple had gotten serious very quickly. Lena had been Johnny's protector from early childhood, and most people who knew him thought that Suzanne and her world outside New York were simply outlets for his grief.

Uncle John wheeled around to face his hosts, his arms spread wide in frustration. "What else could we have done to instill a strong Catholic faith in Johnny? Chaminade is the best Catholic high school for boys. The Marianist Brothers' teachings have guided me all my life, and I thought that it would be the same for my son. You know, we recently met with the board to discuss funding for a new athletic center in Lena's honor. And it wasn't even my idea. It was Johnny's. I know he's a good boy, but he's obviously lost his way. I'm still his father, and I can't let him start his married life outside the church."

"You're preaching to the choir, John," remarked Virginia. "Maybe what you need to do is—"

Sensing that Virginia was on the verge of giving John some advice on being proactive and possibly intervening in Johnny's affairs, Phil quickly stood and approached his guest, standing next to him and putting his arm around his friend's shoulder. "You have to remember that children don't come with an owner's manual," he said. "We teach them as best we can and then send them along, like a kid on his first two-wheel bike."

Virginia rolled her eyes and took a sip of wine, knowing that she'd been pre-empted.

"You've got two great kids," Phil continued. "Phoebe is distinguishing herself in her fellowship in interventional cardiology at New York Hospital. And Johnny has done well at the House of Cirone. Give yourself a little credit. You've obviously done a great many things right."

"Yeah, I know," John sighed. He moved to his left, absentmindedly running his index finger along the spines of leather-bound volumes in one of two built-in bookcases in the den. "But lately I'm reminded of Matthew and Dana and how well they turned out. I'm a bit envious, I suppose. I shouldn't have to deal with Johnny possibly making the biggest mistake of his life."

Matthew Martignetti was Dana's younger brother. A champion surfer who'd mastered the Banzai Pipeline, he was in a graduate program in marine biology at the University of Hawaii.

Virginia rose from the couch and poured herself another glass of wine. She had a few things on her mind and wasn't going to be interrupted again.

"We're certainly fortunate," Virginia said, her voice adopting a more reflective tone. "Dana has made us exceedingly proud, but that doesn't mean we've never had any concerns."

John frowned. "Oh, come on, Virginia. She and Brett have led a fairy tale existence."

Phil knew what was coming. He also knew that it wouldn't be wise to censor his wife a second time, so he, too, poured a second glass of wine and returned to the couch. "Just make it the short version, okay, honey?"

Virginia winked at her husband and nodded. Despite their different temperaments, Phil and Virginia had learned over the years how to make their respective styles complement each other.

"You might remember, John," Virginia began, "that I thought Brett was a bit too spoiled and pampered. I also thought he pushed Dana into marrying him before she was ready. His mother was never really friendly to us, and his father blamed Dana for Brett's decision to take a job on Wall Street after graduating from Penn Law, rather than accept a clerkship in D.C. He thought Dana had coerced Brett to move to Manhattan because of her professional aspirations. You know she would never do something like that. So you see, their marriage didn't begin without considerable friction between the families."

"And then there was the beautiful wedding," Phil said with a smile, as if he were wrapping up a long tale. "Today Brett and Dana have been happily married for eight years."

Phil was aware that Virginia could have added to the history of Brett and Dana, all of which might make Uncle John feel even more frustrated than he already was. In point of fact, Brett had shocked everyone, and infuriated his parents, when he'd sold shares of IBM stock to buy Dana an expensive engagement ring while still a student. Virginia felt that Brett had been like a kid in a candy store, spoiling Dana by throwing around his money. She knew that he had needed to grow up, and marriage was not the place to do that. As for church attendance, Brett went to mass very seldom these days, and the altar at which he now worshipped seemed to be his desk at Davis, Konen and Wright. Most disturbingly, Virginia, never one to let anything go unnoticed, believed Brett's eye lingered a little too long on certain attractive young women when the two families went out for dinner. Was her hotshot son-in-law becoming a little too arrogant, too sure of himself as his influence within the firm spread? Was he rooted in family and faith? Virginia told Dana that she thought the matter needed attention and that she was being too naïve, too trusting. Dana responded, rather unconvincingly to Virginia's way of thinking, that such suspicion was ridiculous.

"I appreciate what you're both saying," John said. "It's just that I believe when you marry somebody, it's for life and you get the whole package. You don't just marry a single individual—you marry the entire family. Their traditions, their quirks, their warmth . . ." He frowned. "Or lack thereof. If Suzanne is pushing the accelerator on the wedding, what is she going to do down the line, for heaven's sake? She's too aggressive for my taste." He returned to the couch and sat between Virginia and Phil.

Phil and Virginia each put an arm around their good friend. "We know it's hard, John," Virginia said as she looked at Phil at the other end of the couch, giving him a nonverbal cue that she was going to keep her advice short. The Martignettis could communicate with each other with their eyes better than most couples could with the spoken word. "Take one day at a time."

Virginia could indeed have gone much farther in her agreement with Uncle John. She, too, believed that marriage was a package deal, and that was precisely why she was so concerned about Dana at present. To her way of thinking, Brett had never matured. She'd been right from the beginning. Sure, he was a hard worker and kept Dana comfortable, but he seemed to be drifting. She felt he was exhibiting the McGarry family aloofness. While he went through all the motions in exemplary fashion, she didn't think the marriage was growing and thriving. Dana shared an apartment with her husband, but not much else.

"I wonder if Dana would mind speaking to Johnny," Uncle John said. "You know how close they used to be as kids. Don't forget that there was a time when we hoped *they* might be the ones to tie the knot. Maybe she can talk some sense into him—make him take a second look at the situation."

Phil laughed and nodded. "True enough, John, but I don't think Dana is going to want to interfere. I think she's going to want to give him space precisely because they were so close."

Virginia thought it was an excellent idea but said nothing.

"I suppose you're right," Uncle John said.

"Let's go out to the dock and get some fresh air," Phil said, escorting Uncle John from the den.

Virginia leaned back into the soft brown leather cushion. She was convinced that Uncle John was right about Suzanne Farnsworth. As for Brett McGarry, the jury was still out as far as Virginia Martignetti was concerned.

Chapter Five

Dana entered the library of her apartment, intending to remind her husband of their dinner reservation at Cheshire Cheese. Engrossed in a phone conversation, Brett held up the palm of his hand, gesturing that his wife would have to wait for a hearing. Rather than dwell on the brusque manner with which her husband dismissed her, Dana turned around and walked into the hallway, summoning Wills for his evening walk. Brett reclined on a plump English club chair and ottoman positioned in front of a bookcase that occupied the entire wall behind him.

Dana leaned over to hook the leash to the spaniel's collar. Brett was constantly on the phone, she thought, always talking with a client, a colleague, their accountant, their investment analyst—always schmoozing and working and laughing as if he had all the time in the world. But when was the last time they'd gone to a movie or enjoyed a quiet evening at home? When had they last talked about their future or having a family?

Dana rode down in the elevator, Wills panting in anticipation of ruling the sidewalk for the next fifteen minutes. She walked through the softly lit lobby, Wills' paws tapping the polished marble floor as he scooted through the door held open by the uniformed doorman. It was twilight, and streetlamps were just winking on as Dana allowed the eager spaniel to take the lead, pulling the leash taut. They had only gone half a block when Wills suddenly bolted forward, the leash going slack.

"Wills!" Dana called. "Come back! Please!" She took the end of the leash in her hand and noticed that the metal clasp that hooked to the collar was worn.

The spaniel sprinted on its short legs, its wide furry ears flapping against its head as it enjoyed newfound freedom on the crowded sidewalk of Park Avenue.

"Wills!" Dana cried. "Please—someone stop him!"

In the distance, Dana could see Wills fast approaching the busy traffic at the corner of 37th Street and Park. Suddenly, a dark figure twenty yards away bent over and scooped him up, cradling him with two arms.

"Wait!" Dana called. "No! That's my dog!"

Dana quickened her pace, trying to make her way through the busy flow of people returning from work or shopping. If the stranger disappeared and she never saw Wills again, she would never forgive herself for not double-checking the clasp on the leash.

Dana stopped in her tracks, breathing a sigh of relief. The stranger was walking in her direction, a smile on his face. Wills was safely bundled against the lapels of his rescuer's wool overcoat.

"I think this little guy belongs to you," said a man in his early thirties. He smiled as he placed Wills into Dana's outstretched arms. He was tall, perhaps six-foot two, and had a friendly smile and light blue eyes.

Dana wrapped Wills, cold and wet from the snow, in her soft cashmere scarf and held him so tightly that the man started to laugh and said, "I didn't save him so you could suffocate him."

"Another second and he would have been in traffic," Dana said as she wiped snow from Wills' face. "I'm sorry. Where are my manners? Thank you so much. You saved his life."

The man shook his head slightly and grinned. "Glad to help. A Cavalier King Charles Spaniel, if I'm correct. A very handsome breed."

"Yes it is. And thank you again. Chivalry isn't dead."

"I should hope not," said the well-dressed stranger. "Besides, we don't own the dogs. They own us. Have a pleasant evening." He slowly walked away, turned to wave, and then disappeared into the brisk sidewalk traffic.

Dana retraced her steps to the lobby of her building, thinking of the brief exchange with the man in the wool overcoat. She couldn't help but think that the stranger had spoken more words to her in the space of two minutes than Brett sometimes said in an hour.

Have a pleasant evening.

It was such a simple phrase, but the four words were warm and comforting. They'd represented a kind sentiment on a dark evening. Dana smiled brightly as Wills looked up at her with big, round innocent eyes. Sometimes, she thought, Christmas angels wore wool overcoats. It had been a bright moment in an otherwise depressing, drab day.

• • •

Dana saw that Brett, his crossed legs stretched before him, had just ended a phone call.

"Just one more," he said, holding up his left index finger. "Five minutes tops."

Dana walked calmly to the chair, took the beige Princess receiver from his hands, and placed it on the cradle.

Brett was speechless, his mouth hanging open. "What are you doing? I have to call Patrick about a case next week."

"Exactly. *Next* week. We have dinner reservations in an hour," Dana said, "and the traffic isn't moving."

Brett wearily got to his feet and picked up his polo coat from the couch, mumbling "Somebody must have had a bad day."

"What did you say?" Dana asked, her tone challenging. Brett's behavior was clashing sharply with the kindness of Wills' rescuer.

"Nothing. You're acting very strange this evening. Can I pour you a sherry?"

"You said 'somebody must have had a bad day,' and as a matter of fact, I did. I got shot down after pitching a new cosmetic section to Bea, and then Bob Campbell told me that I have to throw the teen contest. The winner, to be announced at the Sugar Plum Ball, has already been determined. It's outright fraud."

Brett sank back onto the chair and burst into laughter. "Is *that* what's bothering you?"

"Of course it's bothering me! There are five girls putting their heart and soul into—"

"Calm down, honey. B Altman is practically run by the Archdiocese." He winked mischievously. "You know the rumors—the Catholic Church secretly owns the store, which is why nuns and priests are constantly roaming every single floor. Just look at all the clergy discounts they offer. God will surely look past a little fraud since he's the real CEO. Your place inside the pearly gates is assured."

"That's absurd, Brett, and it's not just a *little* fraud, as you put it. We're talking about people's lives. This contest means everything to the five finalists. What if someone had pulled your article from the law review in your last year and given the space to someone else?"

Brett's laughter was louder this time as he rolled his eyes in disbelief. "You're not seriously comparing the law review to teen models, are you?" He wrinkled his face into a good-natured frown.

Dana paused, put her hands on her hips, and squeezed her eyes shut, not believing what she was hearing. "Yes, I most certainly *am* comparing this to your law review article. These young girls have hopes and dreams, too. You're not the only one, Brett."

"I know that, Dana. It's just that—"

The phone rang, and Brett picked up the receiver before it could ring twice. He listened for a minute and then spoke briefly before hanging up. "Okay. Fine. See you then."

He looked up at Dana. "That was Janice Conlon telling me that my meeting tomorrow was pushed back by thirty minutes."

Dana's jaw dropped. "We're cutting down our Christmas tree tomorrow! The party is Thursday. We've had these plans for weeks."

"Duty calls," Brett said matter-of-factly. "Mr. Heller wants to meet tomorrow, and he's a big client."

"When were you planning to tell me!"

"I've got a lot on my plate, Dana." He balled his two fists and extended his thumbs, proudly motioning to himself. "Don't forget—the next partner at Davis, Konen and Wright is sitting before you."

"I'm not going to dinner," said a furious Dana. "I'm not in the mood anymore."

"We're going," Brett said resolutely. "We can't cancel the reservation at the last minute. I'm going to change now. Are you ready?"

Brett got up and went into the bedroom while Dana took his place on the chair and dialed Andrew's number.

"Andrew? It's Dana. Listen, Brett has to work tomorrow and—"

"Let me guess—you need someone to help you cut down a Christmas tree at the Winterberry Christmas Tree Farm like you've been planning. I'm sure I can convince Nina to come along as well. She's got a VW Bug."

Nina Bramen was the antiques buyer for B Altman.

"You're the best, Andrew. I can always count on you."

There was a pause at the other end of the line, and Dana could sense that Andrew was withholding the phrase "Unlike your husband."

"Thanks, Andrew. See you in the morning."

Dana hung up and tilted her head back. The day had gone from bad to worse. And she was tired of hearing about Janice Conlon. The new litigator got more of her husband's time than she did, Dana thought, as she got up and headed to the bedroom.

"Andrew and Nina will help me cut down the tree tomorrow," Dana informed her husband when she reached the bedroom.

"Nina? B Altman's token feminist?"

Dana lowered her head in frustration at the cavalier use of the word "feminist." "Nina Bramen believes in equal rights for women, as do a lot of employees at the store, both men and women. Is there a problem with that?"

Brett merely smiled. "I get it, honey." He kissed her on the forehead and took her hand. "Shall we go?"

• • •

Brett and Dana sat at the small fifty-seat restaurant, Cheshire Cheese, a wood-paneled establishment with English fare and ambience to match. Brett waited for Cheshire Cheese's famous prime rib to be served, while Dana looked forward to her Dover sole.

Brett McGarry was his charming self, the one Dana had fallen in love with many years ago. Instead of sitting across the small table from her, as was his custom lately, he sat in the chair adjoining Dana's. He also covered Dana's hand with the palm of his own as he spoke.

"I'm sorry I won't be able to help with the tree tomorrow," he said softly.

"Brett, it's not just the tree. It's a day together in the country and lunch at an inn where we used to spend the weekend. You can't even find a few hours on the weekend after Thanksgiving?"

"If the partnership pays off, we'll get the house you want in Bedford, and we can spend *every* weekend in the country. Would you like that?"

"Brett . . . " Dana was about to ask Brett about the distance between them—about the unexplored silences that hovered over their interactions—but the distance had suddenly evaporated. She had his full attention, but was it wise to lose the intimacy of the moment? He was away from the telephone and the office, and he seemed sincerely interested in his wife's happiness and their lives together. He was speaking of their future, and Dana hadn't heard such welcome words from Brett in . . . well, she couldn't recall the last time when he'd been so attentive. Perhaps he'd noticed her displeasure back at the apartment, and now that they were alone and away from all distractions, he was making a conscious effort to be the thoughtful man she'd married. No, she wasn't going to spoil the moment. She felt the same enthusiasm that she'd felt that morning while standing on the sidewalk with Andrew and Mark. Maybe the day would end with a little magic after all.

Dana was on the verge of tears—happy tears—so she took a sip of chardonnay and got up. "Let me run to the ladies room," she said. "I'll be right back."

Dana looked in the mirror of the restroom as she dabbed away the moisture around her eyes. The face staring back at her was ashamed of the suspicions she'd harbored about Brett. She realized that his work was no less demanding than hers. She was worried about convincing Bea, Helen, and Bob that her ideas were sound, but Brett was in the very business of trying to make people come around to his viewpoint, whether it was partners, clients, or judges. Maybe she'd been guilty of underestimating the stress he lived with on a daily basis. She would erase her frustrations and look at this night as a point in time when she realized that Brett loved her and that marriage was often a demanding partnership. Partnership? Dana laughed aloud at the word her mind had ironically conjured to describe her relationship with Brett.

She returned to the table, and for the next hour the couple talked quietly as they enjoyed their meal. Brett said he hoped Phil and Virginia were still coming for dinner the following night. "You know," he said, "your dad just naturally makes people feel good about themselves. And your mom is so much fun to be around."

"They're still coming," Dana said. She continued to be stunned, for Brett hadn't spoken of her parents in recent memory.

"Well, it's been a long day," Brett said after paying the check. "Let's go home."

On this particular night, Dana thought the word "home" sounded especially comforting.

They got up from the table and made their way to the restaurant's front door, walking past a round table with a bouquet of fresh flowers.

"We meet again," said a voice coming from the tall blue-eyed stranger who'd picked up Wills on Park Avenue. "Small world, as the saying goes."

Brett glanced at Dana, a puzzled look on his face.

"This is . . . " Dana paused. She had no name to attach to the kind face.

"Jack Hartlen," the man said. "And this is my wife Patti and my parents, Ralph and Sandy Hartlen."

Smiles and handshakes were exchanged as Dana related events from earlier in the evening. "Mr. Hartlen was kind enough to retrieve Wills when he slipped his leash on our evening walk."

"It was a Cavalier King Charles Spaniel," Jack said, turning to his wife. "And please, call me Jack," he said, turning back to Dana.

"We've been thinking of getting the exact same breed!" Patti said. "Maybe this is a good omen."

Patti was an attractive twenty-seven-year-old woman with dirty blond hair and violet eyes. She always looked everyone straight in the eye when she spoke, a habit some found unsettling.

"Thank you again, Jack," Dana said. "Have a good evening."

"You, too," Jack said as Dana and Brett exited Cheshire Cheese.

Brett glanced over his shoulder at Patti. Her direct gaze had been very penetrating. Such direct eye contact was rare, and he found it refreshing. Janice often looked him in the eye, but she was a lawyer, and body language was very important when questioning someone on the witness stand. Most law students learned its value in Moot Court.

Brett took Dana's hand and they walked towards Fifth Avenue to look for a taxi. Maybe Patti had found him attractive. He'd noticed his reflection earlier that morning at his office, and he'd liked what he'd seen. He had to admit that he was a good-looking man.

Chapter Six

*B*rett brushed Dana's cheek with a kiss before she squeezed into the front seat of Nina Bramen's yellow VW Beetle—Andrew had moved to the cramped backseat—and, wishing them a successful trip, waved goodbye before going back to the apartment. He poured a cup of coffee and grabbed a honey bun he'd gotten earlier from Mary Elizabeth's. He had two hours before he had to be at 30 Rock, so he opened the *New York Times* and engaged in a ritual that was as sacred to many New Yorkers as going to church on Sunday: reading the *Times*. The morning was bright and clear, with sun pouring through the windows of the library, and he paged through the various sections, thinking, as Robert Browning had proclaimed in a poem, that all was right with the world. He had peace and quiet thanks to Dana's day trip to Pennsylvania with Andrew and Nina, and he once again reflected on how well his life was positioned for advancement and personal achievement. He was secretly glad that work had prevented him from making the trip to Winterberry Christmas Tree Farm. And what a motley crew was packed into the Beetle: a gay man and a feminist. "Lord knows what the conversation will be like in that tiny excuse for an automobile," he said aloud. He gazed down at the spaniel resting at his feet. "This is *our* time, right Wills?"

When he'd finished the paper, he went into the bedroom to put on a suit. He supposed he could have dressed down given that it was Saturday, but he was a rising star at the firm, and he intended to retain his competitive edge at all times. He would meet with his client and then take Janice to find some proper attire for the courtroom and office. She was the proverbial handful, but he thought that shopping with her might prove interesting. He would play Professor Henry Higgins to her Eliza Doolittle. It would be great sport.

• • •

Brett stepped into the office of Jacob Heller at 30 Rock ten minutes early. Janice was already waiting for him. She wore jeans and a turtleneck, as she had the day before.

Jacob Heller was a member of the Landmarks Preservation Commission, a client of Davis, Konen and Wright. The previous July, the State Court of Appeals had invalidated the landmark status of the venerable J.P. Morgan mansion on Madison Avenue. The LPC regarded the decision as a major threat to landmark preservation in general in the New York City area. Morgan had been one the richest American financiers in the late nineteenth and early twentieth centuries, and his mansion was history in the truest sense of the word. And that's what was at stake: history. Additional lawsuits had been filed in later months challenging the landmark status of other buildings, and the commission was preparing to fight the movement to undermine the countless treasures in the five boroughs of New York.

Brett, Janice, and Heller looked at briefs for pending litigation as well as files on dozens of landmarks that the commission deemed to be at risk. The entire time, Brett couldn't help but notice that Janice was making frequent eye contact with him, much as Patti Hartlen had done the night before. But Janice's eyes were prettier, he thought. The blue color was deeper, more scintillating.

Jacob Heller droned on about various buildings that he was keeping an eye on: the Seventh Regiment Armory, the Abigail Adams Smith House, the Clarence Dillon House, Grand Central Terminal, the Chester A. Arthur House . . .

"Chester Arthur was a United States president!" said the fifty-six-year-old Heller, his short gray hair and round, rimless glasses giving him the appearance of an archivist. "The domino effect will begin if we don't stop this trend now." He sat behind his desk, removed his glasses, and surveyed the mountain of files before him. "Where does it end?" he asked.

"We agree with you wholeheartedly," Brett said reassuringly, his eyes scanning various documents. He glanced at Janice, who sat beside him on the other side of Heller's desk. She was reviewing several suits filed to revoke landmark status from four sites in New York City.

"The arguments to declassify these landmarks are compelling," Janice stated. "It would save the city an enormous amount of money if some of these non-operational sites didn't have to be maintained at the taxpayer's expense."

Brett raised his right eyebrow, and Janice immediately took his meaning.

"But we feel that history is the paramount issue in these cases," she continued. "Upkeep of certain landmarks can be economized, while many, such as Grand Central Terminal, are fully operational and self-sustaining. Most importantly, however, the city needs to remember how many tourist dollars these landmarks bring in. In the long run, they more than pay for themselves even when minimal municipal subsidies are required."

The truth was that Janice thought the entire matter to be totally frivolous, and she didn't like seeing money squandered on hundreds of old buildings, libraries, and houses scattered around the city. The entire matter of landmark preservation didn't pique her progressive California mindset in the least. But she'd been a good soldier and told her client exactly what he expected to hear. Brett had been impressed as well. She teased him with her initial remark and then followed through with a solid legal argument. With concealed amusement, she watched him exhale and settle back in his chair in relief.

Heller continued to name various sites that he wanted the firm to investigate, assessing the risk for declassification that each one might have. "The Players Club, the Alfred E Smith House, the Andrew Carnegie Mansion, the Dyckman Farmhouse . . ."

The next hour passed slowly, with Brett assuring Heller that they would have the firm's research staff look into the issue in general but that the matter at hand involved certain imminent lawsuits that demanded immediate attention.

Janice placed the fingers of her left hand on top of Brett's right forearm. "We'll do what needs to be done, even if we have to bend a few rules, Mr. Heller. Isn't that right, Brett?" With her head turned sharply to the left, Heller couldn't see Janice's left eyelid quickly wink at her colleague.

"That's correct," Brett replied.

His eyes maintained contact with Janice's for a second longer than would have been normal. *Even if we have to bend a few rules*, Brett thought. She'd been speaking to *him*, not Jacob Heller, and she wasn't alluding to landmarks.

The meeting was over. They shook hands with Heller, left his office, and stepped into an elevator. Brett stared straight ahead and began to speak after the doors had closed. "We need to—"

"Saks is across the street," Janice noted. "Why don't we go there now so you can give me the Davis, Konen and Wright look."

"You've been flirting with me," Brett said bluntly. "Your behavior bordered on the unprofessional, although I don't think Heller noticed."

"It's because you're turning into a landmark," Janice responded without apology. "You're going to grow old before your time. Your entire life is mapped out, and I wouldn't be surprised if you've already bought burial insurance. You want to preserve the status quo as much as you want to preserve those old buildings on Heller's list."

"Is that such a bad thing?"

"Don't you ever want to cut loose once in a while? I've noticed you, Brett. Your eye likes to check out young women. There's a little wanderlust inside you that you keep carefully hidden. Personally, I don't think that's healthy."

Brett shook his head. "If I possessed this wanderlust you speak of, I'd be spending an enjoyable day exploring the countryside in Bucks County, cutting down a Christmas tree with Dana right now. Instead, I took this meeting today and am following up on my promise to Richard to purchase a professional wardrobe for you. This is definitely not my idea of adventure."

Janice nodded her head and smiled. "My point exactly. You could be with your wife right now, preserving McGarry family traditions. But you've opted to buy me new clothes—me, the firm's rebel. We could have scheduled the meeting with Heller anytime during the coming week."

Brett said nothing. The truth was that he enjoyed being around Janice. There was something about her carefree manner that intrigued him whenever the two were together. Years earlier, he showed his independence and defied both sets of parents by insisting he and Dana marry before he graduated from law school and he had a job. Over the years, he'd settled into routines and rituals, but even as he adhered to them to further his career, a part of him liked the idea of breaking the rules—and Janice was definitely a rule breaker.

He knew that Janice sensed his vulnerability, which was a bit unsettling to a man who prided himself on the ability to play things close to the vest. So why *wasn't* he taking the day off to spend time with his wife? Why not have a little fun and get some fresh air with the woman he loved?

He already knew the answer. He wanted to be right here with Janice Conlon at 30 Rock. As much as he wanted to make partner and live up to everyone's expectations, he didn't want to become a fossil. The ever-observant Janice had been correct. He was afraid that he was already being marked for preservation. Brett McGarry: husband, partner, landmark.

"Let's get to Saks," he said flatly.

• • •

A salesperson on the main floor directed Brett and Janice to the Anne Klein department, which carried conservative suits and skirts suitable for a female attorney. As the saleswoman took Janice under her wing, Brett sat in a customer courtesy chair, pondering her words in the elevator at 30 Rock. At Cheshire Cheese the previous evening, he'd spoken of the future and the possibility of buying a home in the country. Today he should have been cutting down a tree in Pennsylvania, but he'd chosen to spend time with the firm's sexy iconoclast. Richard had told him to make sure she was properly attired, so it was technically part of his responsibility to the firm. The problem was that he shouldn't have been enjoying the task quite so much. The more serious concern was that Janice's reference to him as an evolving "landmark" had struck a chord within him.

Janice unexpectedly appeared from one of the fitting rooms. Wearing a blue blazer and skirt, she searched for the saleswoman to help locate a size eight. Janice wore no blouse, however, so that the partially buttoned blazer was low-cut and revealing. Glancing left and right, she attracted the attention of the Saks employee who was putting together her wardrobe and then turned to face Brett. "How do I look?" she asked, flashing an innocent smile.

"Uh, fine," Brett replied. He took a deep breath. Janice's blond hair fell across the navy blazer, and thanks to the bare skin below her neck, she created a stunning image that he knew would be hard to forget. He suspected that her failure to wear a blouse had been solely for his benefit.

The saleswoman and Janice returned to the business of choosing skirts, blazers, and business suits. An hour later, Brett was satisfied that apparel had been selected that would pass muster with the partners as well as prevent embarrassment in the courtroom. Janice's final choice, however, caught Brett by surprise. At the last minute, she'd added a lined red trench coat to her purchases, something that was flashy and more in keeping with her California *joie de vivre.*

Brett simply pulled out the firm's credit card and paid for the garments at the sales counter a few yards away. He knew the coat was her way of asserting independence despite the firm's insistence on conformity of dress, but he wasn't going to take the bait.

"How did I do?" Janice queried, once more dressed in her jeans and turtleneck.

"Mission accomplished," Brett said with little emotion, eyes lowered as he signed the receipt.

Some outfits would need alterations, but the two litigators nevertheless carried four shopping bags between them as they headed for the front doors.

"Hi, Brett," said a female voice.

Brett looked to his left to see Patti Hartlen approaching. He forced a weak smile. "Good afternoon, Mrs. Hartlen."

"Please, call me Patti." She aimed her very direct gaze at Brett, Janice, and then at Brett again. "Doing a little shopping?"

"This is Janice Conlon, our firm's newest litigator. Janice, this is Patti Hartlen." Brett was at a loss for words. How could he explain that he was helping another woman pick out clothes? "Did you and Jack enjoy your dinner at Cheshire Cheese last night?" he asked, groping for words to change the subject.

"Yes, it was excellent," Patti replied. She examined Janice carefully and then addressed Brett. "Tell your sweet wife hello for me."

"I certainly will," Brett said. "Now if you'll excuse me, I need to get to Mrs. John L. Strong's to pick up Dana's order for wine journals." He thought using his wife's name might signal that the shopping excursion was aboveboard.

"Certainly," Patti said. "Have a lovely day."

Brett smiled again and left the store, Janice following him.

"I really need to be going," Brett said. "I think you're set as far as the wardrobe goes."

"Yes, and thanks. But I'd like to tag along if you don't mind. Want some company?"

"That's very kind of you, but it's not necessary. I can—"

"You want me along," Janice said. "Trust me. You may not know it, but your life just changed after those few words with . . . Patti, is it?"

"What are you talking about?"

"Let's go," Janice said. "I'll explain later." She paused. "By the way, did you and Dana have a cozy little dinner last night?"

Brett made no reply. Eliza Doolittle had trumped the superiority of his modern-day Henry Higgins.

They left for the stationer's on the Upper East Side. Brett had a sinking feeling in his stomach. He no longer felt on top of his game.

Chapter Seven

Dana, Andrew, and Nina cruised southwest on I-78 towards Pipersville, Pennsylvania, the home of Winterberry Christmas Tree Farm. Nina Bramen had a heavy foot, and the Bug sped down the Interstate at seventy-five miles per hour. The antiques buyer for B Altman was in her early forties, had short, graying hair, and wore round, dark-rimmed glasses. As Brett had noted, Nina was a feminist, a bohemian by nature since her earliest days growing up on the Upper West Side. Unmarried, she had eclectic interests that sometimes bordered on the eccentric. Smart and opinionated, she was well-traveled, loved Peru, practiced Buddhism, and collected Asian art and objects, especially miniature Japanese sculptures called netsukes. She had found her strong voice and outspoken manner courtesy of the growing women's movement since it matched her fiercely independent mindset. She also had a kind heart and would do anything for a friend.

Dana always felt energized in Nina's presence. Though Dana was diplomatic and chose her words carefully, she nevertheless admired Nina's willingness to speak her mind openly and take chances both personally and professionally. In some ways, she was very much like Dana's mother, a woman who believed in candor and full disclosure. Nina was an honest and forthright individual, and Dana daydreamed of one day being able to set her agenda at B Altman with the same courage and tenacity as the woman who was now driving the VW while speaking animatedly about her travel plans for the near future. She would be journeying to India in search of exotic merchandise for the store's Indian extravaganza, a lavish event planned by Ira Neimark and Dawn Mello to compete with Bloomingdale's Retailing as Theater movement. The movement was the brainchild of Bloomingdale's Marvin Traub, who staged elaborate presentations such as China: Heralding the Dawn of a New Era. Typical extravaganzas featured fashion, clothing, food, and art from various regions of the world.

"I'll bring back enough items to make Bloomingdale's blush!" Nina said confidently. "And I'm not just talking sweaters, hats, and walking sticks. I'll stop first in the Himalayas and prowl the Landour Bazaar."

Andrew grinned at Dana, and she knew exactly what he was thinking. *I'll stop first in the Himalayas and prowl the Landour Bazaar.* Only Nina could utter such a phrase so matter-of-factly and be taken seriously.

"They have three-hundred-odd shops there that sell any and everything," Nina continued. "After that, I'll head to Jaipur just in time for its fairs and festivals filled with bright turbans, ethnic clothes, embroidered textiles, and jewelry. But that's just to set the stage! I intend to bring back other objects as well to really lend flavor to the show—reed baskets, woven carpets, mirrored ceramic elephants, antique brass accessories, Imari porcelain, miniature paintings, and—well, the list goes on. Ira will absolutely love it."

Dana was envious. A teen makeup section paled in comparison to such lavish presentations as the one Nina was going to help stage. The Retailing as Theater concept did not bring in revenue as much as highlight merchandise and whet a buyer's appetite, so why worry about a little free makeup?

Dana looked out the window as the miles drifted past and decided not to spoil such a beautiful day with worries about work or her meetings with Bob Campbell and Bea. She felt that her marriage had been given new hope the night before. Brett had spoken of making their dream of a weekend country home a reality, and if he were truly serious, his sentiments might bode well for starting a family. She needed to remember, as she'd done the night before, that his sacrifices for the firm had been difficult for both of them. Dana had been patient, and now that patience might finally pay off.

Meanwhile, Nina continued to list her itinerary, citing the exotic items from the other side of the world that she would deliver to Ira and Dawn for B Altman's own version of Retailing as Theater.

Andrew laughed at the use of the word "theater." "B Altman will have *plenty* of theater on Monday," he said, "when Estée Lauder arrives to secure a prime location in the new cosmetic department. I was told on Friday that she intends to bring along her husband Andrew as well as her sons, Leonard and Ronald, to make sure she gets exactly what she wants."

Nina laughed loudly. "Oh, she'll get what she wants all right. She's a determined woman." She glanced sideways at Dana. "And we know what a determined woman can accomplish, don't we?"

"Yes, we do," Dana replied. In Nina's presence, the restrictions imposed by Bea and Helen seemed almost trivial. Dana had experienced a single setback, but Nina was a reminder of what real determination and enthusiasm could accomplish.

"Her reputation precedes her," Andrew said. "Ira already told me to give Ms. Lauder whatever she wants."

"Sounds like a done deal," Dana said.

"That's why there's going to be a little drama on Monday," Andrew said, rubbing his hands together in anticipation. "The space she wants has already been promised to Charles of the Ritz."

"My money's on Estée Lauder," Nina proclaimed, pressing down on the accelerator. She smiled broadly and glanced at Andrew in the rearview mirror. "Anyone care to bet against me?"

"Not today or any other day, Nina!" he said.

• • •

Rows of trees extended far into the distance at the Winterberry Christmas Tree Farm. Andrew and Dana began strolling leisurely through the green, full Douglas and Fraser firs. Horses and sheep grazed in a distant rolling pasture, giving the farm a lovely bucolic atmosphere. Dana thought she would love to spend weekends in the country chasing after one or two McGarry offspring.

"Remember the size of my Beetle's roof," Nina reminded them. "Don't make me haul back a sequoia. I'm going to browse in a section over on the right while you two poke around. I smell something delicious!"

"I don't think there's *anything* Nina can't find," Andrew remarked.

Ignoring Andrew's comment, Dana slapped her forehead. "We should have rented a Lincoln. I guess we'll have to settle for a smaller tree. Oh well."

"How tall are your ceilings?" Andrew asked. "If I recall, they're ten feet."

"Eleven. I'll just add more garland on the mantel. The tree doesn't have to be the focal point of the living room this year." She shrugged and walked on.

Andrew touched Dana's arm, halting her progress as she continued down a row of Douglas firs. "Okay, Dana, what's on your mind? You're going to settle on a smaller tree, and Brett's working as usual. And yet you've been beaming all morning."

"Have I?"

Andrew nodded and then stepped back, his eyes round as quarters. "Hey, are you pregnant?"

Dana laughed. "No, silly. But maybe it's in the offing."

Andrew stopped dead in his tracks. "Maybe the fresh air has gone to my head, but something's different. You're thinking of having a baby? I can read your mind from across the store or across Manhattan. Tell me what's going on."

Dana related the conversation over dinner at Cheshire Cheese, Brett's caring demeanor, and the possibility that they might be buying a weekend home in Bedford.

"Sounds like a sea change is occurring in the McGarry household." Andrew put his arm around Dana's shoulder and gave her a squeeze. "I hope things work out. Lord knows you deserve it. And to think I might become Uncle Andrew one day soon."

Andrew didn't believe for a second that Brett had changed, but he wasn't going to spoil his friend's ebullient mood. He made a mental note to observe Dana's husband closely at their annual Christmas party the following week. If something in the relationship had changed, he'd spot it immediately.

"While we're on the subject," Dana said, "you've been in terribly good spirits yourself lately, Mr. Ricci. Is there a special someone in your life at present? Come on—it's your turn to share the wealth."

Andrew's brief hesitation caused Dana to wheel sideways and poke her friend in the chest with her finger. "I knew it!" she said, eyes wide. "Who is he?"

"At the moment, things are a bit . . . challenging, shall we say."

"Does that mean you've got some competition?" Dana asked.

"Aren't these trees magnificent?" Andrew asked.

"Okay, I get the message. I won't press you on it, but I hope this guy knows that he'd be crazy to pass you up."

"Time will tell," Andrew said. "Relationships can be complicated."

"This is the one!" cried Nina from fifteen yards away. "Dana, I've found your tree."

Dana and Andrew hurried to the row where Nina stood proudly, her arm motioning to a group of Concolor fir trees.

"Inhale!" Nina exhorted. "Can you smell that marvelous fragrance?"

"Fresh oranges," Andrew commented. "I'd love to take home every one," he said. "Every shape and size. They complement each other perfectly!"

"Exactly!" Nina declared resolutely, pointing to a five-foot Concolor fir. "And there's the one for Dana."

The short evergreen had long bluish-green needles. Though small, it was full and fragrant.

"It's got potential," Dana admitted.

"I'll send over a round table from the display department before the day is out," Andrew said. "With the right ornament on top—the perfect tree-topper—you'll have a tree that reaches within an inch or two of the ceiling. Use a nice tree skirt and spread some packages around and voilá—you'll have the illusion of height." Andrew pointed to his right eye with his index finger. "The seeing eye knows all."

Dana knew her friend could visualize a display in his mind's eye, complete with every accessory down to the last detail, and she had no doubt that his idea for the McGarry Christmas tree would work well. The Concolor fir was cut and secured to the top of Nina's VW.

"I'm famished," Nina said as they piled into the car. "How about lunch?"

"I know the perfect place," Dana chimed in. "Can we take River Road to New Hope?

Look for an ivy-covered stone house with a big copper pig over the door. It's called the Inn at Phillips Mill."

Nina pressed the clutch with her left foot and threw the Bug into gear. "River Road it is!"

As the VW meandered along the road, Dana recalled what Andrew had said a few moments earlier about the Concolor firs: *I'd love to take home every one. Every shape and size.* The words gave her a sudden flash of inspiration about her dilemmas at B Altman. Maybe she could think outside the box after all. Isn't that what made Nina so distinctive—the ability to see possibilities that no one else could?

Dana didn't know whether it was because of the fresh country air or Nina's infectious enthusiasm, but an idea had materialized out of nowhere, and she thought that Bob and Bea might just go for it. The day was turning out to be the best in a long time.

Chapter Eight

"So what is this earth-shaking revelation you have for me?" Brett asked impatiently as he and Janice walked towards Mrs. John L. Strong on Madison Avenue.

"Just get your wife's . . . wine things, or whatever they are, and then we'll talk."

Brett and Janice entered the store, which provided custom luxury stationery and related products. A legendary establishment in New York City since 1929, Mrs. John L. Strong created its own cotton paper, mixed its own ink, and hand-engraved its stationery according to customer preference. As always, the store was orderly and quiet, its ambience professional and upscale.

"What exactly is this place?" asked Janice, her head turning in several directions as she examined the sedate store. "It looks like an antique shop. Is it safe to touch anything in here?"

"It's exactly what the sign outside says it is," Brett replied. "A stationery store. It has provided stationery, announcements, and gifts for royalty and seven presidential families. It has catered to clients such as the Duke and Duchess of Windsor, Diana Vreeland, Jackie Onassis, Gloria Vanderbilt, and the Rockefellers. That's the short list."

Janice gestured to the display cases on either side of them. "So what are *you* doing here? Dana grooming you for the White House? Wow, she really does have it all laid out."

"Dana picks out gifts for the partners each Christmas," he explained, once again ignoring her sarcasm. "This year she ordered wine journals."

"Wine *what?*"

"Wine journals."

An impeccably dressed man approached Brett and offered a welcoming smile. "Good afternoon, Mr. McGarry. So good to see you again. I assume you're here to pick up your wife's order."

"That's correct, Mr. Stiles."

"I'll be back in a moment, Mr. McGarry."

"And what are wine journals, President McGarry?" Janice asked.

Brett rolled his eyes and pointed to a leather-bound journal on display. "It's for saving wine labels and writing down information on grapes, taste, cellaring, and vintages for wines people have a special fondness for. Don't try to tell me you don't have wine connoisseurs in California, home to Napa Valley and hundreds of vineyards."

"I know merlot from cabernet," Janice said dryly, "and I also know that most people on the East Coast regard California wines as beneath their palates. But saving labels from favorite beverages? That sounds like a hobby for high school nerds who also belong to the chess club. If I like a wine, I'll drink it and buy it again, end of story." She paused as she looked around the store, studying its products. "Is this another grand McGarry tradition—picking out scrapbooks for rich people? And why can't you buy your own presents for the partners? Just get them a great bottle of scotch so they can get snookered and have a good time with the missus."

Brett tried to hold back laughter but couldn't. "I guess that would be simpler, wouldn't it."

"Absolutely! They can drink single malt and then sing the Yale Whiffenpoof Song before doing the deed."

Heads in the shop were turning, and Brett had to lower his gaze and bite his lip to keep from laughing further. Janice's remarks had conjured up several entertaining images in his mind, and he found her humor not so much irreverent as just plain funny.

"Here's your order," Mr. Stiles said, bringing out Dana's order from the rear of the store. "Everything is gift wrapped just as Mrs. McGarry requested. Please don't hesitate to call if you have any questions."

"Excellent," Brett said. "Merry Christmas, Mr. Stiles."

"And to you and Mrs. McGarry." Mr. Stiles took notice of Janice but his demeanor remained entirely professional. At Mrs. John L. Strong, all customers were considered above reproach and were treated accordingly. The shop dealt in quality and service, and an inquisitive look from an employee would have been beneath the establishment's standards.

Brett and Janice left the stationers and stood on the street.

"Let's go to the Polo Lounge for a drink," she said. "We have a few things to discuss in private."

"Why the Polo?" Brett asked.

"Because it's expensive and you're paying."

Brett took a deep breath. "If you insist."

"I most certainly do."

Brett glanced at his watch and decided he could spare a few minutes to listen to whatever Janice deemed to be so urgent. He presumed the matter involved running into Patti Hartlen.

• • •

Brett and Janice sat at a table in the rear of the Polo Lounge at the Westbury Hotel on Madison Avenue and 69th Street.

"I'll have a glass of house cabernet," Janice told their waiter.

"Just coffee for me," Brett said, his arms folded defensively.

"I'd rather have a Georges de la Tour cab, private reserve," Janice declared, "but what's the point if we're not sharing a bottle."

Brett's jaw dropped.

"Don't act so surprised, Mr. Landmark. I know more than people give me credit for. It's just that I don't place a lot of stock in facades and traditions. Consider the wine journals, for example. They're part of yet another tradition, one that I'm sure will be carried on until you retire from the firm. It's just more preservation. Preserve your precious wine labels and then preserve your routines until you turn into stone. Is this really how you want to live your life? I mean, it's all well and good for some people, I suppose, but as a lifestyle, it would leave me cold, as in dead. If that makes me a bad girl from the West Coast with no breeding or social amenities, then so be it."

"I get what you're saying about turning into a landmark," Brett said, looking across the table at his colleague's deep blue eyes. "But even partners at law firms have skeletons in their closets. Nobody's a Boy Scout. Why did you imply back at Saks that my life is going to radically change?"

"Because Patti Hartlen is a very astute observer, and women have been known to gossip."

Brett shook his head as the waiter brought a glass of cabernet and a cup of coffee to the table.

"I've been thinking about that little run-in with Patti. Dana and I don't even know those people. The meeting at Saks was awkward, but there's no harm done."

"What if I told you that Jack Hartlen has a meeting with Patrick Denner next week?"

Brett cocked his head and frowned. Patrick Denner was a corporate associate at Davis, Konen and Wright and a friend of Brett's. "I haven't heard anything about such a meeting," he countered, sounding nonplussed. "You've heard of the Hartlens?"

"It's just a tidbit I picked up," said Janice. "Ears to the ground, as they say. I don't know any particulars, but if the Hartlens plan on retaining the firm's services, then sooner or later they're going to see you or me, possibly together. Whether or not Patti will draw any conclusions is anybody's guess. We were leaving the ladies department together. Makes for interesting speculation."

"There *aren't* any conclusions to draw."

"That's irrelevant when it comes to gossip, and nothing will sink the chances of a partnership faster than salacious gossip. You also might not be picking up any more wine journals for Dana if Patti's the kind to talk." Janice raised her eyebrows seductively as she spoke slowly and deliberately. "But I can provide some cover, shall we say, to prevent any scandal."

"I'd appreciate that," Brett said. "Do whatever you can."

"Ah, my dear Brett, you can be so naïve. Everything comes with a price tag."

Brett narrowed his eyes. "Which is?"

"I want you. In the short term, that is. No kids or picket fences for me. Just a little innocent fun. And don't tell me that you're not attracted to me, or you wouldn't be sitting here. I saw the way you laughed at my remarks back at Mrs. John Q. Whatever's shop."

"You're an opportunistic woman. This is blackmail."

"Is it? You want me with every fiber of your being."

Brett sipped his coffee and thought of the years he'd positioned himself to make partner. He also thought of Dana and how she trusted him. If the Hartlens became suspicious, then his career and marriage might well be in jeopardy. Janice's scenario was a bit far-fetched, but Dana had bumped into Jack, and he had just bumped into Patti. What were the odds? He'd seen more than one career falter due to innuendo or even an ill-timed remark. Should he do what Janice wanted for a month or two to preserve his home and career? Would it really hurt anything as long as he was discreet?

"What kind of protection are you offering?" he asked, hardly believing that the conversation had progressed this far.

"I can get men's attention rather easily. If I'm rumored to be dating someone other than you, people will learn about it and you'll be in the clear. Since we work together, we can schedule a little time for ourselves once in a while without suspicion. Call it a little romantic sleight of hand."

Brett took a deep breath as Janice sipped her cabernet. "It's a no-win situation."

"No, it's just the opposite. You get to have your cake and eat it, too. At heart, that's what Brett McGarry wants out of life. You want it all."

Brett looked sideways and exhaled slowly. "I need to think about this."

Brett excused himself to go to the restroom. He'd broken out in a cold sweat and needed to rinse his face and dry off. A few hours earlier, he'd been happy and confident, content to eat his honey buns and read the *Times*. Now a chance encounter with a virtual stranger had changed everything. Exactly how far was he willing to go to save his career and spare Dana a lot of nasty rumors that she might be inclined to believe?

He exited the restroom to find Janice standing in the dim lights of the dressing room area, empty except for them. She put her arms around his neck and pressed her lips softly against his. He made no attempt to pull away.

"Was that so bad?" Janice asked, stroking Brett's cheek.

"I need to get home," he said, clearing his throat nervously. "I'll leave first. We can't be seen leaving together."

Brett left as Janice smiled broadly. "He's already got the vocabulary down," she said.

Chapter Nine

Nina steered her VW into the gravel parking area on the side of an ivy-covered stone edifice that, when it was built in 1750, had been nothing more than a barn with an adjoining piggery. The three B Altman employees had arrived at the Inn at Phillips Mill. The pre-Revolutionary War estate in Bucks County was now a charming inn with period rooms and fine French dining.

"It's beautiful scenery," Nina remarked, "but give me the city on a day-to-day basis. Or a foreign country with a bustling population and hundreds of side streets lined with shops, stalls, and artisans. I like to feel the pulse of what's going on in the world. I need color, movement, variety."

"What I need now," said Andrew, "is a nice meal and a glass of wine."

"The wine's on me," Nina said. "I was introduced to some lovely vintages last year when I visited the Alsace region."

The trio was escorted to a private dining room with a stone fireplace and a roaring fire. Nina ordered poached salmon, Andrew the baked cod, and Dana the crab salad. Nina ordered a bottle of chardonnay to go with the seafood.

"Nineteen seventy-five has been designated as International Women's Year," Nina said, moving straight from the menu to the topic of feminism. "It's going to be our year, Dana. Thank God New York will soon have a woman as Lieutenant Governor. Mary Anne Krupsak is fabulous! She has already taken a stand for us. She won't attend the Democratic Party's midterm convention because there won't be enough women and minorities in attendance, nor will there be balanced geographical representation. She'll be working closely with Bella Abzug, my congressional representative on the West Side. I know her well, and, of course, Betty Friedan. Betty started the whole idea of an international conference when she met with Kurt Waldheim at the UN last January. The topics we're going to take on will be all-encompassing: equality in the workplace, voting rights, marriage equality, and reproductive rights, to name just a few. We're shaking things up!"

The wine had arrived, and Nina raised her glass in a toast. "To women everywhere!"

"Indeed," said Andrew, lifting his glass.

"This place has an almost hypnotic charm," Dana remarked after the toast. "I think I'm going to ask for a tour when we finish lunch. I bet the rooms are adorable."

"We've already made great strides, thanks to the UN report last year on sexist attitudes around the world," Nina continued without missing a beat. "The report found that the universal image of women was either that of a sex idol needing masculine approval or a merry homemaker fussing over dust mops and laundry. And who do we have to thank for that? The ad men of Madison Avenue! Now that we have all this good information, we can develop a plan of action! We won't be second-class citizens any longer!"

Lunch arrived, and Nina continued to talk about Betty Friedan, her idol and a woman who many considered to be the founder of the modern women's movement.

"Friedan's *The Feminine Mystique* should be given to every college freshman woman!" Nina said, her voice growing louder with each sip of chardonnay. "They'll quickly learn that the Mrs. degree they are frantically working towards is not all it's cracked up to be!"

Andrew smiled, looking at Dana and then at Nina. "We're behind you, Nina. It's good to get these things off your chest, but maybe we should speak a little lower. I think the waiter has been giving us the eye for the past few minutes."

"I'll tell you what I got off my chest today, Andrew. Clothing! I'm not wearing a bra! What a symbol of oppression, as if women need to wear harnesses. Pour me another glass of wine please."

"I think I'll go to the ladies room," Dana said, whispering to Andrew. "She's all yours."

Andrew winked, indicating that he'd try to calm the indefatigable and slightly tipsy Ms. Bramen.

Dana smiled at Nina's passion as she asked the waiter if someone were available to give her a tour of the guest rooms. Brett's birthday was in January, and Dana thought she would surprise him by booking a romantic weekend getaway. It would be a harbinger of good things to come and an excellent way to ease into spending time away from the city. The country life was growing on Dana by the hour. It was exactly what she and Brett needed on a regular basis: some quiet time when neither the store nor the firm could impinge on their life together.

Dana thought that the rooms were irresistible. Her favorite had a brass bed, a colonial writing desk, a window seat with a view of the river, and a ceiling covered with tiny print fabric to give a canopied effect. It was cozy, warm, and romantic. She dreamed of a snowbound Sunday morning in January and breakfast in bed with her husband.

Back at the desk, she learned that the inn was near the James A. Michener Museum and the Peddler's Village, which had seventy specialty shops. Hot air balloon rides were also available just a few miles away. Before returning to the dining room, Dana asked the proprietress if she would please translate the writing over the fireplace. A quotation by the Roman poet Horace, it read, "Ille terrarum mihi praeter omnes angulus ridet." Moved when she heard the meaning—"This corner of earth smiles for me beyond all others"—Dana knew she had found the idyllic getaway and booked the weekend in January without hesitation.

Dana rejoined Andrew and Nina, who were waiting at the front desk of the inn. Andrew had paid the check and convinced Nina to surrender the keys to the Beetle.

"I feel perfectly capable of driving," Nina declared. "The brisk air outside will clear my head immediately. I once drank my fill of rice wine in Burma and then traveled ten miles through the jungle on an elephant."

Andrew didn't doubt Nina's Burma adventure for one second, but he still thought it best that he drive back to Manhattan. Five minutes later, they were once more inside the VW, Nina already sleeping in the backseat, her head tilted against the small side window. Andrew put the Bug into reverse, eased it away from the other parked cars, and then pulled onto River Road.

"Did you reserve a room?" he asked Dana.

"How did you know I was going to do that?"

"Because I'm Andrew. You didn't take that tour for nothing. A weekend here will be bait to get Brett to commit to the country."

"Hey, he was the one who brought up the idea of having a retreat in Bedford," Dana conceded. "I'm just trying to give him a nudge towards domesticity."

She turned around in her seat before the first bend in the road, taking a final look at the Inn at Phillips Mill before it disappeared from view. January couldn't arrive fast enough, she thought.

"One step at a time," Andrew said, as if reading her mind. "We've got a tree to get in the stand today before we go to Lenôtre to select the hors d'oeuvres for your Christmas party."

"So we do," Dana said, facing forward again.

For the first time in many months, that's exactly what Dana was doing: facing forward.

Chapter Ten

John Cirone and his son Johnny entered the opulent marble lobby of the Sherry-Netherland a thirty-eight-story brick and limestone hotel located on the corner of Fifth Avenue and East 59th Street. Johnny was a tall, handsome man who loved to work out and play sports whenever he had the chance. Touch football, squash, tennis, swimming—he loved to work up a sweat, compete, or just have fun, and his muscular, well-defined physique showed it.

"Dad," Johnny said as they stepped into the elevator, "we must have looked at a dozen apartments today. Did any of them appeal to you at all? You find fault with nearly every one. This search for the perfect digs could go on for weeks."

John shrugged nonchalantly. "A few seemed okay. Maybe I'll have a second look at some in a day or two."

"Do you really need to move to the city? You're less than forty-five minutes away as it is."

"I need to be near my beloved opera house," John said as they exited the elevator and entered his suite. "The situation at the Met is dire. At last week's directors meeting, some members suggested we cut the length of next season. I almost had a heart attack. We're expecting a nine-million-dollar deficit this year, and union contracts run out in July. If there was a single room for me at the Metropolitan Opera, that's where I would live until this mess is straightened out."

Johnny knew that the real reason his father was looking at apartments in Manhattan was because he'd grown increasingly lonely in the large family house on Long Island. He'd never completely gotten over the death of Johnny's mother, but he was ambivalent about moving from the family home and hence his lukewarm assessment of the apartments they'd seen. Johnny couldn't blame him because he, too, had not been able to completely overcome the grief of losing his mother. She'd been the glue that held the Cirone family together, a strong, loving woman who always had the right words for any situation. His sister Phoebe, who had a more stoic disposition, had been the only one to heal completely, and Johnny suspected that her ability to do so came from her absorption in the demanding cardiology fellowship.

"You have your work cut out, Dad, but I know you'll turn things around. The Met has an impressive board, and if there's anyone who will know how to negotiate with the unions, it's you. As for the apartment, however, everything we've looked at is near St. Thomas More Church. Maybe we should expand the search a little."

St. Thomas More was on East 89th Street, between Madison Avenue and Park Avenue.

"That's the church I like, Johnny. The priests there give sermons that speak to my heart, and we *always* should listen to our hearts. That's where true wisdom resides."

"Are you trying to tell me something?" Johnny asked with a grin. He knew his father was attempting to broach a subject, either about his impending wedding or his lapsed church attendance.

"Perhaps. Where was your heart when you were growing up, Johnny?"

"With you and Mom and Phoebe."

"And?"

"Okay, I get it. With God."

"But where is it now?"

Johnny hesitated as he walked to the window of his father's room. "God let Mom die," he answered, his tone now somber. "I find that hard to accept even now."

"Nobody misses your mother more than I do, Johnny. But we can't blame bad things on God, as if he were some kind of puppet master. It was her time to go. I ask God a hundred times a day why that was the case, but it's not for me to know the answer."

Johnny turned back to face his father. "I guess that's the difference between us. I *do* need to know."

Johnny sat in a chair on the far side of the room as his father freshened up in the bathroom. Johnny *was* listening to his heart. He was aware that people believed that he'd gotten engaged to Suzanne to numb the pain of his mother's passing, but he genuinely loved his fiancée. In fact, his heart had more invested in his forthcoming marriage than it did in the House of Cirone, although he would never hurt his father by openly confessing such a sentiment. He didn't hate his job, but neither was he passionate about it.

"How are things with Suzanne?" John asked when he returned to the bedroom.

"What kind of question is *that*?" Johnny asked defensively. "We're getting married, for God's sake. Listen, I know you're having a hard time with the idea of an Episcopalian ceremony, but the Farnsworths' traditions are as important to them as ours are to us."

"You're right, of course. Sorry, Johnny. The question just came out wrong. You have to admit that it's all been rather sudden."

"I guess."

John remained silent for several seconds, rubbing his forehead as if considering some weighty matter.

"Johnny," his father said at last, "God's ways are beyond knowing. They're not *our* ways. Events in our lives can be extremely painful sometimes." He paused as he withdrew a manila envelope from the writing desk. "I want you to look at something."

Johnny was growing frustrated. There was something on his father's mind, and he wished he would just blurt it out.

"What are you getting at, Dad? I really need to get going."

"Just a little business, son. It'll only take a few minutes."

"Okay, but it will have to be quick. I'll read it more carefully later." He looked up at his father. "I could do this at the office, you know."

Johnny opened the clasp of the legal-sized envelope, removed a sheaf of papers, and studied them for several moments. John paced the room as his son looked at the documents. Johnny's interest was suddenly piqued as he read several papers a second time. At the end of ten minutes, he looked up, obviously disturbed.

"This can't be right," he said, disbelief straining his usually calm voice. "These numbers just don't add up. This financial report makes no sense at all, and yet my name's on these documents. What should I do?"

"What should *we* do, Johnny. We're family, and we rely on each other, but the first thing we do is pray."

Johnny stood. "Yeah, whatever. May I take these with me?" he asked, returning the financial report to the envelope. "I'll bring them to work on Monday."

"Sure, Johnny. Take time to study them. If you need to talk, just call me."

Johnny, his face pale, left his father's suite without bothering to say goodbye.

John sat on the edge of his bed and looked at a picture of Lena that he kept on the nightstand. He'd weathered the storm of her death two years earlier, and he'd weather this one as well. He wasn't so sure about Johnny, however. He suspected it was going to be a tough few weeks.

"Pray for Johnny, Lena." He picked up the picture, kissed it, and returned it to the nightstand.

"It's up to you, Lord," he said. "It always is."

Chapter Eleven

Patti and Jack Hartlen, together with Jack's parents, were also staying at the Sherry-Netherland. Whistling a tune from Sinatra's "Fly Me to the Moon," Jack was donning a gray business suit while his wife looked at apartment listings supplied by their realtor.

Jack was a tall, lanky man in his early thirties with slightly thinning brown hair and angular cheekbones. His laidback manner matched his pale blue eyes and measured speech that had the barest hint of a Texas accent.

"Where are you off to?" Patti asked, her index finger running down the listings.

"I'm going downtown to see Patrick Denner," he replied while slipping on the coat of his gray Brooks Brothers suit.

"I thought your meeting with Patrick was next week."

"It is, but we thought we'd get together today and tie up a few loose ends. It's been a hectic few months, hasn't it? Are you getting used to New York, honey?"

Patti sighed as she brushed away strands of hair from her forehead. "I can't deny that I'll miss Houston. We have so many wonderful friends there, but I'm sure we'll make new ones. Yes, New York is growing on me after making so many trips here with your parents. I can't wait until we get an apartment though."

Jack worked for his father, Ralph Hartlen, the CEO of Hartlen Oil. The company was opening an office in New York City after the first of the year. Rumors of an impending oil shortage were rampant in the business community, and there was even talk of an oil embargo by certain Arab states that would stop the flow of oil from the Mideast to the United States and Great Britain. Ralph had decided it was time to better position his company if foreign oil production was going to tighten up in the foreseeable future, although Hartlen Oil also had several subsidiary companies. The main subsidiary, Hartlen Response, was run by Jack, who had taken the lead in laying the groundwork for opening an office in Manhattan. Jack's company had certain techniques and equipment—cutting edge technology—not utilized by any other oil company, and Ralph thought that the equipment was going to be needed soon if the movement of oil around the globe was going to strategically change in the next year or two. The techniques and hardware were a well-guarded secret in the oil community, and Ralph had naturally deemed it necessary to obtain first-rate legal representation as a natural part of the move north. Competitors would almost surely attempt to copy the proprietary technology.

Jack picked up his black leather briefcase and headed for the door when Patti spoke up.

"Hold on a minute, Jack." Her tone sounded foreboding.

Jack turned and saw Patti approaching, a worried look on her face. "Is something the matter?" he asked.

Patti drew near, her penetrating violet eyes examining Jack's face and then his shirt collar. Her right hand reached for his tie and straightened the knot. "There," she said, patting her husband on the chest. "It's perfect."

"Nothing gets past you," he said with a grin. "What would I do without you?"

"You won't ever have to find out," she replied. "You're stuck with me."

"Which is my good fortune." He kissed her on the lips and started again for the door.

"Jack?"

He turned around a second time. "Yes?"

Patti was about to speak but stopped, closing her red, sensuous lips. "Nothing. Have a good meeting with Patrick."

Jack gave his wife a second kiss and this time made it through the door.

Patti walked to the window and looked at the crowded city that would soon be her home. She had considered calling Cheshire Cheese to get the phone number of Brett and Dana McGarry since they seemed like the logical place to begin in forming new friendships in New York City. But she'd noticed something unusual in her exchange with Brett at Saks earlier that afternoon. He had obviously been shopping, but not with his wife, which is what she had almost mentioned to her husband moments earlier. As Jack had pointed out, nothing got past her.

Patti walked to the sitting area of the suite, poured herself a cup of tea she'd ordered from room service, and sat in a wingback chair. She hadn't completely adjusted to New York yet, and maybe she was being paranoid. Regardless, Brett was a virtual stranger, and his activities weren't any of her business.

On Fifth Avenue, Jack glanced quickly at his wristwatch and then at the nearest street corner. The offices of Davis, Konen and Wright were downtown. He then pivoted, rapidly walking towards Madison Avenue, looking for a taxi to take him north.

Chapter Twelve

Thanks to a call Andrew had made from the Inn at Phillips Mill while Dana was touring the guestrooms, the round table and its base were waiting in the lobby of 77 Park Avenue when Andrew and Dana returned from the country. Nina had awakened with a clear head and driven off into the heavy holiday traffic, leaving Andrew to carry the tree inside and ride up to Dana's apartment with the table via the freight elevator.

Andrew stood the tree upright in the living room and told Dana, who was holding Wills, to step back in order to render her opinion. "So what do you think?" he asked. "Did Nina pick a winning tree?"

Dana nodded. "We've never had a tree that was this perfect from every angle. I think Brett will love it."

"Then let's get it in the stand," he said. "But I'm warning you—I can put a window display together far easier than I can get a Christmas tree to remain straight in a stand. Darn things have given me trouble ever since I was a kid."

Five minutes later, Andrew and Dana laughed heartily as the tree tilted left and right each time Andrew tightened the wing nuts of the stand.

"Never fails," Andrew said. "You would think that a five-foot tree wouldn't be so much trouble."

"It's *supposed* to be trouble," Dana commented. "It's high up on the list of things that contribute to Christmas stress, like last minute shopping, tipsy relatives, and assembling a kid's bike on Christmas Eve."

Andrew raised his eyebrows and shot Dana a look, which she interpreted immediately.

"Yes," she said, "I hope that one day in a few years Brett will be sitting on the floor with a hundred bicycle parts scattered beneath a Christmas tree. He'll try to read the Chinese directions unsuccessfully and then muddle through as best he can."

"And this will all happen in Bedford, right?"

"That's the blueprint," she said. "Dream big or don't dream at all."

"Uncle Andrew will be there if Brett needs a helping hand," he said, lifting the tree onto the table, where Dana had draped her grandmother's green and gold Fortuny tablecloth. "I wouldn't mind playing Santa's helper for your kids. Meanwhile, I've got to run some quick errands. Meet you at Lenôtre in two hours?"

"Two it is," Dana said.

Andrew left, and Dana stood back even farther to admire the Concolor fir. She thought it was probably the prettiest tree to ever grace their apartment. Its beauty more than compensated for its small size. Nina's VW had been a blessing in disguise. It had forced Dana to think outside the box, and now she had the perfect Christmas tree in her home, freshly cut from the pastures of Bucks County.

Dana felt that it was going to be a good week. In fact, she was certain of it.

• • •

Chateau France, also called Lenôtre, was a dimly lit patisserie with a rich patina on its paneled walls. The small restaurant had brightly lit display cases to highlight delicate pastries, and the European setting was inviting to busy New Yorkers who enjoyed lingering over coffee and an afternoon sweet.

"Did you get your chores done?" Dana asked as she spotted Andrew upon entering the patisserie.

"It was a productive afternoon," Andrew replied.

"You're happy as a clam, Andrew Ricci. You're a man in love."

"And you, Dana McGarry, have your eyes on a country home and taking care of rug rats. Just make sure the rugs come from B Altman's carpet section on the fifth floor."

"That's a given. Now what shall we select for the Christmas party? I was thinking of a mousseline of lobster, a truffled pate, salmon trout tartare, and assorted tartes flambées."

"It's a good thing you asked me to come along and help. First, what about quiche? Are you having a Christmas party or a clambake?"

"A dreadful oversight," Dana said with fake dramatic flair. "Brett hates it, but if he's going to buy a house in Bedford, then he can handle the quiche as well."

"Next, he'll be baking bread and attending Lamaze classes," Andrew joked. "But back to the matter at hand. You have to include gougeres with blue cheese. I insist."

Dana put her hands on her hips and shook her head. "The runner has stumbled. Gougeres with gruyere or nothing at all," she said emphatically.

"Very well," said Andrew. "Boring, boring, boring."

The two friends burst into laughter at the imagined gravity of their conversation.

"We haven't done that in a long time," Andrew observed.

"*Too* long," Dana agreed. "Maybe it's because we're both in good spirits today."

Andrew looked around the patisserie while Dana placed her order. He supposed she was right. He was indeed happy, but he also knew that sometimes happiness came with a price. He wondered if Dana had learned that lesson yet.

Dana rejoined him and they were about to leave Lenôtre when Andrew took his friend's hand and halted. "Come over here for a minute," he told Dana. "I want you to meet a friend of mine. I hired him as a consultant for the installation of the store's American Designer's Gallery."

They walked to a table in the corner where Andrew's friend was sitting with a woman with her back to them. The man looked up, smiled, and stood. "Andrew Ricci! How are you?"

"Great," Andrew said. "Max, this is Dana McGarry. Dana, this is Max Helm, Curator of American Decorative Arts at the Metropolitan Muscum."

"It's a pleasure to meet you, Dana," Max said. "I'd like you both to meet my friend, Rosamond Bernier."

Bernier turned in her chair, smiled, and shook their hands. Dana's heart skipped a beat as she stood inches away from one of New York's most glamorous and adored women.

Rosamond Bernier was a world-renowned art lecturer who was a close friend of some of the most important artists of the twentieth century. When Henri Matisse, for example, was bedridden, he invited Rosamond to his home to show her his new creations from miniature cut-outs. Picasso had urged her to travel to Barcelona and report on a collection of his early work. Her interviews regularly appeared on television, and in 1955 she co-founded the art magazine *L'OEIL*, which featured the works of the masters of the School of Paris. Leonard Bernstein had proclaimed that she had a gift for instant communication, and she had lectured at the Louvre in Paris. She'd begun a career as a lecturer in 1971 and gave yearly sold-out lectures at the Metropolitan Museum of Art. Andrew and Dana had attended her series without fail for the past three years, hanging on her every word. Though seated, she was a tall slender woman. She had a pretty, oval face, an aquiline nose, and a broad, welcoming smile.

"It's an honor, Ms. Bernier," Dana said. "Andrew and I never miss your lectures, and we loved your talk last week on Picasso. And I absolutely adored the Balenciaga that you were wearing—my favorite this season."

"How very kind of you to say so," Bernier said in her inimitable and cultivated voice. "I never tire of talking about Picasso. He helped launch our magazine with his Albrecht Altdorfer drawings based on *The Body of St. Sebastian Recovered from the Water*. What I always found so interesting is that he had no interest in flowers, unlike Matisse," she said with all of the ease she exhibited while lecturing.

"Didn't his dark moods ever intimidate you?" Andrew asked.

"Not really, although they were definitely a challenge. Nor did he always respond to correspondence with punctuality. Quite to the contrary. By the way, I hope you're coming to my last lecture on Tuesday?"

"We wouldn't miss it," Dana replied enthusiastically.

"Then you both must join me at the after-party at Café des Artistes. It's an enjoyable way to end the season."

"We'd love to join you," said Andrew. "We'll be there, and thank you so much."

Andrew said goodbye to Max, and he left Lenôtre with Dana.

"Now *that* doesn't happen every day," Dana remarked on the sidewalk. "It feels like we were granted an audience with royalty."

"New York royalty," Andrew commented. "This has been an incredible day. We found a great Christmas tree, Nina publicly announced that she wasn't wearing a bra, and we just got invited to Rosamond Bernier's after-party."

Dana gave Andrew a big hug as the two parted.

"Thanks for all the help today, Andrew."

"No thanks necessary. Tell your parents hi for me."

"I will."

Ten minutes later Dana stepped into the lobby of her apartment building. She was ready for a relaxing evening at home with family. It would be the perfect end to the perfect day.

Chapter Thirteen

Brett had walked around his neighborhood for more than an hour as he tried to clear his head. It was late evening, and the dark sky overhead was awash with the bright lights of Manhattan. Still, he felt a welcome anonymity as he blended in with other pedestrians as he thought of Janice's proposal and her brazen kiss at the Polo Lounge. He wasn't sure yet how he would handle the situation, although he had an uneasy feeling that Janice was going to leave him with very few options. If he didn't give her the fling she desired, she could ostensibly sabotage his hopes of partnership by allowing gossip to spread through the office, even if she jeopardized her own position with the firm in the process. She might even openly flirt with him. If she were fired, she would no doubt land on her feet at another firm, whether in New York or back in California. She was holding all the cards, and her freewheeling mindset made her all the more unpredictable. He was drawn to her unpredictability, of course, which was a fact he preferred not to think about.

He looked at his watch and realized that he needed to get home since Dana's parents were coming for dinner. He sighed and put his hands in his topcoat pockets. He didn't feel like sitting down and making small talk, and he was well aware that his mother-in-law had a penetrating gaze that rivaled that of the astute Patti Hartlen. It was going to be a very long evening.

He was within six blocks of 77 Park Avenue when he decided that he would take everyone out to eat. The popular folksinger Mary O'Dowd was playing at the Irish Pavilion. It would be best to have everyone focus their attention on the comely and melodic O'Dowd rather than on his nervous demeanor. It would be a classic case of a magician's use of misdirection, and he needed a bit of magic right now to conceal thoughts he found overwhelming. Until he could get Dana's family to the Pavilion, however, he would try his best to appear relaxed and use a little humor. He would pour a scotch, talk with his in-laws, and pretend to be enjoying the holiday season.

He turned a corner and thought yet again of how Janice's lips had felt against his. They'd been warm and inviting, and the kiss had not been unwelcome. Its clandestine nature had caused his heart to beat faster—had caused him to feel alive in a way that he hadn't for several years. Maybe Janice was right. He wanted to have his cake and eat it too. He wanted it all. And it wasn't as if a fling had been *his* idea. The affair was being forced upon him. Wasn't it up to all good husbands to protect their families and jobs by whatever means possible?

Of course it was. Deciding the matter was as simple as looking up precedents in case law. His legal mind told him he was on solid footing.

Chapter Fourteen

Dana found her apartment quiet except for the barking of Wills, who met her at the front door, anxious for his evening walk. Using a different leash, she took him down Park Avenue for a few minutes and then returned to her living room to look at the tree again and recall the pleasant excursion to Pennsylvania with the eccentric but loveable Nina. She thought of Nina's words from earlier in the day: *we know what a determined woman can accomplish, don't we?* Dana would not be fazed by Bea or Helen on Monday morning. She'd done good work and would continue to do so. And she was determined to find a way to keep the teen contest from becoming a farce.

Phil and Virginia arrived fifteen minutes later, and they brought a special guest: Dana's younger brother Matthew. He was a wiry young man who wore his thick brown hair over his ears, and his tan stood in stark contrast to the fair complexions of his parents and sister.

"Matthew!" Dana cried as she gave him a hug. "I didn't think we'd see you until Christmas."

Brett and Dana were with the McGarry family on Thanksgiving.

"I'm meeting some friends downtown later this evening," he replied, "so I thought I'd tag along with Mom and Dad and join you for dinner. I turned in my term papers early, so I don't head back to school until next Saturday. I'll be at your party Thursday night." He turned as Wills' barking demanded his attention.

"Wills!" Matthew exclaimed. "I'm glad to see you, too!" Matthew dropped to his knees and began playing with the excited spaniel.

"Uncle John hasn't called you, has he?" Virginia asked Dana.

Dana frowned. "No. Why?"

"Because he's getting more upset by the day over Johnny marrying Suzanne Farnsworth. The Episcopalian ceremony is like a stake through his heart, plus Suzanne sent out the wedding invitations earlier than expected. Uncle John is beside himself."

"He was hoping that you might speak to Johnny," Phil added. "Uncle John isn't even sure he's going to attend the wedding."

"That's awful, but what could I possibly say to Johnny?" asked Dana. "He's a grown man. I'm not going to get involved in his affairs, although I can understand Uncle John's feelings all too well. I don't think he's missed Sunday mass in his entire life, and he's in the pews on weekdays as well whenever he has a chance. And let's don't forget, Mom, that you insisted that Brett and I have a high mass with three priests to ensure that the marriage was going to be rock solid, as if the ceremony were an insurance policy. I feel sorry for poor Uncle John, but I don't see how I could be of help."

"That's just what I told John," Phil said. "No good can come from interfering with Johnny's plans. All that meddling would turn into a soap opera."

"You could send him to Hawaii for a couple of weeks," Matthew suggested, laughing. "I know a few girls on the beach who might make him think twice."

"I don't think so, little brother," Dana said, kissing Matthew on the cheek.

Not surprisingly, Virginia privately thought Matthew had a good idea. She sighed as she thought of her daughter's wedding eight years earlier. She had indeed arranged for a solemn ceremony in the Catholic Church to impress upon Brett the seriousness of the vows he was taking. To this day, she wasn't sure that he had gotten the message. In retrospect, she might not have minded if someone had taken him on an extended tropical vacation like the one Matthew was jokingly recommending.

Dana noted the concerned look on her mother's face but decided not to disclose details of her dinner at Cheshire Cheese the previous evening or their discussion about a weekend home in Bedford. It was a case of slow and steady wins the race. Brett needed to make partner first, and the romantic getaway at the Inn at Phillips Mill was still more than a month away.

"And just where *is* the other half of this rock solid marriage?" Virginia asked.

Dana rolled her eyes at her mother's wording and intonation.

Wills barked as he ran to the front door, anticipating Brett's arrival.

"What's that saying from the Bible?" Matthew said. "The master cometh at an hour you least expect?"

"Behave yourself," Dana told her brother playfully.

Brett came through the door and saw Dana's family assembled. The observant Virginia noticed that he had a smile on his face even before he'd seen his guests, as if he'd been preparing for his entrance.

"Matthew!" Brett said, giving the young man a hug. "What a surprise! And look at your tan while the rest of us are bundled up and walking through snow storms. Hey, does anyone want a drink?"

"I'm going to open a bottle of wine in a moment," Dana said. "Something special in honor of Matthew."

"I'm going to have a scotch," Brett said. "It'll warm me up quicker."

Dana poured everyone a glass of wine while Brett hung up his topcoat, followed the others into the living room, and poured a tumbler of scotch. He circled the table Andrew had provided as he inspected the tree. "Is that what they call a Hanukkah bush?" he asked.

Brett looked around the room, but only Matthew had rewarded the remark with a chuckle, and he was receiving a sharp elbow from his sister as he did so.

"It's a Concolor fir," Dana informed her husband. "We've never had one before, and since we had to use Nina's Beetle to bring it home, I decided to do something a little different this year."

"Well, it's a wee bit on the small side," Brett said, wrinkling his nose and tilting his head. "Why don't we get a bigger tree and use this somewhere else in the apartment?"

"I like the tree," Dana said, turning to look at the fir again. "I think it looks just fine where it is."

"Oh, it's a beautiful tree, honey! It's just that I thought we'd preserve a little tradition by putting something a little taller here in the living room—something that really says Christmas."

The word "preserve" caused Brett's forced smile to disappear momentarily. Janice had directed sharp barbs at him for trying to preserve his proper, staid way of life, and he was about to acquiesce to her remedy for removing himself from "McGarry landmark status." He realized that attempting to preserve tradition was a visceral response to his anticipated fling with Janice.

"I think that maybe it's time to start some new traditions," Dana said, recalling the time she'd taken to pick out the tree with Nina and Andrew because Brett had to work. "We'll be surrounded by Christmas tree farms in Bedford and perhaps then you can spare an hour so we can pick out a tree together."

Dana had decided the previous evening to remember how hard Brett was working to make partner and to be more understanding of his work schedule. But did he have to criticize the tree within five minutes of stepping into the apartment? If he wanted a bigger tree, then he should have gone to Bucks County.

"Bedford?" Phil said. "Are you two moving?"

Looking confused, Brett sipped his scotch.

"That's pretty cool," Matthew remarked. "Make sure there's a spare bedroom for a marine biologist."

"I propose a toast to the Multicolor fir!" Brett said, reclaiming his smile.

"It's a *Concolor* fir," Dana said, now growing visibly irritated. "And no, Dad, we're not moving. We just think Bedford is the perfect spot for a weekend home."

"Bedford?" Brett said. "Oh yes—the country. Of course! Let's raise a toast to a future home in Bedford!"

Dana was silently fuming. Brett obviously didn't seem to recall their conversation at Cheshire Cheese. Memories of the day's earlier triumphs were fading quickly.

"I think it's time to get dinner started," Virginia suggested nervously. Her daughter was upset, and there was obviously a backstory involved in the exchange between Dana and Brett that the Martignettis weren't privy to.

"Good idea," said the unflappable Phil. "I'm starving."

"I've got frozen crepes ready to bake," Dana said.

"Wait, honey!" Brett said. "It's been a long day, and I don't want you to have to cook tonight. Let's eat at the Irish Pavilion. We can see Mary O'Dowd, the Irish folksinger. We'll have a great time. We can even ask Paddy FitzGibbon to show us a catering menu for the party next week."

"I love O'Dowd," Matthew said. "but she's not playing until next Saturday."

"And Andrew and I have already taken care of the menu for next week," Dana said. "We're using Lenôtre."

"We could always do French next year," Brett said. "Paddy's such a good friend and—"

"I think you've been outvoted," Matthew declared good-naturedly while patting Brett on the back.

"The crepes are now in the oven," Virginia announced a minute later. "No Pavilion tonight."

"Then I propose another toast," Brett said, realizing that his efforts to appear jovial were falling flat. "To family and new traditions!"

Everyone raised their glasses except Dana, who turned sharply and headed to the kitchen. Brett, she thought, was acting strangely. Why did he try so hard to impress her parents whenever they were together?

"Matthew," Brett said as he sat on the sofa, "tell me how the surfing is on Oahu these days." It was the only thing he could think of to talk about.

"Pretty cool," Matthew said. "The waves are some of the best in the world."

Brett nodded and sipped his scotch. "Glad to hear it, Matthew. And I'm happy you could join us tonight."

Virginia glanced at Phil, and in their unspoken vocabulary, Phil knew exactly what she was saying: with Brett, nothing had changed.

• • •

Dinner was peppered with small talk, and Brett confined his remarks to asking questions about what others were saying rather than trying to initiate any conversation of his own. Dessert was served, Virginia helped clean up the kitchen and dining room, and the Martignettis left for Long Island at ten-thirty. The evening had come to an abrupt halt.

Dana decided to take Wills out despite Brett's protest that he would be happy to do the final chore of the evening. "I need some fresh air," she said tersely.

Brett, who'd had wine with dinner, poured himself another scotch. He wasn't drunk, but he'd forfeited complete sobriety by the middle of dinner. He was standing in front of the Concolor fir when Dana returned.

"I think you made a great selection," he said. "We'll serve French hors d'oeuvres in front of the pisher tree."

"What are you talking about?" Dana asked, feeling her anger from earlier in the evening resurface. "You've had entirely too much to drink."

Brett laughed, realizing that she didn't understand his meaning. "Pisher," he said. "Not pisser. It's Yiddish for small."

"It's Yiddish for insignificant," Dana snapped back, "which is exactly how you're making *me* feel! In case you haven't noticed, I happen to like the tree."

"Let's just forget all this," Brett said with a rather silly look on his face. "The goose is cooked."

"Whatever you say, Brett," Dana said dismissively as she started climbing the stairs to the bedroom.

Brett quickly chased after her. "Just a stupid joke, honey! Goose, like Christmas goose. Get it?"

"You got the stupid part right," Dana replied. She suddenly began to cry, realizing that she had been so distracted for most of the evening that she hadn't even told her parents about being invited by Rosamond Bernier to the after-party at Café des Artistes.

Brett put his scotch down in the bedroom and wrapped an arm around his wife's shoulder. "You're right, Dana," he confessed, using his best apologetic tone of voice. "Guilty as charged. I've had too much to drink." He paused. "Say, I forgot to mention that I picked up your wine journals today. They're in the downstairs hall."

"You did?"

"Yes. I had some time after my meeting and thought I'd save you the trouble."

Dana wiped her cheeks with a tissue. "That was . . . very thoughtful. Thank you." She paused for several seconds. "Brett, were you serious last night about getting a weekend home, or were you just trying to placate me?"

"Of course I was serious," Brett answered without missing a beat. "It would be a wonderful place to go on weekends and holidays—and a great place to raise a family. And I'm sorry if I appeared insensitive this evening. Please forgive me."

Dana turned to face her husband. He had gone a step further and pronounced the magic word: family. "Did you have a hard day?" she asked. "Is that why you've been so tense all evening?"

"Yes," he replied. "You have no idea just how hard it was."

"Do you want to talk about it?"

Brett shook his head. "Not really. I'd rather go to bed and make love."

An hour later, Dana felt drowsy. As she'd told Andrew that afternoon, Christmas could be stressful, but the day had ended on a good note. Brett had drunk too much, but he was still serious about their future. She fell asleep with peace of mind.

Chapter Fifteen

After making a call on Sunday morning from the library, Brett discovered Dana in the living room tying red plaid bows to adorn the Christmas tree. She was clearly in love with the Concolor fir.

"Are we still going to decorate the tree tonight?" Dana asked, hoping her husband wouldn't have to review legal briefs before the work week began.

"The tree will definitely be decorated today," Brett said confidently. "And it's going to look nicer than you could possibly imagine."

Dana was pleased that her husband's sincerity and thoughtfulness from their late night talk had carried into Sunday. "Aren't you bright and chipper this morning? Would you like to come to mass?"

Brett held out his arms to indicate that he was dressed for squash. "Next Sunday, honey. I promise. Johnny and I already have a match scheduled for this morning."

Dana stopped tying the ribbons and looked across the room, absorbed in thought. "It's a shame Johnny doesn't want to attend church anymore. He's breaking Uncle John's heart." Dana proceeded to relate the trouble John Cirone was having because of Johnny's upcoming Episcopalian ceremony and the early mailing of the wedding invitations. "Don't tell Johnny I mentioned any of this," she added. "My parents and I have decided to stay out of it."

"Mum's the word," Brett said, picking up the leather bag that held his racquet.

He kissed Dana and left for the New York Athletic Club. He needed to work off more than a little stress because of events in the past twenty-four hours.

Dana found it peculiar that Brett didn't take time for his honey bun and cup of coffee. Perhaps it was the scotch from the previous evening, she thought, although she couldn't recall any time in eight years when he'd passed up his favorite morning pleasure because he'd had a couple of extra drinks. Also, he wouldn't be playing squash if he had even the slightest hangover. The morning was sunny and bright, and she decided to continue tying ribbons for the tree.

• • •

Brett quickly realized that Johnny was definitely off his game. He was losing badly, and Brett couldn't help but notice that the younger Cirone was swinging hard, as if he were angry, but without any finesse or strategy. Brett took the match easily, after which he turned to his partner. "Another?"

"No, not today," Johnny replied with little emotion in his voice. "As you can tell, I'm just going through the motions."

In the locker room, Johnny toweled off and walked over to Brett, who was unlacing his sneakers.

"I guess Dana's told you how badly my engagement to Suzanne is upsetting my father."

"Actually, she did mention something in passing this morning. An Episcopalian service, an invitation snafu—something like that."

"Yeah, but there's a lot going on besides that. My dad's moving to the city because the Metropolitan Opera Board is working overtime with budget deficits and other problems. I don't think I'll get a minute's peace."

"Sure you will," Brett said reassuringly. "Just make sure he doesn't move into the same building as you and Suzanne."

Johnny shook his head and sighed deeply. "I wish it were that easy. Say, would you mind looking at some papers for me? I could use a little legal advice if it wouldn't be an imposition."

Brett waved off the remark. "No problem, Johnny. I'd be happy to."

"I was hoping you'd say that," Johnny said, sitting beside Brett on a bench near the lockers. He reached into his bag and produced a manila envelope. "It's a financial report, and my name is listed inside."

Brett took the folder and began to examine the papers. He surveyed the documents for several minutes while rubbing his chin. "This company is leveraged to the hilt. It's borrowed a lot of capital, but only part of it appears to have been invested. The full amount isn't accounted for." Brett shuffled through the papers and pointed to the top of a page. "My guess is that the money is in these offshore accounts. But look at the salaries for these upper level managers. The amount they're being paid equals the amount of investment capital that is unaccounted for. It's an old trick, although it's hard to prove the dishonesty. The portfolio for company officers is usually complex, making it difficult to track any funds they've received in the event they're audited individually. Did you ever sign any papers that would explain your involvement in the company?"

"I didn't think I had *any* involvement in the company," Johnny answered. "Not like this, that is. I mean, I bought some stock, but that's all I did."

"I'm afraid you may have done more than just purchase stock," Brett said. "You probably signed a lot of papers with fine print, only some of which were stock certificates. You're obviously the majority stockholder since you're listed as the company's Chief Financial Officer for two of its subsidiaries. That makes you responsible for the offshore accounts. In short, my friend, this company is cooking the books and you're in the hot seat if anyone gets suspicious. There's a lot more in this report that doesn't look right, but you get the gist."

"I was afraid of that," Johnny admitted. "What the hell can I do? Is there any way I can get out of this mess?"

Brett smiled. "I know *exactly* what you can do. You want me to handle this?"

Johnny breathed a sigh of relief. "You bet—and I can't thank you enough. My whole life is crashing down around me."

"Keep all this between the two of us. Deal?"

"Deal. Hey, would you like to come over to Cipriani's for lunch? I'm meeting my dad before we start hunting for apartments again."

"Sure. I'd like that."

The two men got dressed and headed to Cipriani's.

Chapter Sixteen

Johnny and Brett entered Cipriani's, the fashionable Fifth Avenue restaurant located off the lobby in the Sherry-Netherland. Harry Cipriani's restaurant was modeled after Harry's Bar in Venice and served Venetian cuisine, which included its signature drink, the Bellini cocktail.

"What's going on over at my dad's table?" Johnny asked, noting that the restaurant was unusually crowded for late morning.

Brett and Johnny walked across the restaurant, noticing that several police detectives and uniformed officers were speaking to guests, including John Cirone and his dining companions. The policemen had just finished their questions and were tucking away their notebooks into jackets and coat pockets as they got up to leave the restaurant.

"What's up, Dad?" Johnny asked as they approached the table. "Is everything okay?"

"It was unbelievable, Johnny," Uncle John said. "The hotel was robbed this morning. The thieves hit the safety deposit boxes. I lost a pair of cufflinks, but Ralph and Sandy Hartlen lost $50,000 in jewelry. Ralph, Sandy—this is my son Johnny and our friend, Brett McGarry."

"We met Brett briefly the other night," Ralph said. "Good to see you again."

Brett and Johnny shook hands with the Hartlens and then sat in the chairs formerly occupied by the detectives.

"That's awful," Brett said. "Do the police have any leads?"

"Fortunately, yes," Sandy Hartlen said. "My daughter-in-law Patti—she and her husband Jack are also staying here—woke up at six A.M. and came down to the lobby to get a piece of lost luggage that arrived last night. She saw two robbers holding guns on the bell captain, concierge, and the main desk staff while a third plundered the safety deposit boxes. They all wore ski masks, but when the three left, Patti noticed everything—their clothing, shoes, height, weight, and what they were saying. She saw the get-away car and memorized the license plate."

"That's simply amazing," Johnny remarked.

"The police said this gang has hit other hotels recently," Ralph said, "and that Patti's information was invaluable. She never misses a thing! We always tease her that she should have been a private investigator. Patti was a bit shaken since she and Jack are moving here in January."

Brett realized that Janice's claim that a meeting between Jack and Patrick was in the offing made a lot more sense now. The Hartlens were moving to New York City, and for reasons he didn't know yet, they were apparently retaining the services of Davis, Konen and Wright.

"But Patti won't be starting any P. I. agency," Ralph laughed. "She's planning to continue her philanthropic work with a corporate foundation. She's been a grant manager with the Houston Endowment."

"That's terrific!" John said, beaming. "Brett, maybe Dana can see if the Altman Foundation is looking for someone. I'm sure she'd be glad to help Patti get started." "Absolutely,"

Johnny declared. "Dana also has good contacts around town through her PR work, right Brett?"

Brett felt numb. Dana and Patti working together? Could the scenario get any worse?

"Brett?" It was Johnny who had spoken. "You okay?"

"Uh, yeah. Just a little dehydrated from our squash match. But yes, I'm certain Dana would be glad to help Patti in any way possible. Where are Patti and Jack now?"

"Looking for apartments," John said, "which is exactly what Johnny and I are going to do after lunch."

""I'm really glad I got to see all of you," Brett said, standing, "but I have to run. Dana and I are decorating our Christmas tree later, and I need to get out the decorations and do a few errands. It was great to see everyone. Have a good lunch."

Brett smiled and left Cipriani's. Outside, he took a series of deep breaths and tried to calm his nerves. He would need Janice's help more than ever. Patti, who had been described as observant as a private detective, had already noticed that he and Janice had been shopping together. The Hartlens were presumably retaining the firm, and Dana had been enlisted to help Patti find a job. Brett began walking without purpose, his mind reeling. He would have to give Janice whatever she wanted—and for as long as she wanted it. He desperately needed her protection—the cover story that she was seeing someone. He had previously thought he might escape with a tryst or two with the bohemian blond, but if the Hartlens were going to become part of Brett's daily routine, he might be at her mercy for much longer.

He regained his composure after several minutes. He would get through it. Children, a house in the country—he would give Dana the life she desired and hope that Janice would tire of New York and leave the firm sooner rather than later.

Meanwhile, he had a special surprise planned for Dana later in the day. She was going to love it. It would be the first of many steps needed to keep home and hearth stable while he was seeing Janice.

Chapter Seventeen

Dana had decided to pick up new decorations for the tree given its distinct character—its shape, color, needles, and fragrance—and returned to her apartment in the afternoon carrying a shopping bag filled with handmade ornaments from the Gazebo. She had found both porcelain and handcrafted wooden pieces representing scenes from *A Christmas Carol*, as well as lampposts and snow-covered cottages. She'd also discovered delicate crystal figurines that would reflect the miniature lights on the tree. The Concolor fir, with the new ornaments and the red plaid bows, would have an elegant yet old-fashioned look that would be perfectly accented by soft candlelight, swags of garland, and baskets of paperwhites. Dana was relieved that Brett had come to terms with the small tree, and it also bode well for what Dana saw as his emerging adaptability.

She stood in her lobby, waiting for the elevator, when she overheard a couple a few feet to her right.

"Isn't that scent of oranges sublime?" a woman asked her husband.

He nodded. "It is" he said, "Do you think it's coming from a candle?"

Dana smiled. "I have a Concolor fir in my apartment upstairs," she said. "I think its aroma may have begun to spread throughout the building. It was cut yesterday at the Winterberry Christmas Tree Farm in Bucks County. Isn't it amazing how a tree can retain its fragrance for so long once it's put in a stand with water?"

"So true," the woman said, touching Dana lightly on the forearm. She took a ballpoint pen from her purse and scribbled "Concolor fir" and "Winterberry" on a page of her day planner. "We've wanted to go to Bucks County, and now we have a good reason to do so," the woman told her husband.

The elevator doors opened and the couple boarded the car, but Dana waved goodbye and moved to the far end of the lobby, where the odor of oranges was the strongest. She and Andrew had brought the tree upstairs using the freight elevator normally used for furniture and large deliveries, and it seemed natural that the odor had lingered throughout the entire service area.

She entered the area and gasped. In a deep rectangular alcove opposite the freight elevator was her five-foot Concolor fir. Some of the branches were bent at odd angles, and a few had broken off completely from what had obviously been rough treatment, as if someone had taken the fir down in the elevator and merely tossed it unceremoniously into the alcove. Bluish-green needles littered the concrete floor, and it was now obvious why the odor of oranges permeated the lobby so thoroughly. The fallen needles and broken branches had allowed the fragrant sap to yield its odor into the air more strongly.

Dana reasoned that Brett surely would not have dumped her tree into the service area, especially after their pointed exchange about the fir the previous evening. He'd even complimented it. There had to have been some mistake. The building engineer had been summoned early that morning to fix a broken light switch on the wall of the library, and Brett had asked him to haul away a few boxes of books that they had decided to donate to charity in order to make room for new additions to the shelves. Maybe the engineer had misheard Brett's instructions and thought he was supposed to take away the tree as well. It was plausible.

Dana retraced her steps and took the elevator to her apartment, pushing the button for her floor multiple times in frustration. She fumbled for her key, opened the front door, and hurried into the living room. Her heart sank when she saw Brett standing on an extension ladder, decorating a ten-foot tree. The table Andrew had provided was nowhere in sight.

"Isn't it a beauty!" Brett said proudly. "It's a Concolor fir, just taller! I called the Winterberry farm this morning to put in a special order and paid a ransom for someone to deliver it by this afternoon. You were right all along, honey. A Concolor fir is the kind of tree I think we should get every year—a new tradition, just like you said." Brett stepped down from the ladder and surveyed the partially decorated tree. "What do you think?" he asked. "I see you went to the Gazebo. Let me see the new decorations."

He walked over to Dana and kissed her on the lips. "I am officially in the Christmas spirit today, and it's all thanks to you."

Dana was once again moved to tears in the face of her husband's thoughtless behavior. Brett, however, appeared puzzled.

"I thought you'd be happy, Dana. It's a Concolor fir! Isn't that what you wanted? I'm confused."

"I wanted the *small* tree!" Dana protested.

"But why? This way, you can have your cake and eat it, too."

Waves of guilt washed over Brett as he uttered the very words that Janice had used to describe his behavior.

"I want us to be on the same page!" Dana replied, almost yelling. "I'm tired of trying to second guess what you want, when you want it, how much time you have, and what is allocated to *us*! It would have taken us three hours to go to Bucks

County and return with a tree, but that was too much for you to spare, even on a holiday weekend. I guess I should be thankful that you showed up for Thanksgiving dinner! That small tree represented a lovely day that I had with my dearest friends, who are there for me time and time again because you are missing in action. The problem is that you can't see beyond yourself and what satisfies you at any given moment. Decisions have consequences, and you decided it was my job to get the tree. The tall tree would have been perfect if *we* selected it yesterday, but today I have my friends' feelings to consider."

"Honey, where are you going?" Brett asked as Dana turned on her heels and started to leave without responding to his question.

Dana rode the elevator down to the basement and knocked on the door of the building engineer.

"Hi, Mrs. McGarry," said a tall man carrying more than a few extra pounds around his waist. "What can I do for you?"

The engineer was in his early fifties and had bushy eyebrows and a thick brown mustache. His tool belt clanged whenever he moved.

"Mr. Janowski, I hate to ask you to help us out twice in one day, but there's a small Christmas tree next to the freight elevator that got thrown out by mistake. I was wondering if you could bring it up to my apartment."

"Give me ten minutes and that tree will be back upstairs," Mr. Janowski said with a smile.

"Thanks," Dana said. "I'll be waiting."

When Dana returned to the apartment, Brett had already left, leaving the ten-foot tree partially decorated.

Mr. Janowski arrived within minutes, holding the smaller Concolor fir by one hand. To the building engineer, carrying the tree was as easy as lifting a potted plant.

"Nice little tree you got here," he said. "Love that smell of oranges."

Dana had the engineer carry the table from B Altman to the library and then set the tree into a stand and place it on the Fortuny cloth.

"Thanks again, Mr. Janowski," Dana said, giving her helper a five-dollar tip. "You're the best."

"Anytime, Mrs. McGarry," he said, leaving the apartment as his tool belt jangled.

Dana decided to decorate the five-foot fir herself, but first she slumped onto the sofa with Wills, who was also clearly upset, and cried for half an hour. She felt conflicted, torn. Was Brett, in his own clumsy way, trying to make amends for years of increasing neglect? Walking home from work on Friday evening, she'd sensed that big changes in her life were in the offing, but not necessarily changes for the better. And then everything had shifted with Brett's tender side suddenly coming to the forefront. New hope had coursed through her veins. She still wanted to give her husband the benefit of the doubt. After all, how much could a man change in just a few hours? He could have gone to any lot in the city to select a replacement tree, but he'd ordered the kind of tree she wanted from Winterberry Christmas Tree Farm and paid dearly to have it delivered. Yes, he was trying. Thinking of weekend homes and children was all well and good, but she had to take one day at a time. The old saying was true: a journey of a thousand miles begins with a single step. Brett had indeed taken that step.

Dana started decorating the small tree, realizing that her head needed to be clear for work on the following day. An entirely different set of challenges awaited her at B Altman, and if she were going to be effective at her job, she needed to trust that her relationship with Brett had at least experienced some movement in the past three days.

She also would be joining Rosamond Bernier at the after-party Tuesday night, and she thought of Nina's words yet again: *we know what a determined woman can accomplish, don't we?* She would need to be focused. It was almost 1975, International Women's Year. If she wanted to live up to the expectations of women like Nina Bramen, she would have to rise to the occasion. If Nina could navigate exotic bazaars in the Himalayas, she could handle a teen contest.

• • •

Brett was angry and his breathing was shallow as he made his way to the street and, as he'd done the previous evening, walked along the sidewalk to gather his thoughts. He had tried to please Dana. He'd found the perfect compromise by getting a taller version of the tree she wanted, but she was not only ungrateful but downright angry, worried more about her friends' feelings than his. Maybe she was the one who didn't have her priorities straight.

He quickened his pace to release pent-up energy. He wanted to preserve his marriage, and by his way of thinking, he'd made several concessions in the past few days. But he was only human. Dana was acting childishly, as if going to Bucks County to get a Christmas tree was a sign of true love.

He spotted a pay telephone up ahead and fished in his pocket for two nickels. He dropped the coins into the slot and dialed Janice's number. When she answered, Brett outlined what the two would be doing in the coming week at Davis, Konen and Wright.

"Sure," Janice said, "but I already know all of that, and you're calling from a payphone. I can hear traffic in the background. Why are you calling? Do you want to come over?"

"Yes. I mean no—I can't come over now. I'm just not in a very good mood."

"Let me guess. You and Dana had a spat."

"Yeah, something like that." He proceeded to relate the fight he'd had with Dana in the living room a few minutes earlier. There was silence on the other end of the line. "Are you still there?" he asked.

"Still here," Janice replied thoughtfully. "This is exactly what I've been talking about. These customs you two have are ridiculous. This is all over the size of a Christmas tree? Frankly, I think you're both a couple of spoiled brats. You're so busy talking about life and the precious little baubles it should contain that you never ever bother to really live *any* kind of life."

"Maybe you're right," said a tentative Brett.

"Of course I'm right. Plan on coming back to my apartment when we have some spare time this week."

"*This* week?"

"Would you like a written invitation? Yes, this week! Have you forgotten about the Hartlens?"

"No. Quite the opposite, in fact. Not only is Jack Hartlen meeting with the firm, but Patti and Jack are moving to New York and a friend of mine volunteered Dana to help Patti get settled when she gets here." He paused for several seconds. "I . . . need your help."

"More than you realize," Janice said. "Hold up your end of the deal, and I'll hold up mine. If you do, the Hartlens won't be a problem."

"Thanks."

Brett hung up and headed back to the apartment.

Chapter Eighteen

Dana sat at her desk on Monday morning feeling a renewed optimism about her work at B Altman. At home, she would adopt her father's patience, giving her marriage the necessary time to find balance and harmony. At work, however, she was ready to use her mother's more aggressive style. She intended to make both Andrew and Nina proud of her drive and innovative thinking. Most of all, she had something to prove to herself. She already knew that she was more than capable of handling tasks far beyond her position, but it was now time to execute her ideas and move on to even bigger ones.

Dana removed a yellow legal pad from her desk drawer and picked up a silver pen. The first order of business was to finalize a rehearsal schedule for the contestants who would be competing at the fashion show luncheon on Wednesday at B Altman's Charleston Garden restaurant. The judges would be given ballots to vote for Miss Altman Teen of the Year, the winner being announced on Friday evening at the Sugar Plum Ball. Dana realized that the ballot was a frivolous exercise, but she had formed an idea about how to put the contest back onto honest footing thanks to a random comment by Andrew on Saturday. Regardless of whether her idea worked or not, she would have a clear conscience about her own involvement in the contest.

Dana looked up to see Andrew standing at the edge of her office.

"So how does the McGarry Christmas tree look?" Andrew asked. "I trust my display skills were able to set the stage properly."

"Let's just say that the tree is alive and well in the library after a bit of horticultural CPR," she said.

"Brett didn't like the small size, did he? What is it about typical guys anyway? Everything has to be bigger and better."

"There's a large tree in the living room now, but all-out warfare in the McGarry household was averted for the time being," Dana said, making light of her situation.

Andrew was wise enough not to ask for any details, especially since he knew that Dana had a full week ahead of her. "We've got a lot going on at the store today," he said, changing the subject, "but remember that we're going to Rosamond Bernier's lecture and after-party tomorrow night."

"How could I forget?" Dana said. "I almost convinced myself that meeting her at Lenôtre was a dream."

"It was surreal all right" Andrew said, grinning. "It's going to be a fabulous Who's Who party. I can't believe we're going. I wouldn't be surprised if Leonard Bernstein shows up. They've been friends for years. Meanwhile, why not come down to the main floor? Estée Lauder is going to arrive any minute. Mark and I have been here since six-thirty adjusting the floor plan to accommodate the Lauder family, but Ira hasn't given us the green light to show it to anyone yet. Things could get tense very quickly, although Mark will be dispatched to use his charm to make sure everybody is on their best behavior."

Dana shut her eyes tightly. It was tempting—she'd love to see how everything played out, but she had her own job to do. "I'm going to beg off, as much as I'd love to join you. Too much on my plate, but give me all the juicy details when it's over."

"Okay," Andrew said, "but if I get wounded in battle, I'll be disappointed that you weren't there to help with the triage."

Dana put her pen down and stood. If she were going to learn how to get things done, she wanted to be an eyewitness to how deals were cut, especially in the cosmetic department, plus she wanted to see how Andrew and Mark's plans would allegedly appease all parties involved. She might learn something valuable. Getting involved—it's what Virginia would do.

• • •

Dana and Andrew arrived just in time to see the Lauder family make a grand entrance onto the main floor of B Altman from Fifth Avenue. Ms. Lauder and her husband Andrew were flanked by their sons, Leonard and Ronald.

"A formidable group of people," Dana whispered.

"Indeed," said Andrew. "The company is a veritable empire. Wish me luck. And hold these floor plans while I greet our guests, if you don't mind."

Dana took the rolled-up plans and moved to the side.

Andrew stepped forward, introduced himself, and extended his hand to Mr. and Mrs. Lauder.

"Good morning," he said. "My name is Andrew Ricci, display director for the store. "Welcome to B Altman."

"It's a pleasure, Mr. Ricci," Ms. Lauder said, "but where is Ira?"

"He'll be here any minute," Andrew said reassuringly.

Estée Lauder raised her eyebrows, glanced at her husband, and smiled thinly. She'd expected to be greeted by the executive vice president of the store, not a display director. She immediately began to pace around the wide aisle, surveying the layout of the main floor. Her attention was drawn to the first display on the left, which was what shoppers saw upon entering the store from Fifth Avenue.

"Mr. Ricci," she said, "this location is preferable for obvious reasons. I think this will do nicely."

"And it's exactly where we're hoping to place your display," Andrew said.

"Hoping?" Ms. Lauder said. "I was expecting something more definitive this morning."

Dana looked at Andrew, knowing that he had been cast in a difficult diplomatic role for the moment. The following exchange, she thought, would be very interesting.

"Yes," Andrew said. "That's exactly why we were happy you requested this private meeting. We're still in the design stage and want your input before we finalize the other companies' locations. We have a few options for you in the prime section that you want. We'll also be joined shortly by the president of the Tepper Display Company, who wants to hear firsthand how you want the fixtures designed. You're sharing the cost, and we want everything to be perfect for you."

In reality, Andrew was aware that Ira was in the process of trying to obtain a release for the desired space from Charles of the Ritz. The eyes of all four family members were on Andrew, who nevertheless remained calm under their scrutiny.

"And where exactly is Revlon going to be?" Ms. Lauder asked, turning in a circle. "I'll need to know before I finalize anything."

Andrew was temporarily at a loss for words.

"Leonard!" came a familiar voice five yards away. It was Mark Tepper, who had stepped into the main aisle, confidently walking towards the group with a disarming smile. "It's been quite a while. How have you been?"

"Mark!" exclaimed Leonard Lauder. "Great to see you! I'm sure you remember my family."

Andrew wandered over to Dana, who'd been standing several yards away from the impromptu meeting on the main floor. "The cavalry has arrived," he said. "Mark and Leonard were classmates and good friends at Wharton for a few years. As I mentioned upstairs, Ira, who was out of town for the holiday weekend, decided to dispatch him as a diversionary tactic while he tries to get that release. Mark's timing couldn't have been better."

"It seems as if the diversion is working," Dana said. "Interesting gamesmanship."

Clasping his hands behind his back, Andrew smiled almost imperceptibly. "True, but what counts is Estée Lauder walking out of here with what she wants. It's not easy making everyone happy."

Andrew's words resonated with Dana. She was supposed to follow the orders of Bea, Helen, and Bob on a daily basis, and each of them had different temperaments and tastes. And she was, according to Bob, supposed to be creative and innovative in the process, but there was literally no formula for accomplishing certain goals, a fact that was driven home all the more as she watched Estée Lauder anxiously examining the main floor while her son and Mark lightened the serious mood with their nostalgic talk of college days.

Estée Lauder was born Josephine Esther Mentzer in Corona, Queens. Growing up, she was more interested in her uncle's work as a chemist than her family's hardware store. She named one of her uncle's chemical blends Super Rich All-Purpose Cream and sold it to friends. Her uncle, Dr. John Schotz, also made other products, such as Dr. Schotz's Viennese Cream, which she sold to beauty salons, beach clubs and resorts. Founding the Estée Lauder Company in 1946, she later introduced the enormously popular bath oil and fragrance known as Youth Dew, and the first allergy tested, dermatologist-created cosmetic brand, Clinique. A perfectionist, Lauder kept a watchful eye on every aspect of her luxury brand, choosing pale turquoise for the packaging because it looked good in any color bathroom. Her instincts for promotion and marketing were just as keen, introducing the successful concept of "gift with purchase." One of her most famous quotations was, "If I believe in something, I sell it, and sell it hard."

To Dana, the story of Estée Lauder's success was an incredible and inspirational tale. She had seized opportunities and worked aggressively to pursue "what she believed in." There had been no prescription or formula for success other than following her interests and working hard when opportunities presented themselves, and it had all begun with a simple interest in her uncle's chemical creations. Maybe that had been Bob's underlying message in the conference room on Friday: keep your eyes open and look for advantages that others might not perceive. It's certainly what Estée Lauder had done.

It was clear that Estée Lauder did not wish to be kept waiting any longer, and Andrew once again approached the group when it seemed as if Mark had exhausted pleasantries with Leonard.

"I really should wait until Mr. Neimark arrives before I show you what Mark and I have been working on," Andrew stated, "but—"

"Mr. Ricci," Ms. Lauder began, "there's really only one issue here. May I have the first display on the left, assuming you can tell me where Revlon will be positioned?"

"Are you prepared to give us this space?" Andrew Lauder asked straightforwardly.

Dana saw that the moment of reckoning had come. The Lauder family expected an answer. They clearly perceived Andrew had been stalling for time.

"Good morning, everyone," said a smiling Ira Neimark. "I'm so sorry I was detained with an international call. Now, what's all the fuss about?" he asked matter-of-factly. He looked innocently from Andrew to Ms. Lauder, as if puzzled by the impasse.

"I'd like the first space on the left," Ms. Lauder said. "It's the most strategic display since it gets traffic from the main aisle."

Ira clapped his hands together and beamed. "The space is yours, of course, Estée!"

Dana came forward and handed Ira the floor plans Andrew and Mark had worked on early that morning. Ira unrolled them, glanced quickly at what he already knew would be there, and spoke confidently. "Charles of the Ritz will be to your left, towards the wall. We'll remove the sofa and palms against the wall to extend its counter. You will, therefore, have the first display on the left and receive the volume of traffic from the main aisle."

The Lauder family looked visibly relieved, as did Andrew and Mark.

"But no one has yet told me where Revlon is going to be," Ms. Lauder said.

"That's currently being discussed," Ira said, still wearing his conciliatory smile.

"Well, let me know when it's decided," Ms. Lauder declared.

Andrew glanced at Dana, clearly worried. Estée Lauder and Revlon had always maintained a fierce rivalry, and Dana could read Andrew's mind: *defeat is about to be snatched from the jaws of victory.*

"Mother, I don't think there's any better location than the one you've chosen," Leonard said. "It's perfect."

Estée Lauder looked around pensively, not uttering a word for over a minute. The tension was palpable as people waited for her reaction with suspended breath.

"I agree," Ms. Lauder finally announced. "The space will be fine."

"Splendid," Ira said. "Andrew, make it happen."

Andrew nodded as the Lauder family politely thanked Mr. Neimark and left B Altman.

"Thanks for helping out," Ira told Mark. "I was on the phone, and it took forever to get the final thumbs-up from Charles of the Ritz. Nice work, everyone."

Ira turned and walked away, leaving Andrew, Mark, and Dana to survey the plans.

"Do you mind if we sit on the sofa against the wall?" Dana asked, taking the plans from Andrew.

"Not at all," Mark said.

The three relocated to the sofa, Dana seated in the middle with the plans spread open in her lap. She borrowed a pencil from Andrew and made a quick sketch on the edge of the floor plan.

"What are you doing?" asked Mark.

"I guess you might say that I'm going to try to sell my uncle's all-purpose cream," Dana said.

Andrew frowned. "What are you talking about?"

Dana put pencil to paper again and wrote two words next to her sketch.

"Interesting," said Andrew. "Are you going to sell this . . . uh, cream, as you call it, to Bea, Helen, and Bob?"

"I think you definitely should," Mark said. "Go for it."

Andrew laughed. "Next, you'll be asking for an expense account to travel to the Himalayas."

Dana returned the floor plans to Andrew, stood up, and looked at her companions. "I've got a contest to schedule," she said, winking before she left for her office upstairs.

Chapter Nineteen

Brett sat in the conference room of Davis, Konen and Wright on Monday morning, Janice seated across the table. Richard Patterson delivered a broad outline of what was in the offing during the coming week. He assigned new cases to litigators, announced postponements in pending cases, and confirmed the time for the firm's annual Christmas party, which would be held in ten days. Before concluding, he spoke of the firm's newest client.

"I'm pleased to announce that Davis, Konen and Wright will be representing Bertelli Imports, an international beverage company," Richard said proudly. "And I want to give a special nod to our corporate associate, Patrick Denner, for landing this latest client."

Patrick smiled as a round of applause erupted around the table. New clients were always good news, but an international client usually translated into large profits for the firm.

Brett shifted uneasily in his chair. As a litigator, he didn't have many opportunities to bring in new clients. He'd been feeling very confident about his prospects for making partner, even tying plans with Dana to his anticipated advancement. After hearing Richard's announcement, however, a tinge of doubt crept into his thinking. The current economic climate was tough, and it wasn't beyond the realm of possibility that he might get passed over in favor of those who could generate revenue for the firm by soliciting new clients. Janice noted the sober look on Brett's face as he glanced across the table, but he quickly shifted his gaze from the seductress.

"Along the same lines," Richard continued, "we are currently negotiating with Jack Hartlen of Hartlen Response, a subsidiary of Hartlen Oil. Mr. Hartlen is opening an office in New York City after the first of the year."

"So they haven't officially retained the firm yet?" Brett asked, his curiosity instantly piqued.

"No," Richard answered. "The sticking point is that Hartlen Response developed revolutionary equipment and techniques to deal with oil spills, which have become a growing problem. They're literally the only manufacturers of this equipment. Maybe it's because I'm such an avid competitive sailor and am fond of the water, but I'd like to see Davis, Konen and Wright approach this from a wide perspective. What I'm proposing is that Hartlen Response be part of a consortium to become first responders to oil spills along the eastern shoreline."

"Why do you think they're delaying?" Patrick asked.

"Because of the proprietary nature of their new technology," Richard answered. "They are currently unwilling to share their techniques for obvious monetary reasons. Personally, I think they could still retain a decided financial advantage through leasing options I've proposed in relation to their equipment, but thus far they're balking. They're impressed with the firm, however, so I'm hopeful."

As the meeting adjourned, Brett realized that he might be the perfect person to bring the Hartlens into the fold. If he succeeded in doing so, he thought his chances for partnership would increase exponentially

• • •

"I can see the wheels turning," Janice said as she sat in Brett's office after the meeting. "You believe that you can get Jack on board, don't you? What happened to maintaining your distance from Patti?"

"The best defense is a good offense," Brett countered. "If you hold up your end of the bargain, I'll go straight to the Hartlens as if nothing is wrong."

Janice raised her eyebrows in surprise and smiled broadly. "Very aggressive move. I like the new Brett McGarry. This kind of talk is a definite turn-on."

Brett shrugged matter-of-factly, although he secretly relished the compliment. "As lawyers, most of what we do involves taking risks. If you give me the protection I need, I see no reason why such a bold move might not reinforce my position rather than jeopardize it."

Janice had stood and was walking around the office while Brett spoke. "Speaking of my protection," she said as she picked up a photograph on the credenza behind Brett, "this is the person I want people to think I'm dating."

"You've got to be kidding," he said. "This is a bold move in itself."

"No, I'm not kidding at all," Janice said. "Just make sure that he's at your party on Thursday."

"He'll be there, but *you're* not on the guest list."

Janice smiled as she left the office. "But I am now. And make sure that the Hartlens are invited as well so they can witness my new dalliance."

It was an interesting gambit, Brett thought. It just might work. His adrenaline was pumping. Having an affair now seemed like good strategy, and strategy is what he used when preparing to litigate a case. It was his strong suit.

• • •

Brett picked up his desk phone and dialed the number for the Sherry-Netherland and asked to be connected to John Cirone.

"Good morning, John. It's Brett. Any word from the police on the hotel robbery?"

"As a matter of fact, yes. They called hotel management this morning and think they might have a lead on where the gang is fencing their stolen property. I told Ralph and Sandy that they might just get their jewelry back after all. They were naturally delighted to hear the news."

"I'm sure they were," Brett said, wondering to himself what kind of people traveled with such expensive jewelry. He, of course, knew the answer to his question: wealthy people he wanted to become clients of Davis, Konen and Wright. "Listen, John, I hope I'm not speaking out of line, but Johnny showed me the financial report you gave him after we finished our squash match yesterday. I told him to keep our discussion private, but I thought I'd tell you confidentially that I can help Johnny out of this mess. I know you must be worried as hell. When I'm finished, your son won't be connected with *anyone* in that company. In fact, they'll probably be glad to get rid of him since they'll know he's onto them."

Brett could hear a heavy sigh of relief on the other end of the line.

"You're a godsend," John said. "How can I ever thank you, Brett?"

"Don't give it a second thought, John. I'm glad to help. By the way, I was wondering if you could set up lunch with Jack and Patti Hartlen tomorrow. I'd like to extend a welcoming hand since they're moving to New York. They look like fine people."

"I'd be happy to," said a relieved John. "Consider it done."

"Thanks, John. Give my best to Phoebe, and in the meantime, I'll meet with Johnny later in the week to help him extricate himself from this mess."

Brett hung up, feeling pleased. Disaster had turned into an unbelievable opportunity. Brett would deliver Hartlen Response into the lap of Richard Patterson, and his negotiation with Jack—it would be brief and to the point—would be done right in front of Patti. He'd invite them to his party, reiterate the promise of Dana's help with Patti's future endeavors, and allow them to see Janice work her special brand of deceptive magic with her most unusual choice of a suitor. He had to admit that he and Janice made a great team. He now realized that she'd been right. He'd been restricted and fearful, stuck in a rut of his own making. He was now willing to take some risks to accomplish his goals, both professional and domestic. Grabbing for the brass ring was not for the faint of heart.

He clapped his hands together and smiled at the empty office. He was on top of his game again. He felt invincible.

Chapter Twenty

With a definite spring in her step, Dana walked through the executive suite of B Altman, headed for Helen's office. Helen's assistant buyer brushed past Dana, almost knocking her over before bolting into the office a few feet away. Dana advanced and stood in the doorway.

Clearly upset, Helen's assistant buyer was out of breath. "The shipment of fringed suede miniskirts hasn't arrived!" she said.

Helen looked up and slammed the pen she'd been using to her desk. "What!" Helen exclaimed. "The ad ran in the *Times* yesterday! Get the manufacturer on the phone and put the call through to me immediately! They'll never see another order from me as long as I live!"

"Right away," said the assistant, who turned and hurried from the office as quickly as she'd arrived.

Helen returned to making notes, not bothering to acknowledge Dana's presence.

"Helen," Dana began, "I really would like to speak to you about—"

"Not now, Dana! I've got too much to deal with."

The light on the desk phone was flashing, and Helen grabbed the receiver from its cradle. The manufacturer was already on the line.

"Excuse me, Helen," said Dana, hoping to get in a few brief words before Helen began to speak. "The five teen finalists are coming in this afternoon for their fittings, and I need a room where I can organize their racks of clothing. I was wondering if I could use your conference room."

Dana's words fell on deaf ears as Helen's raised voice demanded an explanation from the manufacturer of the suede miniskirts. The heated exchange had already lasted for over two minutes when Dana realized that Helen was in a foul mood and would therefore be unapproachable for the rest of the day.

Dana, however, was in especially good spirits after witnessing the meeting with Estée Lauder. She reminded herself that when one door closes, another usually opens, a saying that both of her parents had often quoted when she was growing up. It was the bridge between Phil and Virginia's two different approaches to life. Dana spotted Bob Campbell walking down the corridor and decided that he might just be that open door.

"Bob, I need a conference room large enough to hold the fashion show merchandise, and Helen has her hands full," Dana explained.

"Use mine for as long as you need it," Bob said. "In fact, I'll pop in to tell your contestants hi before going downstairs. I'll be on the selling floor most of the day. The room is yours."

"Thanks," Dana said as Bob continued on his way, hardly breaking his stride.

It was a typical day at B Altman, and Dana could feel the energy of the store, from customers to employees. Even better, she herself was a part of that pulse of high energy. Everything was in motion, and not even Helen's harsh words or bad mood could dampen her enthusiasm. She sensed all parts of her personality working together, from her father's quiet confidence to her mother's proactive posture.

It was shaping up to be a great day.

• • •

Dana distributed handouts detailing the events for the fashion show to the five teen contestants seated nervously around Bob Campbell's conference table. She looked at the face of each girl, knowing that she was looking at five sets of hopes and dreams. If all things remained constant, she was also looking at four faces whose hopes were utterly futile. Dana, however, did not intend for things to remain constant. She had thought of Friday's conversation with Bob many times over the weekend, and she was more convinced than ever that his logic was terribly flawed. The fact that Kim's parents were divorcing was tragic, but it was wrong for the other four contestants to pay for whatever difficulties Kim Sullivan's parents were encountering. If 1975 was going to be International Women's Year, a year advocating equality and fairness rather than preferential treatment for some over others, then that ideal needed to apply to all. To Dana, the year of equality was going to start a few weeks earlier if she had a say-so in the matter. It would unofficially begin at the Sugar Plum Ball with an announcement based on fairness.

The girls listened intently as Dana started to explain the program, each contestant hanging on her every word.

Lisa Gelber was a vivacious and ambitious girl who wanted to be a jewelry designer. Although her parents thought she should attend Syracuse after high school, Lisa was determined to leave school at the end of her junior year to enroll in the Division of the Arts at Simon's Rock College in the Berkshires, the first early college in the country.

Japanese-born Mari Kimura was a quiet girl who was interested in science. She had a healthy mischievous streak and had not yet decided on what she would do after high school. Her home life was very eclectic: her mother gave violin lessons and her father had recently opened a world-class sushi restaurant in Midtown.

Robin Flowers, the youngest of three children, was playful and fun and could best be described as a "girl's best friend." Her time was spent improving her grades and preparing for the SATs—and trying to convince her mother, a high school economics teacher, that she herself was not interested in the teaching profession and wanted to study at the New York School of Interior Design.

Kate Daly, who lived in Forest Hills Gardens, home of the West Side Tennis Club, was, not surprisingly, an avid tennis player and a top competitor on the court. A natural-born leader and organizer, she always strived for perfection—except in the classroom. Her mother, who regretted not launching a career before marrying Kate's father, encouraged her daughter to improve her grades and get into a good college while at the same time acquiring more feminine interests to balance her life on the court. Entering the teen contest at B Altman had naturally gone a long way in accomplishing the latter goal.

Kim Sullivan was oblivious to the fact that she had been slated to win the competition, nor would anyone have guessed the pressure she was under as her parents went through the divorce process. She was introverted, thoughtful, and loved the arts despite parental pressure to major in pre-med. Always eager to please, she listened attentively as Dana ran down the luncheon schedule.

As coordinator for the contest, Dana knew the backgrounds and personalities of each girl so thoroughly that she could literally put herself into the shoes of all contestants. All were worthy, and all represented the very best of their generation. It was sobering that their fates had been placed in her hands, especially after the news that Bob, who did not know the girls as Dana did, had decided the outcome of the contest.

As promised, Bob stopped in to greet the contestants personally. He waved to everyone and then proceeded, to Dana's mortification, to approach Kim and give her a warm smile and kiss on the cheek. The other girls looked at each other, not knowing what to make of the gesture. He then stood at the head of the table, officially welcomed everyone to the store, and wished the contestants the best of luck.

"I assure you that all the girls are working extra hard to make their families and B Altman proud," Dana said, hoping that Bob would understand the rather overt reference to the position she had taken on Friday.

Bob merely continued smiling. "I'm sure they are, Ms. McGarry, and I want each of them to know how important they are to the Sugar Plum Ball benefit. We appreciate their participation and hard work."

The conference room door had been left slightly ajar by Bob, and the unmistakable sound of Helen's voice could clearly be heard in the hallway. Dana surmised that Helen's phone call had not gone well. "I'll just be a minute," she was telling someone. "I'll be in and out."

Helen entered the room but immediately halted. Bob had lent his conference room and his personal time to Dana's contestants. She vaguely recalled Dana standing in her doorway earlier, but the public relations and special events coordinator had been quickly dismissed. How had she merited the time of the store's vice president and general manager? There were a dozen problems that needed Bob's attention, all more urgent than Dana's teen contest.

"I'd love to stay and talk with each of you personally," Bob told the girls, "but as you can see, duty calls. Once again, good luck to all of you."

Bob began turning towards Helen, but stopped. "By the way, Dana—congratulations on the approval of your teen makeup section. Ira and Dawn looked at the floor plans Andrew brought to them after the meeting with Estée Lauder, and they loved your penciled sketch indicating a small section in the alcove that the sofa is now blocking. It won't get in anyone's way, and the new addition will help us find out whether we can address the teen market as aggressively as Biba."

The mouths of both Dana and Helen dropped open simultaneously.

Bob leaned in close to Dana. "Way to go," he whispered. "I knew you could do it. The indirect approach was a smart move."

Bob was out the door before Helen could consult with him on her latest problem. Helen turned sharply to Dana, red-faced and angry. "Outside. Now!"

The contestants looked at each other, not knowing what to think.

"Everyone stay seated, please," Dana said, following Helen into the hall.

"I expressly told you not to broach the subject of a teen makeup section with anyone!" Helen said. "You went behind my back and got Ira's permission!"

"But I didn't," Dana countered, standing her ground. "I simply made a sketch on some plans Andrew and Mark had drawn up. I was just brainstorming. I didn't talk to Dawn or Ira or Bea about it. I'm as surprised as you."

Helen was about to reply, but didn't. She clenched her fist, turned, and walked down the hall with the speed of a marathon walker.

Dana smiled, feeling totally elated—and more than a bit puzzled. She'd thought that her idea for putting the teen section in the alcove might perhaps be considered in the coming days or weeks. She'd planned on approaching Bob or Bea when she thought the time was right since the meeting with Estée Lauder had resulted in the alcove space being freed up, a space that, despite its small size, would be perfect for the new section.

The fact that Ira and Dawn had seen her sketch so soon and immediately decided that it was a great idea came as a shock, albeit a pleasant one.

As Dana reentered the conference room and looked at the teen contestants, she knew that her plan to make the contest honest would now work. The teen makeup section would give her the leverage for what she had to do.

Chapter Twenty-One

Dana left her apartment Tuesday morning to rendezvous with Brett at Mary Elizabeth's. The two were going to attend a neighborhood association meeting, the goal of which was to discuss petitioning local officials to sponsor an anti-loitering bill that would prohibit curbside prostitutes from soliciting motorists at the approach to the Queens-Midtown Tunnel. The solicitation of motorists in their slowly-cruising automobiles, "all with New Jersey plates" according to one local resident, was deemed an assault on the neighborhood and its tranquil lifestyle. Brett had agreed to handle the matter pro bono for the association and had already drafted the petition. Hopefully, Brett and Dana could further outline the problem and begin to collect signatures.

Dana was feeling on top of the world. She had accomplished so much the previous day, and she now hoped to make further progress on the home front. The petition and the legislation it proposed aimed to make the neighborhood cleaner and safer. It was not only the responsible thing to do, but it was also an action that sought to foster community-related values. It was, Dana thought, an activity not that far removed from the kind of steps people took when raising a family. If Brett could take time out from his busy schedule with the firm, Dana reasoned that he might be open to attending a PTA meeting or volunteering to coach a Little League team. This morning's assembly at Mary Elizabeth's was one more step in the right direction.

Dana arrived at the bakery and tearoom at 6 East 37th Street, three blocks from her apartment building, and saw that several dozen people had already gathered, although she did not yet see Brett among the people milling about and talking as they ordered coffee, tea, and pastry. He'd gone into the office early that morning so that he would be able to free up two hours in his schedule to attend the meeting.

Dana walked through the tearoom, thinking that Brett might be in a corner speaking with someone—and, of course, enjoying a honey bun. He was nowhere to be seen. Instead, she was approached by a tall blond wearing tight jeans and a sweater.

"You must be Dana," the attractive woman said. "I've seen your picture in your husband's office. I'm Janice Conlon." The woman extended her hand.

"But . . . where's Brett?" Dana asked, taking the blond's hand in a tepid gesture. She was confused. Janice Conlon had no connection with the neighborhood association.

Janice cocked her head and gave Dana a forced yet encouraging smile, as if she were breaking bad news to a client. "I'm sorry, but Brett was called to court at the last minute. I told him I'd be happy to stand in for him at your little gathering this morning."

Little gathering? The phrase sounded condescending to Dana.

"But Brett has the petition," Dana said. "He was prepared to explain what steps would be taken after we get enough signatures."

"I've got the petition right here," Janice said, holding up a legal folder. "He's outlined the entire matter for me." She motioned to the people in the tearoom. "If you don't mind, I'd like to begin. I've got a busy afternoon planned."

Dana was certainly aware that Brett's schedule was subject to change on any given day, but Janice Conlon was not exhibiting a great deal of interest in the meeting. Judging by her hurried manner, it seemed to be an imposition more than anything else.

Dana moved to the front of the tearoom and motioned for people to give her their attention. "Good morning, everyone," she began, "and thank you for coming. As most of you know, my name is Dana McGarry, and my husband is Brett McGarry, a lawyer who will be handling this matter for us. Unfortunately, he was not able to make it this morning, so an associate from his firm will walk us through the initial steps we need to take."

Janice moved through the crowd and stood next to Dana. "I'm Janice Conlon," she said with a noticeable lack of enthusiasm, "and I'm told you wish to submit a petition in the hopes that legislation will be introduced to stop the solicitation by prostitutes of vehicles entering the Queens Tunnel."

"It's the Queens-Midtown Tunnel," Paddy FitzGibbon said politely. He looked at Dana and winked. She was glad to have a friendly face present in the absence of Brett.

"Yes, the entrance to the tunnel," Janice continued. "Quite simply, you need to get the signatures and submit the petition to the councilman representing that municipal district and then follow up with a phone—"

Janice paused unexpectedly, a troubled look crossing her face as she surveyed her listeners. "Excuse me," she said, "but may I offer a personal observation?"

"Of course," said a middle-aged woman. "That's why you're here, isn't it?"

"Thank you," Janice said. "Are you really sure you want to go through with this action?"

"Why wouldn't we?" asked a man in his early thirties.

Janice shifted her weight to one leg and folded her arms. "Do you really think you're going to curtail prostitution anywhere in New York City? Even if you succeed in shutting down undesirable activity near the tunnel, the streetwalkers will simply relocate to a different neighborhood and become someone else's problem. What you're doing here is rather like sweeping the problem under the carpet, but it's not going to go away."

The people in Mary Elizabeth's turned to look at each other in consternation. A few mumbles expressing discontent drifted through the room.

"But it's what we came here to do," the middle-aged woman said. "Can we please just move forward?"

"Of course we can," Janice responded, "but before I instruct you how to go about this, I feel constrained to point out that this proposal of your association is completely regressive in nature. Does anyone here recall that prostitution is the oldest profession on earth? For that matter, is it really your place to tell women how to conduct their sex lives?"

"I wish Brett were here," Paddy whispered to Dana.

"I think she's right," said an attractive twenty-something mother holding a baby. "Now that I think about it, it's a bit naïve to think we'll ever stop prostitution. And why should we just pass the buck to a different neighborhood?"

Janice smiled, knowing that she was causing confusion as Little Miss Priss, in her cashmere sweater set, stared at her in disbelief.

Dana leaned close to Janice. "I'd appreciate it if you'd adhere to the association's agenda," she said in a no-nonsense voice. "This is not the way Brett would have handled the meeting, and to be quite honest, this matter isn't any of your business."

"This is outrageous!" protested the man in his early thirties. "Either help us, Ms. Conlon, or get Brett McGarry down here."

"No, I want to hear more," said an older gentleman in the rear. "I think she makes a valid point."

Tempers were starting to boil over, and a majority of the crowd now voiced their opinion in unison. "We want to sign the petition!"

"I think we should at least have some debate," said the young mother.

Paddy stepped forward and raised his hands for silence. "I think we may all be a bit tense because of the holiday season. We're all very busy, and maybe we should reconvene in January, when Brett can be present." He smiled and held out his hands, waiting for a response.

"I'm going home," said the middle-aged woman. "This was a waste of time."

The crowd began to disperse as Dana turned to Paddy. "Thank you," she said. "Things were getting a bit tense."

"Blessed are the peacemakers," Paddy said with his always reassuring smile and thick brogue. "Give my best to your husband. I'm sure he'll get things straightened out for us in a month or so."

Dana approached Janice, who, oddly enough, seemed as if she were waiting for Dana to comment on her controversial handling of the brief and ineffective meeting.

"Did Brett know you were going to make these remarks this morning?" Dana asked sharply. "Your . . . performance, shall we call it, was inexcusable. It was not your place to precipitate a debate on prostitution or freedom of sexual expression."

Janice pursed her lips and looked sideways, as if considering Dana's harsh words. "You know, I tend to be a plainspoken woman, but I guess I get carried away sometimes. I really owe you an apology. I don't even live near here, and I allowed my own beliefs to get in the way. Please forgive me. I'll tell Brett about the mess I made."

The sudden apology caught Dana completely off guard. She felt as if she'd been watching staged theater—or courtroom theatrics.

"Thank you," Dana said curtly as she started to leave.

"By the way," Janice said, "I really love the wine journals you picked out for the partners. You have impeccable taste." Her voice was suddenly filled with the warmth of a friend, encircling Dana like a genie and stopping her dead in her tracks.

Puzzled, Dana turned around slowly. "Where did you see the wine journals, if I may ask?"

"At Mrs. John L. Strong. Yours, of course, were already wrapped, but I saw many on display. Brett and I stopped there after he purchased my new wardrobe at Saks."

Dana was speechless. "Yes, of course," she stammered, not wishing to look as if Janice's words constituted startling news. "I'm glad you like them."

"Have a nice day, Dana," Janice said cheerily. "I'll be going now."

Dana made her way to the nearest chair and sat, feeling weak. She'd known that Brett and Janice had scheduled a meeting with a client on Saturday morning, but he hadn't spoken of buying clothes for Janice or that she had accompanied him to Mrs. John L. Strong. When she'd been upset at his behavior after dinner Saturday night, he had softened her mood by reminding her that he'd saved her time by picking up the wine journals himself. As for choosing Janice's wardrobe, buying clothes for another woman was not something husbands did.

The weekend had been a rollercoaster, with Dana's emotions vacillating between hope that her marriage was on the mend and disappointment over Brett's thoughtless behavior. She'd decided to give him the benefit of the doubt and concentrate on her challenges at B Altman, which had thus far been met with overwhelming success, buoying her spirits. She was now devastated, however. She could not imagine Brett giving her a satisfactory explanation for spending time with the brassy blond from his office, and yet she would have to broach the subject head-on.

She took a couple of aspirins from her purse and quickly swallowed them with a glass of water. She didn't believe that having a successful career and marriage should be this difficult. She nevertheless decided to take life one day at a time . . .

. . . or one hour at a time, if need be.

• • •

Janice had accomplished everything she'd set out to do at the meeting upon learning that Brett had been summoned to court at the last minute. Brett's decision to go after the Hartlens and take a few personal risks in the process was something that had frankly surprised her. And yet she had always sensed a bit of the rebel inside Brett—sensed that he was, to some extent, a man who did not want to be constrained by the buttoned-down existence he'd grown accustomed to. His fear of turning into a stodgy landmark had given her the opening she needed, and she had gotten what she wanted—as she usually did. But now Brett held a greater fascination for her. She didn't think he was cut out for the institution of marriage, and his boldness was a trait she thought she might be able to cultivate. She now desired a relationship that went beyond a casual fling, and she had therefore intentionally planted a few weeds in the garden of his marriage. And she had relished every minute of the contentious meeting. Women like Dana, with their pearls and pretentious manners, still irritated her just as they had when she was growing up.

She walked to the subway, intending to ride to the Village. She was expecting a visitor at her apartment in the afternoon.

Chapter Twenty-Two

Jack and Patti Hartlen were already seated when Brett, running late, joined them at their table at Cipriani's early Tuesday afternoon. He was given a menu and ordered a club soda with lime.

"Good to see you again!" Brett said enthusiastically, as if he'd known the couple for years. "Thanks so much for meeting me today."

"It's our pleasure," Patti said.

After inquiring how the Hartlens' moving plans were proceeding, Brett informed them, in the manner of an afterthought, that he was a litigator at Davis, Konen and Wright. Perhaps he could be of professional assistance as well. A look of surprise immediately claimed the expressions of both Jack and Patti. Neither, however, volunteered that Hartlen Response had been speaking with the firm.

"To be honest," Brett said, "one of our junior litigators mentioned that you were meeting with Patrick Denner."

"Are you here on Patrick's behalf?" asked a curious Jack Hartlen.

"No," Brett admitted, "but I thought that since we've become acquainted through John Cirone and Dana that you wouldn't mind if we spoke. And believe me when I say that

Dana and I are looking forward to helping you feel at home in any way we can once you've finished your relocation."

"Fair enough," Jack said. "What's on your mind?"

"The firm is always interested in obtaining stellar clients such as you, although I was told there was a sticking point regarding Richard's idea that Hartlen Response become part of a consortium of first responders in the event of an oil spill."

"True," said Jack, not willing to commit to any explanation about prior negotiations until he knew exactly what Brett was driving at. In truth, he regarded the lunch meeting to be a little unorthodox, but he had indeed already met Brett and Dana, and John Cirone had been a most welcome and helpful friend after the robbery. He considered John to be above reproach.

"May we speak off the record?" Brett asked.

Patti gave her husband a serious look that was clearly tendered as a warning. Exactly what was Brett's agenda, she wondered.

"Very well," Jack said. He had worked tirelessly for months to open the company's New York office, and if Brett were going to help facilitate matters with Davis, Konen and Wright, he was willing to listen.

"It's only a matter of time before other companies copy your technology or develop versions of their own," Brett began. "For that matter, simple news coverage of an oil spill will give the R&D departments of other oil companies a good idea about what you might be doing, and then you've got some serious competition."

"It's a possibility we've considered," admitted Jack. "Go on."

"Any member of a possible consortium is going to get good press at a time when oil companies are perceived to be the bad guys. They'll want to join even if they have to accept a few terms they might normally reject."

"Which are?"

"Here's what I propose to take to Richard. Any response to a spill would be led by Hartlen, with limited assistance from other companies. These companies would sign a two-year non-compete clause in case your technology gets some exposure during a crisis. After that, they would have to agree to lease your equipment and become equal partners in any response for the following three years. They would be free to start developing their own response technology, but they couldn't use it until the three years are up. By that time, Hartlen will have built a solid reputation for being eco-friendly, and that's going to position Hartlen Oil as a leader in the responsible use of energy. You get to be out front as the good guys, and increased profits for Hartlen Response are assured for five years. Without this arrangement, there's a huge risk that another company, maybe one already on the verge of developing similar response equipment, might cut into both your profits and image far sooner than it normally would."

Jack Hartlen inhaled and leaned forward. "It's an intriguing idea, and not without its merits. You make a compelling argument, Brett, but I'll naturally have to discuss this with my father."

"Of course," said Brett. "It goes without saying. But I don't want to see Hartlen Response get scooped in another year or two. I can get Patrick on board with this, and the firm can arrange everything I've just outlined."

Jack nodded. "I'll get back to you in the next day or two with a preliminary answer after I've spoken with my father. He may have some questions. Is that okay?"

"Absolutely," Jack said.

They were served lunch, and Brett left the restaurant feeling as if he had just made a superior closing argument to a jury. The deal he was proposing would be more than acceptable to Richard, and the logic of the proposal made good business sense for Hartlen Response.

Brett smiled and straightened his tie. He was now on his way to Janice's apartment in Greenwich Village. He wasn't nervous at all. On the contrary, he was excited. When he'd been called to court at the last minute, he had sent Janice to Mary Elizabeth's to explain the petition, which he thought had been a masterful move on his part. Dana certainly wouldn't suspect his own messenger of any impropriety. What could possibly go wrong?

Chapter Twenty-Three

Dana decided that in order to retain her ability to focus on her job at B Altman—indeed to keep her sanity after being humiliated by Janice Conlon—she needed to get through the rest of the day without deviating from her schedule. She had an afternoon appointment with her hairdresser at Kenneth's, the 1897 Renaissance Revival townhouse at 19 East 54th Street that had been redesigned as a salon by Billy Baldwin. At the request of Kenneth, the lavish décor was inspired by the Brighton Pavilion, and five hundred yards of paisley and nine hundred yards of Indian jungle flower cotton in circus shades of red and yellow were draped in such a fashion so as to create a fantasy palace.

As much as she enjoyed being pampered, Dana was in no mood for such luxury after leaving Mary Elizabeth's. Janice's bizarre words echoed in her mind again and again. The woman was impertinent, and her totally unexpected public tolerance of prostitution had managed to sabotage an issue that was important to the Murray Hill Neighborhood Association. But the failure of the meeting was now the least of Dana's worries. The idea of Brett purchasing a wardrobe for someone was bad enough, but that he had done so for the brash and tawdry Janice was something that made Dana's mind reel. And then there was the matter of the wine journals. Janice had no more business being with Brett to pick up the gifts Dana had selected than she did attending the neighborhood association meeting. Their client had offices at 30 Rockefeller Plaza, not at Mrs. John L. Strong.

Dana entered Kenneth's and was escorted to the chair at the station of Mr. Gino, her personal stylist. Mr. Gino was talking animatedly to Dana about what she wished to be done on this particular visit, but Dana didn't hear a word. She was rehearsing the questions she would ask Brett later in the day. He was good at thinking on his feet after years of standing in open court and handling unanticipated situations, and she wondered what answers he would tender when confronted with the information she had learned from Janice at Mary Elizabeth's. The one glimmer of hope that Dana entertained was that it made no sense for Brett to send a woman to the meeting who could offer compromising information on his recent activities. Why would he intentionally incriminate himself?

Perhaps the woman was just abrasive, and Brett would have a perfectly legitimate explanation for his activities on Saturday. For that matter, Janice Conlon might not even be telling the truth. Her histrionic manner and unwillingness to help with the petition had made it clear that she was not someone to be trusted. Dana's impulse was to pick up the phone immediately, call Brett and clear the air for good or ill, but she wanted to confront her husband face to face. People's body language sometimes said far more than the spoken word. If Brett flinched the smallest bit when Dana requested an explanation, she would know that something was amiss.

Until the opportunity presented itself, however, Dana decided to relax in Kenneth's peaceful sanctum while she reveled in Monday's triumph at B Altman. There was going to be a teen makeup section, and Helen wasn't going to be able to block it, regardless of her adamant opposition to the concept on Friday. The air would be chilly for the foreseeable future when the two women encountered each other, but Helen would eventually come around. She might even end up, at some point in the future, speaking of what a wonderfully creative move it had been for the cosmetic section to incorporate a teen makeup counter so as to be seen favorably by Ira and Dawn. Dana knew that everyone was capable of using revisionist history to their own advantage.

Dana was finally beginning to tune into Mr. Gino's words when the receptionist approached his station and handed her a slip of paper torn from a message pad. Dana read the words and turned to her hairdresser. "Sorry, Mr. Gino, but I have to run back to work. I'll need to reschedule."

Dana was out on the street in a matter of minutes. Kim Sullivan's rack of clothing had been sprayed with water from a pipe being repaired in an adjacent dressing area. Dana would need to make another selection of clothing for the contestant. Before leaving Kenneth's, Dana had called the Sullivan's residence and asked the housekeeper to rush Kim to her office for another fitting as soon as she was out of school.

As Dana taxied back to the store, she mentally rehearsed everything that needed to be done before the luncheon. For the moment, her thoughts were no longer on Concolor Christmas trees, the Queens-Midtown Tunnel, wine journals, or Janice Conlon. There was a contest to run, and she was going to see it done correctly—and fairly.

Chapter Twenty-Four

Jack and Patti had returned to their room after lunch to discuss Brett's proposal that Hartlen Response retain Davis, Konen and Wright, gradually phasing in an amended version of Richard Patterson's plan for Hartlen Response to join a consortium of oil companies to participate as first responders to oil spills along the East Coast.

"So what did you think?" Jack asked his wife.

"I thought the entire lunch was rather strange," Patti confessed. "Why didn't Brett tell your father that he was with the firm?"

"Well, maybe he did and Dad forgot to mention it to me."

"Perhaps," Patti said. She, of course, had a different explanation. Brett had probably learned that Ralph and Jack were considering using his firm and perhaps thought he could land a new client courtesy of his convenient and accidental connection to Jack. To Patti, the proposal seemed a bit too opportunistic.

"He did make some excellent points," Jack conceded. "Hartlen Response may be taking a huge risk if we don't protect our interests in the short term."

"I tend to agree," Patti said thoughtfully, "but I would have thought that he would bring such a proposal to Richard Patterson or Patrick Denner first rather than straight to us."

"That did cross my mind, but maybe he's just trying to be friendly. For all we know, Patrick may have told him to approach us since we've been reluctant to become part of a consortium thus far. This could be their counterproposal, with Brett sent as their point man since he'd already made our acquaintance."

Patti sighed. "You could be right, but I just get a bad feeling when I'm around him."

"Well, I've learned never to ignore your sixth sense. I'll talk with Dad this evening about the proposal."

Patti kissed Jack on the lips and then stepped back. "Are you feeling okay? Maybe coming down with something? You seem distracted."

"I'm fine. I'm still a little shaken from the robbery here at the hotel. It's not the best way to be introduced to New York City. I can't believe the real estate agent told us residents don't lock their doors in the co-op building we were in the other day. I won't take any chances."

Patti nodded her head. "I've had the exact same feeling, but I'm sure things will be okay. Change is always hard."

"No argument there," Jack said.

Chapter Twenty-Five

Dana arrived at her office and saw Kim Sullivan already waiting for her. Kim, who had short brown hair, a petite frame, and warm brown eyes, was dressed in her Dominican Academy uniform.

"Thank you for getting here so quickly," Dana said to Kim.

"Our housekeeper arranged for me to miss my last period, which was study hall." Kim paused, clearly anxious. "What happened to my clothes? Are they the only ones that were affected? Is there time to make a new selection? I mean . . . do I still have a chance?"

Dana smiled reassuringly. "We've got *plenty* of outfits to choose from. In fact, new shipments came in Monday afternoon. A pipe burst in one of the fitting areas set up near the kitchen of Charleston Garden, where we will have the luncheon and fashion show. Unfortunately, the leak was aimed at your rack. Let's go down to the Junior Department. I saw a red corduroy skirt you might like."

Dana thought of the irony of Kim's remark. *Do I still have a chance?* She was visibly upset even though Bob had clandestinely arranged for her to win. Dana, however, had clandestine plans of her own regarding the competition.

Dana laughed when she saw the suede fringe miniskirts. Helen could be a bear, but she was a bear who got results. Dana pitied the supplier who suffered Helen's wrath when the shipment hadn't arrived on time. The miniskirts caught the attention of Kim as well, who inhaled sharply as she ran her fingers tentatively along the brown suede.

"I . . . love these," Kim said softly, as if she were afraid to be heard.

"Let's find your size and try one on," Dana said. "This is more fun than red corduroy."

Kim lowered her head. "I don't know. Maybe you should tell Lisa Gelber that the skirts are here. She came to the fitting yesterday looking for them because she saw the ad in Sunday's *Times*. I know she'll be upset when she sees me wearing one instead of her."

"Lisa already made a great selection," Dana said, "and I know she's happy with her choices. Let's see how the suede skirt looks on *you*. It's a nice change from your uniform, and I think your parents will love you in it. "

Kim hesitated. "If they come to the luncheon, that is."

Dana looked puzzled. "Why wouldn't they?"

"Oh, they certainly plan to attend," Kim replied. "It's just that they're both doctors. My mother does research in molecular biology. My dad is the head of the Children's Eye Tumor Clinic at Columbia-Presbyterian Medical Center. Our housekeeper Vera, who was my nanny, looks after me a lot since my mom works late pretty often and my father lectures out of town. But now . . ."

Dana waited for Kim to continue. The girl clearly wanted to share something disturbing.

Kim looked down as a tear formed in the corner of her eye. "But now my parents are divorcing. I'm trying to be strong, so I want to make them proud of me."

Dana put her arm around Kim's shoulder. "I know you will, Kim. Take everything one step at a time. Meanwhile, why don't we get some ice cream at the restaurant upstairs? We can come back and finish the fitting later. I think you'll like a tan poplin pantsuit I have in mind, and maybe a striped tunic sweater with a pleated skirt."

Kim forced a smile. "Thanks, Mrs. McGarry."

Dana quickly responded, "Please, call me Dana."

Dana thought of the advice she'd given Kim: take one step at a time. It was the only way that she, too, was making it through the day.

• • •

Charleston Garden, on the eighth floor of B Altman, was bordered on one side by the full façade of a Charleston-style mansion, complete with stately white columns that looked as if it could have been copied directly from the pages of *Gone with the Wind*. Murals on the other three walls simulated outdoor gardens. Dana and Kim got their ice cream and seated themselves at a table.

"Do you have siblings?" Dana asked, hoping Kim would continue to discuss her family situation since she was clearly worried.

For a brief moment, Dana felt as if she were talking to a daughter of her own in the distant future, and she realized how precious and delicate those times would be—and how important it was to get it right.

"No," Kim answered. "It's just the three of us. And Vera, of course, who's part of the family. I know my parents and Vera are concerned about me."

"Are you holding up okay?" Dana asked.

Kim shrugged. "I think so. But when we talk about it, I react differently to each of them. I'm calm and listen when my mother discusses the divorce, but it's easier to tell my father of my sadness and my fears. The funny thing is that they're so much alike and yet so far apart. If that makes any sense, that is."

Dana thought of how different her own parents were from each other, although they had been able to build on their differences and turn them into strengths. Not all couples were so fortunate. Dana nodded. "Yep. Makes sense."

"We really love each other," Kim continued, "and no matter what, we'll always be a family. Mom's a very analytical person, devoted to her work, and she's going to join the faculty of the University of Zurich to work on a cancer drug called interferon. I'm supposed to visit her for three months this summer in Switzerland."

"Sounds pretty exciting," Dana commented.

"I guess. But Mom will be working, and I won't know anyone there. Vera's coming with me, but I'll miss my friends—and definitely my dad. We talk a lot. Sometimes I feel good simply because we're together reading in our library at home."

Dana knew exactly what Kim was describing. When she was growing up, being around Phil had always made Dana feel secure and safe, even if he didn't say a single word.

"I read in the essay you submitted for the contest that you're planning on pre-med when you get to college," Dana said. "You certainly have the grades for it. Your parents must be very happy that you're following in their footsteps."

"*Too* happy," Kim said while eating a scoop of vanilla ice cream. "I'm supposed to test for the advanced placement course in chemistry next year, but I'd rather study European art history."

"Have you shared this with your parents?"

"Yes, but they want me to think about it. They say that I can enjoy the arts in my leisure time. I guess I . . . " Kim paused and cocked her head to the side. "Dana, have you ever read a poem called 'When I Heard the Learn'd Astronomer'?"

"It sounds familiar, but I don't remember it. Whitman?"

"Exactly! The narrator listens to a lecture filled with charts and numbers and diagrams and then goes outside to look at the beauty of the night sky and appreciates astronomy in a totally different way. That's me. I like to look at things from a different perspective."

"I love art history myself," Dana said. "I always attend Rosamond Bernier's lectures at the Met."

"Really?" Kim's entire face radiated enthusiasm. "Did you know that Michelangelo used to dissect corpses to prepare for his sculptures, especially the David?"

"He certainly did. In fact, he had to do it in secret."

"Yes! This is the problem with me and my parents. They're like that astronomer. They're fascinated with the science and the numbers and the anatomy—all those endless details. I'm more like Michelangelo. The anatomy is okay, I guess, but I appreciate the big picture. I can spend hours looking at the David or the Pieta and be inspired by the beauty—but not the blood and guts underneath, like my parents."

Amused at the colloquial allusion to dissection, Dana was nevertheless amazed at how articulate Kim Sullivan was. She was remarkably self-aware, and the contrast she'd drawn between Whitman's astronomer and Michelangelo expressed the difference between herself and her parents perfectly. In fact, Dana herself could relate to the poem on a personal level. She was discovering that while she was disciplined and diplomatic—important traits for success in a structured corporate setting—the politics of placating colleagues and superiors was becoming boring and stifling, inhibiting her creativity. Like both Kim and the narrator in Whitman's poem, Dana had a different perspective on achieving success and happiness, and she was determined to find her own way. The more she got to know Kim, the more she liked her. Looking at Kim in her Dominican Academy uniform, Dana felt as if she were speaking to a version of herself thirteen years in the past.

Lisa Gelber sat at an adjoining table with her mother. Lisa naturally recognized Dana and gave her a wave as she began an animated conversation with her parent.

"Just remember, Kim," Dana said, "that it's okay to love yourself, not just your parents. Keep telling them how you feel."

Dana could see that Kim's entire disposition had changed in the last half hour. She had been sullen and quiet while upstairs in Dana's office. She had now opened up, speaking with enthusiasm, daring to allow her own dreams to peek through the very specific expectations her parents had for her future.

Lisa and her mother were engaged in a rather loud conversation, with Lisa obviously complaining about something.

"It looks like Lisa has more on her mind than suede miniskirts," Dana remarked. "What's all that about?"

"Lisa wants to leave school at the end of next semester," Kim said, lowering her voice. "She's only a sophomore but wants to enroll at Simon's Rock College, an early admissions college in the Berkshires. It's in a beautiful spot, but rural. I can't picture Lisa anywhere outside Manhattan. I'd love to know why she's in such a rush."

"It looks like her mother is asking the same question," Dana observed, looking at her watch. "Let's get back to the Junior Department. We've got a lot of work to do."

As they got up to leave, Lisa caught Kim's eye, raised her eyebrows, and smirked, as if to say, "Nice work hanging out with Dana."

In the elevator on the way to the main floor, Dana wished she could help Kim more and knew that the teen trusted her.

More than ever, Dana wanted a family. But would she ever get the chance? The word "family" brought back all the conflicting events of the past few days and the questions she needed to ask Brett.

Dana and Kim spent the next hour selecting clothes for the luncheon. Afterwards, Kim left in good spirits, and Dana returned to her office, still tempted to call Brett. The temptation was cut short when Andrew appeared at Dana's door. His face looked tired and drawn.

"What's the matter, Andrew?" asked Dana. "You look like you haven't slept in a week."

"I have too much on my plate to begin with," he answered, "and I just learned that my dad has been hospitalized. He had a heart attack."

"That's awful," Dana said. "What's his condition?"

"He's stable for now. I'm heading over to Flushing to hold his hand, which means I won't be able to join you for Rosamond's last lecture tonight, or even the after-party."

"Don't give it a second thought. I'll ask Brett to tag along. Meanwhile, hang in there and take care of yourself."

"Thanks, kiddo. You're the best."

Andrew left, leaving Dana to ponder that Andrew already had problems with a new and difficult relationship. He certainly didn't need to deal with a sick parent.

Dana said a silent prayer for her best friend and then headed home to get dressed for the lecture. She felt that she had accomplished a lot with Kim Sullivan and looked forward to a relaxing evening at the Met.

Relaxing? After Brett answered her questions, she might not feel like attending the event, although Rosamond Bernier was expecting her. She knew that the next few hours might well determine the course of her marriage.

As was often the case, she could hear her father speaking in her mind: *Don't borrow trouble, Dana. What Janice told you is second-hand information. Give Brett a chance to explain things.*

As usual, her father's wisdom was a comfort.

Chapter Twenty-Six

Dana arrived at her apartment, walked Wills, and called Brett's office. His secretary informed her that he'd left for the day. That was good news as far as the lecture was concerned, but she had butterflies in her stomach. Would she ask for an explanation about his exploits with Janice on Saturday straight away, as was her inclination, or would she wait until they got home from the after-party so as not to spoil the evening. She didn't know how much longer she could wait to get conclusive answers. Her quandary was resolved, however, when the phone rang.

"Honey, it's me," said Brett. "I have to work late this evening."

"Is there any possibility you can get away?" Dana asked plaintively. "I'm going to a lecture at the Met to hear Rosamond Bernier, but Andrew can't make it. His father had a heart attack."

"That's too bad about Andrew's dad," Brett replied, "but I can't. I should be home by the time you get back, so save me a kiss."

Dana said goodbye and hung up. She was saving questions, not kisses. But how could he be working late if he'd already left for the day? Dana picked up the phone and dialed Davis, Konen and Wright, asking for Brett McGarry's office.

"Brett McGarry," said the voice on the other end of the line.

"It's me. I called a little while ago and was told that you'd left for the day."

Brett laughed. "Patrick and I stepped out for a quick bite before we came back to tackle a brief. Is anything wrong? I guess Alice didn't realize we were just taking a break."

Alice was the secretary for three of the firm's litigators.

"Could you pick up a carton of milk on your way home?" Dana asked. It was the only excuse that she could think of for calling him back to check on his whereabouts.

"Milk? Sure. No problem."

"Thanks."

Dana got dressed in her favorite Calvin Klein black wool jersey dress, feeling somewhat relieved that Brett was indeed at his office. She'd had visions of Brett and Janice having an intimate dinner, Janice dressed in a new outfit her husband had purchased at Saks or Bloomingdale's. At least *that* possibility had been eliminated.

Dana wished that she could take Kim Sullivan to hear Rosamond Bernier speak on Toulouse-Lautrec. The girl needed a confidant, and if anyone would appreciate the lecture, it would be Kim, but it would be an overt show of favoritism on Dana's part.

Dana left, hoping that the lecture could help her get through another four hours before she could finally speak with Brett.

• • •

The seven-hundred-seat Grace Rainey Rogers Auditorium at the Metropolitan Museum of Art had been sold out months in advance, as it always was when Rosamond Bernier was scheduled to lecture. The art world was appropriately dressed in its finery for Bernier's season finale as it filed into the auditorium.

Bernier's lectures were popular, in part, because she was able to create the atmosphere of an intimate conversation with her audience as she chatted about artists she had known so well, artists such as Picasso, Miró, and Matisse. This evening, she spoke of the great post-impressionist, Henri de Toulouse-Lautrec, who'd lived from 1864 to 1901.

Toulouse-Lautrec, Bernier explained, had shown unnatural artistic talent as a child after his parents separated, a time when he began to sketch in a workbook, being especially fond of drawing horses. What the average layperson envisioned in his mind when the name Toulouse-Lautrec was mentioned, however, was a short, disfigured man. When still a teenager, Lautrec fractured both his left and right thigh bones, leaving him for the rest of his life with short, malformed legs attached to an adult torso. To compensate for his hardship, he immersed himself in his art, later spending much of his time in cabarets and brothels of the bohemian Montmartre district of Paris. There, he would produce now-famous sketches, paintings, and lithographs of the bawdy and colorful dancers and prostitutes who inhabited the district. Not surprisingly, most of his adult life was marred by alcoholism, and the great artist died at the age of thirty-six. His greatness had come at a high price.

As Ms. Bernier lectured, Dana could not help but think of the subjective ways in which people defined greatness, with each person willing to make different sacrifices to achieve what they regarded as excellence in their lives. Her colleagues at B Altman were truly gifted people, all driven to attain their personal best. Kim Sullivan's parents were likewise driven by their careers, and their daughter was equally driven by her desire to achieve a different kind of success, perhaps as an academic in art history. Nina Bramen was unmarried, but traveled the world without regret.

Dana's parents, on the other hand, had modeled a very personal brand of achievement. Her father, for example, was truly great in her eyes, and yet achievement for him had been represented by loyalty to his employer and devotion to family. Greatness, it turned out, was a relative term. Some people wanted fame, while others sought success closer to home. Some reveled in details, while others appreciated what Kim termed the big picture.

For Dana, so much had coalesced around the events of the day. She felt that each life was itself a work of art, and she agreed with Kim Sullivan's perspective: finding a big picture that was both beautiful and simple seemed to be the one worth pursuing. Putting a teen makeup counter in an alcove had turned out to be an easy solution to her problem at B Altman, and yet the politics of her job—having to mince words with Helen, Bea, or Bob—suddenly seemed annoying. Dana was a disciplined woman who knew what she wanted and, more importantly, how to get it. Sometimes, however, life pushed back. It certainly had with Toulouse-Lautrec, and forces were currently pushing against Kim Sullivan, who didn't want to follow in her parents' footsteps. In Dana's personal life, the question came down to whether or not Brett would "push back." Since their dinner at Cheshire Cheese, she'd thought that he was again sharing her long-term goals—the big picture for the next phase of their lives together. But was he so immersed in concerns of his career that he would forever be a man who could only address his advancement with the firm? She didn't begrudge his success, but did he have the ability, like her father, to leave work behind at the end of the day to enjoy his family? Would he lend moral support when she was worried about the children, or would he dismiss her concerns as he had done in recent years?

She refocused her attention on Toulouse-Lautrec and his tragic death. He had concealed alcohol in his walking cane so that his next drink was always available. Was there anything Brett was concealing?

• • •

Café des Artistes was located in the lobby of Hotel des Artistes at One West 67th Street, a part Gothic, part Tudor revival co-op building that originally opened as artists' studios. The restaurant, opening in 1917, had been a favorite of many artists of all genres, from Marcel Duchamp to Isadora Duncan. Dana entered the restaurant and was getting a glass of wine when Max Helm approached her with his wife, recognizing her from the day they'd met at Lenôtre.

"And where is Andrew?" Max asked. "He's coming, isn't he?"

"His father had a heart attack today," Dana answered. "I'm afraid he won't be joining us."

"That's terrible news," Max said. "I'll have to give him a call tomorrow. I hope everything turns out okay."

As Max and his wife walked Dana around the small bistro, discussing the history of the enchanting Howard Chandler Christy murals—thirty six flirtatious nudes inspired by the all-American Gibson Girl of the 1900s—he introduced her to many of the guests. Dana made a mental note to tell Andrew the following day about the fascinating people she was meeting.

Dimly lit and cozy, Dana thought that Café des Artistes was the perfect place to be on this wintery December evening. After her various epiphanies during the lecture, she found that she was not star-struck to be around such illustrious company, but rather grateful that she was learning more and more about how to live life on her own terms. She was thrilled, of course, to be in the company of Rosamond Bernier—that hadn't changed—but her definition of greatness had been modified. She realized that her personal satisfaction for creative ideas and a job well done was more important than approval from colleagues and senior executives. She loved the city, with its vibrant pace and cultural richness, but she would also enjoy watching a star-filled sky from a country home. Greatness didn't have to result from tragic circumstances or an obsession with one's career.

Noting that Bernier was talking to only two people, Dana approached while carrying a small arrangement of tuberoses and a thank you card to express her appreciation at being invited to the after-party. Before she could get close enough, however, a woman dashed over to Rosamond with raised, outstretched arms, breathlessly declaring, "The lecture was divine! Dee-vine!"

The woman was Diana Vreeland, the high priestess of fashion and legendary fashion editor of *Harper's Bazaar* and editor-in-chief of *Vogue*.

Dana paused, eyes wide. Well, perhaps she was a bit starstruck after all. During her forty-year career, Vreeland had revolutionized fashion and publishing with her innovation, vision, and style. She discovered Lauren Bacall and became fashion advisor and mentor to Jacqueline Kennedy. Her list of famous friends, from Cole Porter to Warren Beatty, was endless. In 1971, at the age of seventy, her talents were center stage in the newly-created position of special consultant to the Costume Institute at the Metropolitan Museum of Art, revitalizing the institute with lavish, three-dimensional exhibits that drew blockbuster crowds.

From behind, Max's hand gripped Dana's elbow and guided her closer to Rosamond Bernier. "Get in there and say hi," Max whispered. "Don't be shy."

"Dana, how wonderful that you could make it!" Bernier said. "I hope you enjoyed the lecture."

Dana was flattered that Bernier remembered her name, and she offered her the flowers. "I enjoyed it more than you'll ever know. Thank you very much for inviting me."

"You're welcome," Bernier said, turning to Diana Vreeland. "Diana, I think you should consider having Dana join your volunteers at the Costume Institute to work on next year's *American Women of Style* exhibit. I think she would be perfect."

"I agree," Max volunteered. "Andrew Ricci thinks she can walk on water."

"And what do *you* do?" asked Vreeland, examining Dana with piercing x-ray eyes.

"I'm public relations and special events coordinator for B Altman," Dana replied.

Diana Vreeland's expression lit up immediately. "What a coincidence! I just heard that Tony is having his show at B Altman next year? Is it true?"

"Yes," Dana said. "B Altman is underwriting Lord Snowdon's photographic retrospective for the benefit of the Association Residence for the Aged."

Tony was none other than Antony Armstrong-Jones, first earl of Snowdon.

"What a coup!" Vreeland said. "He's such a fabulous man."

"We learned of Lord Snowdon's interest in aging in the TV documentary 'Don't Count the Candles,'" Dana said.

Diana Vreeland laughed and said, "That, my dear, is the first rule of living happily ever after. Don't count the candles! And I'd love to have you join me at the Costume Institute."

Dana smiled and thanked Vreeland. She was beaming, but she also realized that her personal theme of the night had surfaced yet again in the saying "don't count the candles." That, too, was an expression of the big picture—not to look at a single year or event, but at the totality of one's life. As Kim might have said, why count individual stars when there was an entire night sky that comprised the Milky Way? Wanting to advance her career was all well and good, as was becoming a partner in a prestigious law firm. Both pursuits, however, were part of a larger tapestry.

Chapter Twenty-Seven

Dana arrived home in a pleasant mood thanks to her unexpected introduction to Diana Vreeland. Working at the Costume Institute at the Met would be enjoyable, not to mention another impressive achievement for her resume. She had not forgotten the conversation she needed to have with her husband, however, one she had been dreading for most of the day. Brett was sitting in the living room, eating a bowl of ice cream.

"How was the lecture?" he asked nonchalantly. "Did you have a good time?"

Not bothering to answer the question, Dana sat in a nearby chair and decided to ask her questions directly, with no preface as to the subject she was going to broach. "Speaking of having a good time, did you and Janice have a good time picking out a new wardrobe?"

Brett rolled his eyes. "No. It was miserable. The woman is incorrigible." He continued to eat his ice cream, not bothering to look at Dana.

"Brett, what in the world were you doing buying that woman clothes? Don't you think I deserve some kind of explanation?"

"Huh?" Brett looked at Dana for the first time since she'd entered the room. "Clothes? Oh, the trip to Saks on Saturday.

Richard asked me a few weeks ago to pick out a professional wardrobe for Janice. The partners are cringing when she wears miniskirts to the office or court. I tell you, it's downright embarrassing."

"How come you never mentioned it to me?"

Brett shrugged. "I guess it never crossed my mind. It's just something that needed to get done. Why? Is something wrong?"

"A lot of things are wrong, Brett. If this woman needed to get a new wardrobe, don't you think I would have been the logical person to pick it out? I do, after all, work in a department store, and I'm more than aware of what kind of apparel is suitable for lawyers, male or female. I think it was inappropriate for you to go with her to buy clothes." Dana folded her arms and waited for a reply.

"Inappropriate? I sat in a chair while a saleswoman selected business suits and such. I was the one with the company credit card. I was ready to pick up the wine journals after the meeting at Rockefeller Center, but Janice suggested we purchase the wardrobe since Saks was right across the street. It seemed as good a time as any."

Feeling a headache coming on, Dana rubbed her temples with the first two fingers of each hand. "Let's talk about the wine journals. Why was she with you when you picked them up?"

Brett put the bowl of ice cream on the table beside the sofa, leaned forward, and clasped his hands. "She tagged along after I left Saks. I think she was walking to a subway stop, and she simply followed me into Mrs. John L. Strong." Brett shook his head and started laughing. "You would have thought the woman had never been into a stationery store. I don't think she had the slightest clue as to what wine journals are. I couldn't wait to get out of there!"

Dana couldn't hold back her tears any longer. "Do you realize what this woman did at the neighborhood association meeting? She practically gave a lecture advocating prostitution! We got nothing accomplished. She was rude and insulted many of the people who'd come to sign the petition."

Brett nodded. "I was afraid something like that might happen as soon as she left for the meeting. She told me this afternoon what happened and seemed pretty contrite. She thought I might be really angry with her."

"And were you?" Dana asked, raising her voice. "If not, you should have been."

"It wasn't my place. She didn't go to the meeting on behalf of the firm. But not to worry. I called the association and scheduled a date for a new meeting in January. I'm terribly sorry, Dana. It must have been really hard listening to Janice. She rarely censors what comes out of her mouth except in the courtroom, and sometimes not even then. That's what's so frustrating. She obviously can talk the talk when she's focused, but that California mindset—whew! What a handful she is."

"Brett, I don't like you being around her. She's nothing but trouble."

Brett's expression turned to one of consternation. "You mean you don't trust me with silly old Janice?"

"It's Janice I don't trust! And she's not old. She may be too flashy for my taste, but she's attractive."

"I hadn't noticed," Brett said.

"Come on!" Dana exclaimed. "Don't tell me you haven't noticed her!"

"She's pretty, I guess, but it's not something I really pay attention to since I'm with her several hours a day sometimes. Whether at court or at the office, my mind is on work. I have to admit that she's a damn good litigator, and that's all I really care about."

Dana was now openly sobbing. "She was so sarcastic this morning. And I felt that she was somehow trying to convey that she has her sights set on you. When she mentioned picking up the wine journals with you, it was as if she were rubbing it in my face."

Brett rose from the sofa, took Dana by the hand, lifted her from the chair, and put his arms around her. "Like I said, Janice isn't terribly diplomatic on a personal level, and she's even been known to cause judges to raise their eyebrows. There's absolutely nothing to worry about, although I can understand why you're upset. Meeting Janice for the first time without being prepared for the culture shock can be disorienting."

Dana felt foolish. Brett's responses were perfectly reasonable. The small voice in her mind representing her father had been correct: she'd been borrowing trouble all day, but everything had had a simple explanation. Her head resting on Brett's shoulder, Dana nevertheless wondered why her instincts had been on alert for the past several hours. She had fully expected to catch Brett in a lie and to learn that he had allowed himself to fall into a compromising situation.

A compromising situation? Who am I kidding, Dana thought. *I was sure he was having an affair. But I was right earlier when I thought that Janice was a troublemaker and not to be trusted. She was toying with me.*

"Why don't you go up to bed?" Brett suggested. "I'll clean up down here and be up in a few minutes. Okay?"

Dana climbed the stairs to their bedroom, tired from a long, emotionally draining day. So much had happened since the meeting at Mary Elizabeth's. She'd gone to Kenneth's, worked with Kim for much of the afternoon, and then attended the lecture at the Met before going to Café des Artistes. Through it all, she'd suspected that her marriage was hanging in the balance. Her headache was getting worse, and she was in bed and asleep within ten minutes.

•••

Brett rinsed his ice cream bowl and put it into the dishwasher. He then leaned against the counter, his arms folded, as he thought of his exchange with Dana. He had dodged the proverbial bullet. In actuality, Janice had mentioned nothing about causing confusion at the meeting, although in retrospect he shouldn't have been surprised that she'd been vocal on her true feelings about the proposed legislation to move prostitutes away from the Queens-Midtown Tunnel. But mentioning the wardrobe selection to Dana, as well as their joint foray to Mrs. John L. Strong—that was perplexing. Why would Janice give Dana anything to be concerned about? After a moment of reflection, he thought of several reasons.

The first possibility was that it was Janice being Janice. She liked pushing people's buttons, and Brett was aware that Janice regarded Dana with disdain. Dana represented a traditional way of doing things, which was anathema to the California transplant.

The second possibility was that Janice had been intentionally honest with Dana so as to prevent further suspicion in the future. Why not simply tell Dana the truth instead of creating lies that might haunt them both somewhere down the line? Wasn't it always the little white lie that came back to expose an affair? Telling the truth was sound strategy from a lawyer who knew strategy like the back of her hand.

The third possibility was a bit more unsettling. Maybe it had indeed been strategy, although not of the benign kind. What if Janice had, to use Dana's own words, rubbed her time spent with Brett directly into Dana's face, knowing that the prim and proper Mrs. McGarry would surely demand explanations from her husband? If this were the case, it might be a way of sending Brett a clear signal that she wielded the power in their clandestine relationship. Knowing that Brett could explain their Saturday activities without a great deal of trouble, Janice might nevertheless be telling Brett that she had many cards to play if he didn't do everything asked of him.

He would speak to her about the matter, but he didn't foresee any problems. They had struck a bargain in what was a quid pro quo affair. Tonight had been a minor bump in the road that he had handled deftly. He was confident that things would go smoothly from here on out.

He went upstairs and got into bed, glad that Dana had fallen asleep.

Chapter Twenty-Eight

Johnny Cirone sat in Brett's office, nervous but hopeful that Dana's husband could help extricate him from all affiliations with a company that was using him as a front man for illegal activities. Brett sat behind his desk, shuffled through some pages, and then handed Johnny a document to sign.

"This tenders your resignation from the company as of today," Brett explained. "Once you've signed your letter of resignation, we'll walk down the hall and have it notarized. I've arranged for it to be hand delivered to the company's main office later today."

"Why hand delivered?" asked Johnny.

"We're giving them a one-two punch," Brett answered. "I want the resignation and stock sale to hit them simultaneously. They were able to make you CEO of a subsidiary by virtue of your majority holdings. I want to make sure that the company officers don't try to reinstate you with further trickery. On your behalf, I'll relay the sell order to my broker for your shares the moment I've been informed that the letter of resignation has been delivered. After that, you're a free man."

Johnny shook his head and grinned. "Wow, Brett. I can't thank you enough."

"Glad to help," Brett said. "As insurance, I've made a discreet call to people I know with the Securities and Exchange Commission, as well as the IRS, to let them know that they should look into the company's finances. As your counsel of record, my notification will demonstrate good faith in your not wishing to be part of any illegal activities. Otherwise, the company might just say you got out because you got cold feet or had perhaps already made a profit and stashed some money offshore."

"You think of everything," Johnny said.

"The people who got you into this mess, of course, won't be very pleased," Brett said.

"I'm counting on it, Brett. I'm counting on it."

• • •

Johnny had been gone for thirty minutes when Brett received the call he'd been waiting for from Jack Hartlen.

"Brett, I spoke with my father last night about your proposal. While he was very intrigued with it and appreciated the thought you put into our situation, he has decided to pass on it."

"I appreciate your quick response, Jack, but may I ask what your father's reasons were for passing?"

Jack paused before responding. "We've registered our patents for the response technology in question, and the status is currently patent pending while the government processes our request, which naturally entails an assessment of the technology itself. Dad thinks that we'll be duly protected once the patent is granted."

"It's a valid point," Brett countered, "but I assume you know that patents sometimes take a very long time to be granted—even years—and until the government officially issues one to Hartlen Response, your company would not necessarily be protected under present law. There's also the issue of rival patents to consider. If other people have begun to develop their own response equipment, your request for the patent could be tied up in the courts indefinitely, with no guarantee that you would win the case. With a consortium, however, rival companies would have to sign the stipulations we put forward. Waiting for the patent might be a roll of the dice given that oil spills are becoming a big concern to the growing environmental lobby."

"We've already considered the issues you've mentioned and are prepared to take the time necessary for the patents to be issued," Jack said. "We believe the benefits and potential profits outweigh the risks."

"I understand," Brett said. "If you or your father should have a change of heart, please don't hesitate to call. And I sincerely hope that you and Patti will join us tomorrow night for our annual Christmas party. We first meet at Rockefeller Center for the tree lighting. I'll have Dana call Patti with the details. There won't be any shop talk—I guarantee."

"Patti and I would love to, Brett. And my dad and I will stay in touch with Richard. Again, I appreciate your interest in Hartlen Response. Meanwhile, I look forward to the party tomorrow night."

As he hung up, Brett looked up to see Janice standing in the doorway of his office.

"Sounds like the Hartlens don't want to play ball with the firm," Janice remarked.

"And I suppose you have a clever plan, as always, to reel them in."

"Actually, no."

"Then Hartlen Oil may not even use the firm, meaning Patti isn't a concern anymore."

Janice closed the door and approached Brett's desk. "Are you saying you want out of our arrangement?"

Brett smiled. "If you'd asked me last week, I might have said yes. But now . . ."

"But now you're enjoying this, aren't you?"

"If the truth be told, yes. I can't be allowed to turn into a landmark, now can I?"

"I'm glad you've come around," Janice said, "but for what it's worth, I'm told on the sly that Richard is willing to forego the condition that Hartlen Response become part of a consortium. He doesn't want to lose their business. Patti will most likely remain in the picture."

"Interesting."

"What's interesting," Janice continued, "is that if you can find a way to bring Hartlen Response aboard under Richard's original proposal, or even the slightly altered one you advanced, then you'll be sitting in the catbird's seat when it comes to partnership."

"I haven't given up yet," Brett said. "I'm going to be looking for an opening. I need to get to know the Hartlens a little better."

"Very cunning," Janice noted. "You're becoming more of a turn-on with each passing day."

"By the way, why did you talk to Dana about the wardrobe and wine journals?"

"The more truth we give her, the less cause for suspicion she'll have."

"That's what I suspected. It sounds like you have some experience in these matters."

"My dear Brett, I am experienced in so many different ways that it would boggle your mind. Stick with me, and I'll teach you a few things."

Janice left the office, leaving Brett to sigh and wonder what his new teacher had in store for him.

Chapter Twenty-Nine

Dana arrived at B Altman Wednesday morning, ready for the luncheon. There were dozens of details she and her assistants needed to attend to: last-minute seating for guests, greeting the judges, local media coverage, and making sure all of the contestants were present and ready for the final stage of the competition. She was satisfied with Brett's explanation about his activities the previous Saturday, so she was totally focused on the luncheon.

Although Dana had a plan to circumvent Bob's decision to automatically declare Kim Sullivan the winner, her strategy hinged on allowing the luncheon to proceed normally. She genuinely hoped that each of the five teen finalists would turn in a stellar performance and wow the judges. That was the beauty of her plan: all she had to do was encourage each girl to do her very best. Not even the judges, who would naturally assess the girls fairly, knew what Dana had up her sleeve. A trouble-free fashion show, without alteration of the program in any way, would make her plan easier to implement when the time came to announce a winner at the Sugar Plum Ball.

Mark and Andrew stopped by Dana's office in the morning to wish her good luck. Mark dispensed his usual enthusiasm, assuring Dana that the event would be an overwhelming success. Andrew reminded her of the triumph regarding the teen makeup counter and told her that it was an omen of continued good fortune, including the fashion show in the afternoon.

"Success breeds success," Mark interjected.

"Thanks, guys," said Dana. "How's your dad, Andrew?"

"Stable. The doctors say that he'll recover, although he'll have to watch his diet and take it easy from now on. Unfortunately, I won't be able to make your Christmas party. I'll be at the hospital on and off for the next week, maybe longer. This is all pretty new, so tomorrow night I'll have hospital duty."

"I'll be at the party," Mark said as he left for the main selling floor. "Take care, Andrew."

"As much as you'll be missed, Mr. Ricci, I'd be surprised if you did anything but take good care of your father."

"Thanks, and congratulations on working with Diana Vreeland next year. If things keep going like this, I'll be able to say I knew you when."

"Let's not get ahead of ourselves," Dana said with a laugh. "Right now, I have a contest to run."

• • •

The stage for the luncheon was set up in front of the columns in Charleston Garden, with the runway extending forward, tables arranged on each side. By now, everyone—and every *thing*—was in place, and Dana, who had always been an accomplished public speaker, stepped onto the stage with a hand-held microphone to begin the program.

"Good afternoon," Dana began with a warm smile, "and welcome to B Altman's annual Teen Recognition Luncheon and Fashion Show. While the program that led to this afternoon's fashion show originally started out in 1965 as a teen charm school, it is now a twelve-week program that has evolved over the years to address the challenges and interests of contemporary teens. The classes, therefore, range from the benefits of diet and exercise to creative design and writing. Our five finalists, all exceptional, are Kate Daley, Robin Flowers, Lisa Gelber, Mari Kamura, and Kim Sullivan."

Dana paused as the audience applauded at the mention of the names of the finalists. She knew that parents, relatives, and friends of the girls comprised a large part of the gathering, and she was happy to learn that both of Kim's parents were in attendance.

"Each contestant brings a unique style, energy, and enthusiasm to the competition, which I know you will enjoy," Dana continued. "The finalists will be judged in three categories. The first is fashion design, which includes a collage of pictures featuring their concepts of the perfect high school wardrobe. The collage boards are on display near the judges' table, so I hope you'll stop to look at the amazing fashion pictures assembled by our teens before you leave today. Secondly, each finalist wrote a 500 word essay on a current trend, although it didn't have to be on clothes or fashion. The essays were submitted to the judges on Monday. Finally, before lunch is served, each contestant will present a three-minute speech on someone they've never met but who has greatly inspired them. The fashion show will begin after coffee and dessert are served. The winner of the contest will be announced at the Sugar Plum Ball on Friday evening."

Dana then motioned to the table directly below the stage at the front of the audience. "I'd now like to introduce our distinguished panel of judges. They are, from left to right, Shelley Hack, supermodel and Revlon's Charlie girl; Kathy Jones, creative director for Anne Klein; Ilaria Porett, senior accessories editor for *Vogue*; Judy Goodwin, president of the Fragrance Foundation; Mary Corderos, director of public relations for

Balenciaga, and Kendra Ballard, vice president of development for the Fashion Institute of Technology."

A new round of applause came from the audience after the introduction of the celebrity panel of judges.

Dana, who needed to get backstage quickly in order to ensure that each contestant was ready to present her speech, introduced keynote speaker, Marlo Thomas, who walked up to the stage to a new round of applause. Thomas, who had been named director of women's interests for the McCall Pattern Company the previous day, spoke of her coming travels around the country to lecture on the role of contemporary women, with a focus on career choices for young girls, as well as business opportunities for women returning to the work force.

With the girls presenting alphabetically, Dana approached Kate Daley, who would be the first to give her speech after Marlo Thomas had finished. Dana wished her good luck and told her to stand by—her second assistant would cue Daley when it was time to walk on stage.

The girls' alphabetical appearances turned out to be a godsend, for when Dana turned back to the other contestants, she saw Kim Sullivan in tears. She took Kim to the ladies lounge and asked what was wrong.

"I just want to go home," Kim said, almost choking on the words. "It was a mistake to have entered the contest in the first place. I heard Lisa telling Mari how she saw us having ice cream yesterday. She said I was nothing but . . . a . . . a . . . suck-up for spending time with you." Kim paused and buried her head in her hands. "I can't please anyone. Not my parents, not Lisa, not anyone!"

"That's not true," Dana said. "You're a finalist in the contest because you've already impressed a number of people. And I think you're pretty special, too. But you have to remember that the first person you need to please is yourself."

Kim looked at Dana, puzzled. "But . . . isn't that selfish?"

"It would be if you were out to please *only* yourself. But you can't please others until you have self-esteem and confidence. There's nothing wrong in treating yourself well. It's okay to be you, Kim, just like it's okay to want to major in art history or wear the suede miniskirt."

Kim wiped away her tears with a tissue offered by Dana. "I know, but it's really hard to remember all that sometimes."

"It is for everybody," Dana said, "but you can do it."

Dana knew that her words applied to herself as much as they did to Kim. Dana had been moving to a point in her life where she needed to take care of herself. She was willing to compromise with anyone who wished to work with her constructively and in good faith, but she now understood that there was nothing wrong with wanting happiness for Dana McGarry. Andrew had been telling her for years to take better care of herself, and she was only now beginning to understand at a deeper level what he'd been driving at. Being a team player was necessary in almost any endeavor in life—Bob Campbell was correct on that point—but there came a point where being too conciliatory resulted in a self-effacing attitude.

"Don't worry, Kim," Dana said. "I'll handle this. I'm sure you're going to do great—and also make your parents very proud today. Just remember to be proud of yourself, too."

Dana walked into the center of the dressing area and spoke to the other finalists, making sure to make eye contact with Lisa and Mari. Kate was already onstage. "I want everyone's attention for a moment," she said. "I know you're very busy, but a water pipe burst yesterday and ruined Kim's outfits. I called her to come into the store for a new fitting, and we took a break to have some ice cream. The same thing could have happened to any one of you."

Kim returned to the dressing area and stood by the brown miniskirt, which instantly drew the attention of Lisa Gelber.

"But *I* wanted that skirt," Lisa protested. "I saw it in Sunday's ad and decided then that it was my first choice."

Dana turned to Lisa and spoke sharply. "I understand that, Lisa, but the shipment didn't arrive on time. It was on display yesterday, however, when Kim came in for her second fitting. It's just the way things worked out. Everybody here has picked out a great wardrobe for the show, and I don't want to hear any more complaints. How you handle adversity offstage is just as important as how you perform in the contest. It's a measure of who you are, which is what this entire competition is all about."

Lisa rolled her eyes and mumbled "whatever" under her breath.

"Lisa," Dana said, "your behavior is unprofessional and you're on the verge of disqualifying yourself. Do I make myself clear?"

"Yes, Ms. McGarry," replied a chastened Lisa Gelber, who suddenly realized she could miss an opportunity for a *Vogue* internship next summer. "I'm sorry."

Dana nodded. "Good. I want to wish everyone good luck. Stay focused and you will all do fine. Do your best and let the results speak for themselves."

The girls resumed their preparations, looking at their speeches one last time and checking on their outfits. Dana's speech had had the desired effect. The girls were focused on the contest rather than on each other. Robin was preparing to follow Kate, who was finishing her speech.

How you handle adversity is just as important as how you perform onstage.

This, too, was a philosophy of Virginia Martignetti. Dana was more grateful than ever to have had parents who demonstrated that life wasn't black and white, yes or no, all or nothing. That was *their* big picture. You worked to help others, but at the end of the day, you needed to strive for personal happiness and contentment regardless of what life brought your way.

As the afternoon progressed, Dana saw that the luncheon and contest were running smoothly. The girls had performed admirably thus far, and Dana knew that she'd done a great job. She also knew that she'd do a great job announcing the winner at the Sugar Plum Ball, where she would reveal her unique solution to the conundrum caused by Bob ordering her to rig the contest.

It had been a busy week, one filled with highs and lows, worries and triumphs. As she watched the girls put on their outfits for the fashion show, she felt an enormous sense of peace.

She didn't have to know how everything in her life would work out. All the answers she needed were on the inside.

Chapter Thirty

Dana was tired as she settled into her desk chair at B Altman, but she was more than satisfied with the way the luncheon and fashion show had gone earlier that afternoon. All five girls had done a spectacular job, and Kim had pushed away her self-doubts and recriminations in order to turn in a stellar performance. When the fashion show was over, Dana noted that Kim had eagerly sought out her parents in the crowd of people admiring the collage boards. Her mother and father had embraced her, each showing great enthusiasm. Such days, Dana thought, were worth far more than any paycheck. She had given Kim the necessary confidence to finish the contest, and hopefully her words would stay with the girl in the days and weeks ahead. After the results were announced on Friday, Dana intended to tell Kim that her door would always be open in case she wanted to talk.

As Dana was basking in the day's success, Bea Savino's assistant materialized next to her cubicle, looking very concerned. "Bea wants to see you immediately, Ms. McGarry."

"Do you know what it's about?" Dana asked.

"No, but she said that it's urgent."

"Okay," Dana sighed, rising from her chair. "Let's go."

Dana was frequently summoned to Bea's office, but whenever the words "immediately" or "urgent" were attached to the request, it usually signaled some impending crisis. Couldn't she have ten minutes to herself to enjoy the day's accomplishments?

Dana followed the assistant to the executive suite on the fifth floor and went directly to Bea's office. "You wanted to see me, Bea?"

Bea waved Dana in and motioned for her to sit. She lit a cigarette, sat back in her chair, and stared straight at Dana before her entire expression unexpectedly changed. "Congratulations! You got the teen makeup section, plus I hear that the fashion show was a great success. Great work!"

"But I thought you cautioned me not to push the teen makeup idea." Dana was confused. She'd expected to be chastised for some faux pas, but Bea was effusive in her praise for Dana.

"And that's the beauty of it. You *didn't* push it, but you nevertheless made it happen."

"Thank you, Bea. I appreciate your support. Unfortunately, I don't think Helen will be kindly disposed to recent developments."

Bea inhaled deeply on her cigarette, blew out a perfect column of smoke, and leaned forward. "Don't worry about Helen. She'll come around—she always does. Is she going to your party tomorrow evening?"

"I certainly hope so."

"I'm sure she will, and I bet she'll be as cordial as can be. She's a class act." Bea paused as she crushed her cigarette in her ashtray. As she did so, she remarked casually that "You might want to think about taking your career in another direction. Your instincts are good, Dana. You may want to move into a line department. If you get buying experience, you can be a candidate for the fashion group and work with Dawn. Ira is revolutionizing the store, and there are many new opportunities. Keep your eyes open."

Surprised, Dana raised her eyebrows.

"Thank you, Bea. I'll give your advice serious thought. I did major in merchandising, although I certainly enjoy working with you. You have taught me so much."

"Don't get me wrong—I'm not trying to get rid of you," Bea confessed, "but here's a secret. The learning never stops. Even Helen knows that, although she might be reluctant to admit it." Bea lit another cigarette and laughed. "The very name of Biba makes her tremble, and yet she's smart enough to know that change is inevitable."

"A few days ago," Dana said, "you claimed that the teen makeup section would have to wait because Helen had too much on her plate."

"Quite true, but Ira thought otherwise. He knows change is a fact of life—and of business."

"Change—that's been the theme of the week," Dana commented in an almost philosophical tone.

"It's the theme of life, kiddo, and don't let anyone ever tell you otherwise."

• • •

Dana was walking into Bob Campbell's office when she saw Helen out the corner of her eye. Helen had picked up her pace and was proclaiming, just as she had a few days earlier, that "He's expecting me!"

The office door closed, leaving Helen standing in the outer office. "I hope they're not meddling with my department again," she said with exasperation.

"I don't think Ms. McGarry will be long," the secretary said. "She only asked for a few minutes." Helen paced anxiously, holding a bound report in her right hand. Five minutes later, Dana emerged with a grin on her face.

"He's all yours, Helen. Sorry if I kept you waiting."

Dana disappeared down the hall, not looking back.

Chapter Thirty-One

Brett and Janice exited the courthouse in lower Manhattan after filing several motions on behalf of the Landmarks Preservation Commission. They walked down the street under gray, cloudy skies, both carrying briefcases.

"Does your wife know I'll be attending your party tomorrow night?" Janice asked.

"No," Brett replied. "And I don't plan on telling her. You and I will arrive together at the tree lighting at Rockefeller Center. I'll simply tell Dana that we're coming from work, which will be the truth. Dana and I have arranged with John Cirone to have his bus take everyone from the tree lighting to our apartment. John purchased the bus to take family and friends to and from games when his son played football for Villanova. Just get on the bus with everyone else and everything will be fine. If Dana asks any questions, I'll tell her that I can't very well order you not to come to the party since it would be rude."

"Very well thought out," Janice said. "You've grown especially sharp these past few days. Even your confidence level is way up."

"It shows?"

"Very much. And what about the Hartlens? Have you made sure they'll be attending as well? If I'm going to put on a show, I want to make sure I have the right audience."

"I asked Jack on the phone yesterday. He and Patti are definitely coming. So is Patrick."

"Even better. We'll have all of our bases covered. I've also bought a very nice vintage cabernet as a way to reiterate my apologies to Dana for disrupting the neighborhood association meeting on Tuesday."

Brett looked sideways. "Don't tell me that you're really sorry?"

"Hell, no. Trying to keep hookers away from a given location is ridiculous. They'd be back within a month, and I doubt the city council would even pass such legislation. The wine is simply a good tactical move."

"Tactical? That's a rather sterile term."

"I suppose it is," said a thoughtful Janice. "Does your comment indicate that you regard our relationship with a certain degree of warmth?"

Brett merely smiled and looked straight ahead.

"I'll take that as a yes," Janice said.

She was succeeding faster than she'd anticipated. She'd originally presented the affair as a way for Brett to keep from turning into a stuffy socialite, offering him a fling and nothing else. But her goals had changed. She wanted more. Thus far, she had managed to ruffle Dana's feathers and engender some measure of feeling within Brett for her unorthodox view of life. She had no doubt that he still loved his wife—they all did, didn't they—but time and persistence might change that. Brett was a bigger challenge than most, however, and she wasn't going to take for granted that she could lure him from his eight-year marriage.

Janice loved a good challenge.

Chapter Thirty-Two

At four o'clock on Thursday evening, the skies above Manhattan were already turning dark as Dana made her way to Paddy FitzGibbon's VIP section in Rockefeller Center for the annual Christmas tree lighting in front of the GE building. On the edge of the crowd, she was handed a cup of hot chocolate by an employee from the Irish Pavilion.

"You always think of everything," Dana said as she located Paddy near the front of the gathering, just yards from the stage below the bronze-gilded statue of Prometheus. "And just how do you secure such an amazing location each and every year?"

"It's the luck of the Irish, Dana, plus a few kind friends with whom God has blessed me."

"In other words, you pull a few strings," Dana said, grinning.

"Every string is absolutely legal," Paddy said, "although it doesn't hurt to contribute to law enforcement and other agencies every now and then. It's my civic duty!"

The two laughed as they sipped their hot chocolate.

Paddy turned to greet other new arrivals with his warm, welcoming manner, his Irish brogue easily heard above the sounds of the city and the growing crowd.

Phoebe Cirone waded through the huddled overcoats and gave her childhood friend a big hug.

"New York Hospital actually let you out for a few hours?" Dana asked as they embraced.

"My rotation for December puts me in the cath lab, and since I'm not making rounds, I could get away early. Did Dad tell you that I'm sticking it out another year? As soon as I heard the name of the new director of Interventional Cardiology, the decision was made. He shares my research interest in aortic valve disease."

"Phoebe, you have been dedicated to medicine and saving people's lives since we were kids, and you never gave up," Dana said as she gave her friend another hug. "You'll reach your dream in a little more than a year. I'm so happy for you."

"Speaking of saving people's lives," Phoebe added, "my father and brother are so grateful to Brett for saving Johnny from disaster. My father has been in church, praying for Johnny twice a day, and now he's walking on air. Your husband is a miracle worker."

Dana's face reflected her ignorance as to what Phoebe was referring to. "What exactly did Brett do?"

"You mean he didn't tell you that—"

"Hello, everyone!" Brett interrupted. He was being ushered into the section by a police officer, followed by Jack and Patti Hartlen—and Janice. After kissing Phoebe on the cheek, he made introductions all around. Dana and Janice exchanged forced smiles that were as cold as the late evening air.

"Welcome!" Paddy said to the latest arrivals, shaking Brett's hand as he continued to circulate among his guests. "And you must be Jack and Patti. I hear you're moving here next month! I want you to be guests at my restaurant as soon as the move is complete. And if there's anything you need, I'm glad to help. Dana and Brett know how to reach me. We're neighbors in Murray Hill."

"He's not kidding," Brett said. "Paddy's our go-to man for just about anything. In fact, his friend, who works at St.

Patrick's Cathedral across the street, is watching John's private bus that will take us to the apartment after the tree lighting."

"Come with me," Paddy said to the Hartlens. "Let me get you as close as possible to the stage."

Dana looked around, but no longer saw Janice. "Where is she?" asked Dana, as if she were looking for a predator.

"Who?" Brett asked innocently.

"Miss California. I just saw her a minute ago."

Brett looked around and pointed his finger at two people to their rear. "She's right over there. And it looks like she's made a new friend."

Dana turned around to see Janice standing next to her brother Matthew.

"I don't believe it," Dana said, lowering her head. She took a deep breath before asking, "Brett, how could you invite her without discussing it with me?"

"We were leaving court, and she reminded me that this is her first Christmas in New York. She's never seen the tree lighting before, not even on TV." Brett held up his hands and shrugged his shoulders. "I can't stop her from coming to a public event."

"Okay, but keep my brother off her wish list," Dana demanded. "I mean it, Brett."

"They're just talking, honey. Relax and enjoy the ceremony."

"Dana!" Mark Tepper called out. "My meeting with Revlon wrapped up earlier than expected, and I knew where I'd find you before the party. I hope you don't mind my barging in like this."

"I'm glad you could make it," Dana said. "You're a welcome gate crasher, which isn't necessarily true for everyone in the VIP section

While Mark and Brett exchanged pleasantries, Paddy arrived with hot chocolate for Mark, engaging him in a discussion about the stage design.

"You've done a tremendous job getting ready for the party later," Brett told Dana. "You did a luncheon yesterday, and today you're ready to host our annual party. You're the McGarry household's special events coordinator." He kissed her softly on the lips.

"If you're trying to get on my good side," Dana said, "you're succeeding. I didn't even expect you to show up."

"We finished early and I remembered that I haven't been able to get to the tree lighting for the past two or three years. I have no doubt that it's going to be a great night."

"Brett, what did you do for Johnny? Phoebe says that you . . . saved him."

Brett smiled broadly. "Johnny asked for some advice after our squash match on Sunday, so I—"

At the podium, Mayor Abe Beame officially welcomed everyone to Rockefeller Center on behalf of the City of New York. He then introduced Marlo Thomas, who presided over the ceremony, featuring The Voices of East Harlem singing "Sisters and Brothers" and other popular tunes from Thomas' Emmy award-winning children's TV special *Free to Be . . . You and Me*. The songs were also part of a larger project sponsored by the Ms. Foundation for Women, which had published both an album and illustrated children's book that rejected gender stereotypes in children's literature. The central message was that both boys and girls could achieve anything.

The ceremony naturally concluded with Christmas carols sung by a choir and the lighting of the iconic tree above the statue of Prometheus.

"Now it's the Christmas season!" Paddy declared. "Forget the Macy's Thanksgiving Day Parade. For me, it doesn't officially begin until those lights go on!"

"I agree, Paddy" said Mark. "It's a spectacular display!"

As Dana and Brett, hand in hand, made their way to a nearby exit and walked quickly across the street to the waiting bus on 49th Street—a definite perk to being in the VIP section—Dana noticed that Janice, accompanied by Matthew, was already boarding John Cirone's bus.

"She's not invited to the party!" Dana complained.

"Honey," Brett said, "I can't very well tell her she's not welcome and that we want her off the bus. Besides, Matthew seems to like her."

"That's even worse than her coming to the party!"

"Matthew can handle himself. Stop worrying."

"She's a cunning shark, and she's too old for him."

"He's a surfer, Dana. All surfers know to look out for sharks."

Dana couldn't help but laugh. "I still don't want her in our apartment or near my brother."

"*You'll* have to do the dirty work," Brett responded, knowing Dana would not ask Janice to leave. "In the meantime, you should be thinking about your guests."

"You're right," she said. "We need to concentrate on the party."

Still holding hands, Brett and Dana boarded the bus. All of their guests seemed to be in fine spirits. Brett and Dana sat in the first seats, Janice and Matthew huddled close together and talking animatedly in the very rear.

Chapter Thirty-Three

The guests were still filing into Brett and Dana's apartment when Nina Bramen and Patrick Denner arrived back-to-back.

"A few handmade ornaments for your tree," Nina said as she handed Dana a Christmas shopping bag. "I got them last year in Peru. Hand-carved, hand-painted gourds made with pumpkin. Perfect size for a baby tree. Let's hang them now before you get busy."

"Um…well, we have to go upstairs to the library," Dana said as she put her arm around her friend. "Brett thought the ceiling was too high in the living room for a table tree."

"And what did *you* think?" Nina asked indignantly.

"Dana loved the idea of having two Concolor firs in the apartment," Brett quickly responded as he and Mark, only a few feet away, removed their overcoats.

"I don't believe that for a minute," Nina snapped. "*I* was there and I know how much she loved *that* tree."

"Nina, it's fine," Dana said, her eyes pleading with Brett to say something kind. "Actually, the tree made the library very cozy. You know it's my favorite room."

"The fault is all mine, Nina," Brett said in a conciliatory manner. "I should have rented a car for the trip. I'll plan better next year. In fact, we'll all go to Bucks County and make a day of it!"

Nina, infuriated by Brett's patronizing and insincere remarks. responded with a cold stare.

"I propose a toast!" Mark interjected as he handed glasses of champagne to Nina, Brett, and Dana from the server who was exiting the kitchen. "To our gracious hosts!"

Those standing nearby raised their glasses.

"Thank you," Dana mouthed silently to Mark.

Mark smiled and gave Dana a thumbs-up as the staff from Lenôtre passed trays of hors d'oeuvres.

• • •

Brett joined Patrick, who was speaking with the Hartlens in the dining room.

"Jack and Patti were just telling me that you know them apart from the firm," Patrick said to Brett.

"That's right," Brett said as he shook hands with Jack. "I ran into Jack and Patti at Cheshire Cheese, and Patti at Saks." Brett thought the allusion to Saks was bold enough to indicate that he had nothing to hide from Patti. "And as luck would have it, Dana ran into Jack while walking our dog on Park Avenue. Wills slipped the leash, and Jack was his savior. What's the old lyric? It's a small world after all?"

Patrick pointed to Janice, who had not left Matthew's side since arriving at the apartment. "That's Janice Conlon, by the way. She's our newest litigator."

"And that's Dana's brother Matthew she's talking to," Brett was quick to point out.

Brett thought that things were evolving with clockwork precision. Patti now understood that he and Janice worked together, and she could also see that Janice seemed quite enamored of Matthew. Janice had wasted no time in orchestrating her plan. She and Matthew were thoroughly engrossed in conversation, and her body language was overt. She touched him on the arm every few seconds as she stood close by his side.

Brett motioned to Dana to join the conversation. "Honey, why don't you introduce Jack and Patti to Matthew?"

Dana paused for a split second. "Of course. And I'm so glad you could make it tonight. Matthew is the family's budding scientist, as well as an expert surfer, if you can believe that." Dana relished the opportunity to intrude on her brother's conversation with Janice.

With Brett and Patrick left standing alone, Patrick moved closer to Brett. "Richard wanted me to thank you for trying to get the Hartlens to agree to his consortium proposal."

"I hope he's not upset that I didn't consult him first. I was having lunch with them and the opportunity presented itself to broach the subject. I thought I could show them the advantages of joining a consortium rather than waiting for a patent to be assigned."

"You did the right thing, and Richard was very impressed. It showed initiative." Patrick paused as he looked around. "Say, where is that nice odor of oranges coming from?"

Brett laughed. "Why am I the only person who can't smell it?"

• • •

"I brought something for you," Janice said as Dana approached Matthew with the Hartlens. "Let me run and get it. I put it on a table in the corner."

As Janice retrieved her peace offering, Dana went through the formalities. "Jack and Patti Hartlen, this is my brother Matthew. He goes to the Uni—"

"Here," Janice interrupted, handing Dana the wrapped bottle of merlot.

"Thank you," said Dana. "Janice, Jack and Patti are moving to New York very soon."

"I just moved here myself," Janice said. "From California."

"She loves the ocean," Matthew said, "so I'm going to teach her how to surf."

"He's mastered the Banzai Pipeline," Dana said with yet another forced smile. "Now if you'll excuse me, I'll see how they're doing in the kitchen."

Dana walked away, trying to maintain her composure. Janice was loving every minute of monopolizing Matthew's time. Dana wasn't sure what Janice was up to, but whatever it was, she didn't like it. She was also fairly certain that Janice had had no interest in the tree lighting at Rockefeller Center. Her attendance had been a way to crash the McGarry annual Christmas party, and Matthew had been a shiny toy she'd discovered under the tree.

• • •

Dana knew she could do nothing about Janice and Matthew while the party was in progress, but she intended to find out what Brett and Johnny had been up to during the week. Brett, playing the gracious host, was now speaking with Johnny and Phoebe in the dining room.

"I've got some shocking news!" Johnny told Dana.

"It's good news, I hope. Don't keep me in suspense."

"I'm a free man. Dad was right to be worried about my marriage to Suzanne. It's off, and I have Brett to thank."

Dana's mouth fell open. Had Brett meddled in Johnny's affairs? She had counseled her own mother to steer clear of the situation, so how had Brett entered the picture?

Brett could tell what Dana was thinking, so he immediately tried to explain.

"Don't jump to conclusions, honey. All I did was—"

An excited Phoebe couldn't contain herself. "All he did was learn from documents my father received from his attorney that the Farnsworth family was using Johnny as an officer in Farnsworth Textiles in Philadelphia, in addition to other family companies—and without his knowledge. Can you believe it? They're apparently hiding offshore assets and were willing to let Johnny be the responsible party by allowing him to be a majority shareholder."

"I dodged a bullet," Johnny declared emphatically. "Brett thinks a lot of their business dealings are questionable at best. I'm convinced that Suzanne's parents urged her to send out the invitations early before I had a chance to learn what they were doing."

Dana was speechless for several seconds. "And what did Suzanne think of all this?"

"Oh, she thinks it's all ridiculous. She said that her parents are honest people who would never do such a thing, and if I suspected them of being criminals, then she never wanted to see me again. I don't think Suzanne herself is dishonest, but her family is certainly opportunistic."

"All in a day's work," Brett said with a Cheshire cat grin.

"Thank you," Dana said, putting her arm around her husband's waist.

"Matthew has invited me to visit him in Hawaii since I won't be taking time off for a honeymoon," Johnny said. "By the way, Dana—I have a surprise for you. It's upstairs in the library, and it won't wait."

"Let's take a look," Phoebe said excitedly. She obviously knew what waited for Dana upstairs.

"Right now?" said Dana. "Maybe later. I've got to keep my eye on things down here. Guests are still arriving and I haven't yet seen the salmon trout tartare. I need to check with the kitchen."

"It will only take a minute," Phoebe said. "Brett looks like he has everything under control."

"Indeed I do," Brett said proudly. "Go ahead, honey. I'll ask one of the servers about the tartare."

Johnny, Phoebe, and Dana climbed the stairs and entered the library. Matthew and Janice were sitting close together on the couch, Matthew's arm around her shoulder. Their lips were just inches apart.

"Um, sorry to interrupt," Johnny said, "but I left something on the desk for Dana."

Johnny picked up a brown box from the House of Cirone and he handed it to Dana, who slowly removed the cover, eyes wide. Lying on top of her slim black wool crepe gown was a black silk Chantilly lace shawl. "That's why we kept telling you the alterations weren't ready," Johnny explained as Dana unfolded the delicate wrap. "The lace was delayed in clearing customs, and we had to rush to have the shawl made by tonight."

"This looks just like the vintage lace in Chanel's last collection," Dana said in awe.

"Well, I don't know for sure, but it's from Chantilly, France, and it's vintage," Johnny explained. "We're using white and black lace in our holiday collection next year."

"I love it," Dana said as she hugged both Johnny and Phoebe. "It's more than a shawl. It's a beautiful heirloom."

Janice, who was still seated with Matthew on the sofa, observed all the fuss from a distance. "It's so nice," she stated blandly, thinking that wearing an old piece of lace was hideous.

"Matthew, would you run down and remind Brett to have the servers prepare plates for the door staff," Dana asked. "I want to call and thank Uncle John." Dana wanted to get Matthew and Janice out of the library—and apart—by any means possible.

"Say hi to Dad," Phoebe volunteered. "I'm heading downstairs, too. I'm so tired of hospital cafeteria food! I'm starving!"

Janice, Matthew, and Phoebe left the library.

Johnny walked leisurely around the room, looking at family pictures that spanned the Cirones and the Martignettis over many years and holiday gatherings. His attention was suddenly drawn to a photograph on one of the bookshelves. "Hey, here we are at Villanova's May Ball," Johnny said to Dana. "You know, that looks like the same dress I just brought you, only yellow."

Dana laughed wistfully. "I still have that dress, and it still fits, but yellow? I don't think so." Dana paused. "Johnny, are you really glad to be free from Suzanne?" she asked.

"It was a bit of a shock to learn I was being used," Johnny confessed, "but once I called the engagement off, I felt nothing but relief. Suzanne and I weren't really suited for one another, but sometimes opposites attract, right? But I guess I needed the diversion more than anything else. Dad sensed it all along, and I know he was itching to say more than he did, but he knew I had to make my own decision in the long run."

"Your dad is a wonderful man," Dana said. "And he spoils us terribly!"

"I know," Johnny said. "And to tell you the truth, I'm glad he's moving to the city. Now that the wedding is off, I'm going to spend more time with him aside from work. I'll even try to like the opera! Well, at least I'll make an effort to join him now and then. I know that would have made mom happy. In fact, he's at the opera tonight, so don't bother calling."

"You're pretty special, Johnny, not to mention a great son."

"What about you?" Johnny asked. "You've been looking a little stressed out lately."

Dana sighed. "Does it show? I'm not surprised. It's been an incredibly difficult week."

"Dana, you know I'm always here for you. Is everything okay between you and Brett?"

"Yes. We have our issues like everyone else, but we're working our way through them."

"I'm glad," Johnny said as they hugged. "You deserve to be happy. From what I've seen this week, Brett is one of the good guys with the white hat. He really helped me out of a jam."

"Let's go down and join the rest," Dana suggested, not wishing to speak further about her marriage. "I don't want Matthew and Janice unsupervised for too long."

"She's pretty strange," Johnny said as Dana took his arm.

"Strange doesn't even begin to describe it."

"By the way," Johnny said. "Nice little tree there."

Dana could only smile at Johnny's attentiveness. "Let's go," she said.

Dana and Johnny left the library.

• • •

When Dana reached the bottom of the stairs, she heard Nina's unmistakable voice talking to Bea and Helen, who had just arrived. She was relating the size and location of the original five-foot Concolor fir.

"It's okay, Nina," Dana said. "We had such a good time. Finding the tree was just *part* of the day. What about our lunch at the historic inn? I'd say we had a few liberating conversations there and in the car."

"That reminds me," Nina said. "I hope everyone will join NOW to help with the March 8th rally to celebrate International Women's Year."

"Nina, come with me," Dana said quickly before Nina had time to start a sign-up drive in the living room. "You remember my friend Phoebe Cirone? She's planning a wine tour of the Alsace region in the spring, and I thought you would have a few suggestions for her. Bea, why don't you and Helen relax on the sofa. I know it's been a long day. We'll be right back"

"Bea, let me ask you an honest question," Helen said when Dana and Nina left. "What is Dana up to with those kids in the contest? I'm highly suspicious. She keeps scooting into Bob's office, and I can't help but think that something's up."

"Are you still upset over the teen makeup counter?" Bea asked, lighting a cigarette.

"Counter? That's all it is? I can live with that. But don't quote me."

"Dana does have a way with Bob," Bea remarked, "but all I know is that he gave his blessing regarding something to do with the contest. He told me before I left the store that it's going to be a huge surprise, so I have no idea what it is."

"Well, whatever it turns out to be, it will need my blessing as well if it has anything to do with the Junior Department," Helen said. "I won't have my twenty-five years of buying experience run over by those teenagers of hers."

Bea raised her eyebrows and lit another cigarette. She knew Dana well. She also knew that underestimating the young woman's abilities would be a mistake.

• • •

Brett stood in the center of the living room, a champagne glass raised in the air.

"I'd like to propose a toast to all of our good friends. Thank you for coming, and may you all have a Merry Christmas, a happy holiday, and a prosperous New Year!"

"Hear, hear!" several guests said, their voices and glasses raised.

Dana looked around for Matthew and saw him kissing Janice on the lips as Brett finished his toast. Well, she would speak to Matthew the following day, although she noticed that Patti

Hartlen was also taking a great interest in the couple, which made the situation all the more embarrassing for Dana. Patti seemed to notice everything, for that matter. She'd been eyeing Brett, Janice, and Matthew ever since arriving. What was she looking for? Dana advanced towards her brother.

"Matthew has another year and a half at the University of Hawaii," Dana told Janice. Dana thought that the physical distance between them in their everyday lives might pose a severe impediment to their forming an actual relationship. It was worth emphasizing.

"Yes!" Janice said. "Brett is giving me a couple of days off next week. I'm flying back to Hawaii with Matthew on Saturday so he can give me those surfing lessons. And I suggested that we drive up to New England when he returns for Christmas break."

Dana nodded her head. "That's . . . interesting." Dana could see that Janice was aware of how upset she was that Matthew had become an object of romantic interest. Janice was relishing every second of flaunting that interest in front of Dana.

"Johnny is going to fly out after Janice leaves," Matthew said.

"So I heard," Dana said.

"Brett told him that the islands might help him get over the cancelled wedding. I know a few friends who might help him relax a bit and take his mind off things."

Dana rolled her eyes. "I'm sure you do," she said. "Just remember that Uncle John is moving to the city and needs him."

"No problem, big sister. Johnny is just coming out for a quick visit. He'll be back in time for Christmas."

Dana smiled and circulated among her guests, her eyes continually searching for Matthew and Janice. The pair remained inseparable.

Chapter Thirty-Four

Brett and Janice emerged from a meeting with Richard Patterson and Patrick Denner at ten o'clock the following morning. The two litigators suppressed smiles at the news that had been disclosed in Richard's office, news that would profoundly affect their careers and personal lives.

"This is incredible!" Brett said when the two were seated in his office a few minutes later. "We're going to San Francisco!"

"For six months!" Janice said. "The gods have smiled upon us. We really have a sweet deal, my dear Mr. McGarry. How do you think Dana will take the news?" Janice asked, shooting a finger at a picture of Dana in the sitting area on the far side of the office.

Brett leaned back in his chair and clasped his hands behind his head. He appeared both calm and relaxed, as if he were considering a golf game rather than his career and marriage. "She's not going to like it initially—not at all—but if she wants the life she's been talking about lately, she doesn't have much recourse but to accept the arrangement."

During the previous hour, Richard had updated Brett and Janice on a case they'd been working on. The firm's client, owner of an office building in lower Manhattan, had sued a construction company with offices in San Francisco and New York for installing asbestos in the ceilings of the Manhattan building. In the past ten years, asbestos had been linked to several lung diseases, such as emphysema and asbestosis. Many workers in the building, owned by an insurance company, had been diagnosed with lung illnesses and were seeking compensation, so the insurance company was, in turn, suing the builder for failing to disclose the presence of asbestos and provide a safe work environment. Precedent had been set in such cases as early as 1964. During the past six months, during which time Davis, Konen and Wright had represented the insurance company, the paper trail had led to the builder's San Francisco office, where the decisions on construction materials had been made when the building in Manhattan had been erected in 1962. The company had also ignored medical research conducted in California, research warning of the health risks involved from exposure to asbestos. While many pertinent documents were held by the construction company's New York office, more than half the files were at corporate headquarters in San Francisco. The judge had ordered a change in jurisdiction and that all relevant New York documents be sealed and shipped to the West Coast. Brett and Janice would remain on the case and live in the Bay area for the next six months. The defendant was suing for one hundred million dollars in compensation, and the fee for Davis, Konen and Wright more than warranted the presence of Brett and Janice in California.

"It sure is easier than sneaking around," Brett said, "although we'll have to maintain separate apartments since the firm is picking up the tab. They'll no doubt be checking in on us frequently, but three thousand miles is a pretty good buffer."

"We'll have enormous freedom," Janice proclaimed. "Amazing luck!"

Janice was even happier than Brett realized. The separation from Dana that would be imposed by the case might represent the final breaking strain on Brett's marriage. Additionally, she would have at least six months, maybe longer, to indoctrinate her lover in the more laid-back lifestyle of California. To Janice, the news represented a win-win situation.

"I guess your flirting with Matthew wasn't necessary after all," Brett theorized.

"To the contrary," Janice said. "It has thrown everyone off the trail—Dana, Patti, and Patrick for starters. There's no better way to begin our adventure than to have deflected any suspicion about you and me. It was the perfect prologue."

"It was quite a performance last night," Brett admitted. "Dana, Patti, and Richard couldn't take their eyes off you."

"You think I'm a naughty girl, don't you?"

Brett thought for a moment. "Reckless," he said. "Refreshingly reckless."

"Be careful," Janice said. "After California, you may never want to give me up."

Brett smiled thinly. Could Janice's words be true? Was he in over his head?

Brett shook off the thought quickly. He was in control. He was *always* in control. He would go along for the ride, so to speak, but he would never leave Dana. Sooner or later, his pleasant diversions with Janice Conlon would have to end.

But not yet.

Chapter Thirty-Five

Dana had asked Matthew to meet her for lunch at Charleston Garden at twelve thirty on Friday.

"Ready for the Ball tonight?" Matthew asked. "You've put an awful lot of effort into this contest."

"It always requires a lot of work," Dana admitted, "and this year's contest was more taxing than most. But it has been worth every second. I hope I've helped the contestants acquire even greater maturity and confidence. They're all terrific. There's one girl in particular who really needed this experience."

"I'm sure you helped her. You'll be a great mom when the time comes."

The remark caught Dana off guard, and Matthew immediately picked up on Dana's hesitation. "Anything wrong?"

"Brett and I have been discussing starting a family for the first time in a long time. I really feel I'm ready. We have the money, and I'm not getting any younger."

"Is Brett on board with this?"

Dana raised her eyebrows. "He says he is, and from what I've seen these past few days, I believe him."

"Good. You've been a wonderful wife, and I think it's time for the next phase of your life to begin."

"Speaking of new phases in life, where are *you*, Matthew? Anyone special out in Hawaii?"

Matthew leaned back and folded his arms after sipping from a glass of iced tea. "What you're really asking is if I'm serious about pursuing a relationship with Janice," he said with a grin. "I saw you staring at us last night as carefully as a private detective."

"Guilty as charged," Dana admitted. "It's just that . . . well . . ."

"You disapprove, but you don't want to interfere with my life, right? Just like Johnny and Uncle John with all the wedding drama before the ceremony was cancelled."

"You're exactly right, Matthew. Frankly, I find Janice's personality more than a little abrasive. At a neighborhood meeting on Tuesday, she actually—"

Matthew held up his hand, causing Dana to pause in mid-sentence. "Don't worry," Matthew said. "She came on awfully strong last night, but it's a moot point. She called me this morning to say that the firm has dumped a lot of work in her lap. She won't be coming to Hawaii with me next week. In fact, she said that the little trip she suggested to New England over Christmas break would have to be cancelled as well. I think it's for the best. It was fun to flirt, I suppose, but she was moving way too fast for me."

"Whew!" Dana exclaimed, lowering her head in relief. "Music to my ears."

"Hey, you were really worried about me, weren't you?"

"I think she's bad news, Matthew. It's hard to put my finger on it, but she looks to me like a schemer. I don't trust anything about her."

"Her call this morning caught me off guard," Matthew said. "I got the impression last night that she was genuinely interested in spending time with me, but her calling it quits before anything developed—that's strange. I've been dumped before, but never in less than twenty-four hours."

Dana and Matthew both laughed.

"Maybe she found someone else this morning—Janice Conlon's fresh catch of the day," Dana suggested. "I don't think she has any concept of boundaries, and she probably pursues whatever she wants without hesitation. Trying to figure her out would be a waste of time. The important thing is that I don't have to worry about you getting tangled up with the likes of her."

"You don't, but I appreciate the concern."

"I'm *always* concerned about you, Matthew. So are Mom and Dad. We're a close-knit family, and that won't ever change."

"Like the Cirones," Matthew remarked. "Uncle John is so relieved that Johnny's wedding is cancelled that he's taking Mom and Dad out tonight to celebrate. He's also donating ten thousand dollars to Chaminade High School."

"Uncle John is the best. I'm glad everything worked out."

"Just like a Shakespearean play," Matthew said. "Everybody ends up with the right person at the end."

They both laughed again, but Dana knew that confusing situations didn't always resolve themselves in the manner of the famous bard's comedies. Finding the right person—that was sometimes a difficult task. She had prayed very hard during the past week that her marriage and career were on the right track. She felt that her prayers were being answered.

Chapter Thirty-Six

After lunch with Matthew, Dana made sure that all last-minute preparations had been taken care of for the Sugar Plum Ball, which would be held in the ballroom of the Waldorf Astoria. She left work early, returned home, and got dressed, changing into the black gown from the House of Cirone. As she looked in the full-length mirror in her dressing room, she added a few ropes of pearls, pinned a white silk camellia, and draped the Chantilly lace shawl. In that moment, Dana thought of fashion's most enduring icon who created this elegant and alluring style, and the happy personal life that eluded her. Mademoiselle Chanel died in 1971 at the age of eighty-eight while working on her spring collection, but her passion for work did not fill the void of marriage and children. Her success was costly, but clearly the choice of an uncompromising woman determined to achieve greatness on her own. She had once said, "I never wanted to weigh more heavily on a man than a bird."

As she checked her makeup one last time, Dana wondered what Helen would think when she announced the winner of the contest. Bob had thought her idea to be absolutely ingenious, but the solution would affect other departments in the store, especially Helen's. In the long run, Helen's reaction would not affect Dana's announcement or, for that matter, her future actions at the store. She had proven herself this past week, and had shown her colleagues that she was more savvy than they had given her credit for. She respected the executives who had paid their dues for many years, but if Ira were going to pursue the emerging youth market, then she would continue to speak up when she felt she had something to contribute.

"You look beautiful," Brett said as he finished donning his tux.

"Thank you," Dana said as she turned and straightened Brett's tie. He had been a charming host the night before, and he had surprised her with his invaluable assistance to Johnny. The old Brett, self-absorbed and distant, would not have taken the time to help her childhood friend extricate himself from a potentially damaging situation that would also have led to a marriage of questionable merit. He was still distracted at times, but Dana felt that she had indeed, to paraphrase her brother at lunch, found the right person.

"You do know how to wear a tux, Mr. McGarry. You look quite handsome."

"I bet you say that to all of the lawyers who are in line for partnership," Brett said.

"Only the thoughtful ones."

• • •

The Sugar Plum Ball was a black tie event preceded each year by a cocktail reception at six o'clock at the Waldorf. When it was time for the ball, the guests were seated as the finalists' fathers escorted their daughters, all wearing white gowns, into the winter wonderland ballroom. The first dance between father and daughter was to "The Way You Look Tonight." Later, the contestants were seated at tables with their respective families. Seated at the B Altman table were Dana, Brett, Andrew,

Helen, Bob and Bea, each with their spouses. At Brett's invitation, Davis, Konen and Wright was supporting the charitable event, and Jack and Patti Hartlen were seated at the firm's table. Brett surmised that Richard was still tenaciously trying to get the Hartlens to retain the firm.

Opening remarks were made by John S. Burke, Jr., the chairman of B Altman and the president of the Altman Foundation. Burke welcomed the guests and thanked them for their support of the Eighth Annual Sugar Plum Ball for the benefit of the Children's Aid Society. Burke explained that in 1913, under the provisions of Benjamin Altman's will, the Altman Foundation was established to support charitable institutions that benefited the people in the city of New York. Committed to that mission was the Children's Aid Society, founded by Charles Loring Brace in 1853, when orphanages and "poor houses" were the only services available to homeless children on the streets of New York. Brace introduced "Orphan Trains," which took tens of thousands of abandoned orphans from city slums to live with farm families across America. Currently, the Society, together with dozens of other agencies, provided foster boarding care, adoption programs, and community centers offering healthcare and leadership training. The Society was also a founding member of the Boys & Girls Club of America.

Champagne was poured before coffee and dessert as Dana rose from her seat and made her way to the front of the ballroom to make the much-anticipated announcement. As she faced the audience, she was distressed to see Brett get up and leave the ballroom. This was her moment! Where could he possibly be going? In fact, Andrew had also left the table. She'd worked for three months on the contest. Where were her biggest supporters?

• • •

Brett had deemed this the perfect time to step out of the ballroom and call Janice. Dana was occupied and hopefully wouldn't notice his absence. He'd be back within five minutes. He entered a phone booth in the empty cocktail area and closed the door.

"Have you told her yet?" asked Janice.

"No. She'd get pretty aggravated if I hit her with a bombshell before her presentation. I'll wait until we get home."

"Are you prepared for the storm? From what I saw at the Murray Hill Neighborhood Association Meeting, she's feistier than I thought."

"If she wants a country home, she'll have to accept it. What are you doing tonight, by the way?"

"Packing for San Francisco."

"Are you making an itinerary to show me the sights?"

Janice laughed heartily. "You've got to be kidding! And we're not starting a photo album either, although you might be interested in the scenery at Black Sands Beach."

"What's so special about Black Sands Beach?" Brett asked.

"No East Coast inhibitions, if you get my drift."

"I'm intrigued," Brett said, "but I have to run before my absence is noticed. Bye."

As Brett placed the black receiver in its cradle, he looked out the glass panel in the phone booth door and saw Andrew and Jack in a heated conversation. Andrew, visibly upset, turned and started to walk away as Jack grabbed his arm. Andrew resisted and continued to the men's lounge.

As Jack straightened his tuxedo jacket and began walking back into the ballroom, Brett hurried out of the phone booth, approaching Jack just as he was opening the door.

"This town gets smaller by the minute!" Brett exclaimed as he touched Jack's shoulder.

Jack froze in his tracks like a deer caught in the headlights. A look of panic seized his face.

"I can't believe that you know Andrew, too!" Brett continued. "He's Dana's best friend. They work closely at B Altman. They're always together running around town, doing something or other. He practically lives at our apartment. Has Patti met Andrew?"

Jack's stare was frozen with fear and guilt, and Brett played it for all it was worth.

"Listen, let's all get together for a holiday dinner," Brett suggested.

"Certainly," Jack managed to whisper, the blood draining from his face.

"And with the wives," Brett said. Handing Jack his card, he added, "Let's hammer out the details on the consortium first. Call me next week and let's get it done."

Brett clapped Jack on the shoulder. "Shall we get back to the party?"

The men re-entered the ballroom.

•••

"It's always the highlight of our evening," Dana said, "when we introduce the five outstanding finalists who started competing a year ago for the title of Miss B Altman Teen of the Year. The girls joined our twelve-week program last September and were selected among forty contestants for their excellence in writing, fashion design, and public speaking."

As instructed, the girls rose when their names were called.

"As we observed these exemplary young women during the competition this year," Dana continued, "we recognized their unique and diverse talents, personalities, styles, and interests, and we saw a wonderful opportunity for each of them, as well as for B Altman."

Helen sat up straighter at the B Altman table, wondering what Dana was about to say.

Dana paused, looking out across the tables and the anxious audience members. There was complete silence in the ballroom.

"It gives me great pleasure to announce B Altman's very first Teen Advisory Board, consisting of Kate Daley, Robin Flowers, Lisa Gelber, Mari Kamura, and Kim Sullivan. Or to put it another way, all of our finalists have been declared winners. The young women will serve as ambassadors for B Altman. Each will receive a monthly shopping bonus for the Junior Department, hostess in-store events, model junior fashions throughout the store, and will provide Ms. Helen Kavanagh, B Altman's junior buyer, monthly reports about what their peers are wearing and doing. This will support the store's new focus on the growing and diverse youth market as will shortly be seen by the addition of a teen makeup counter. I'd like all five winners and their families to join me on stage, and I ask that you now congratulate them on their hard work and success," Dana said, putting her hands together.

The ballroom erupted into applause as everyone got to their feet. The five contestants looked as stunned—and as pleased—as everyone else. The finalists were handed roses and Tiffany necklaces by the contest staff, after which Dana prepared to make a final announcement.

Dana had gotten the idea to make all the girls winners at the Winterberry Christmas Tree Farm when Andrew had looked at the many sizes and shapes of the trees, noting that he could use all of them in one way or another since they complemented each other perfectly. And if they were all winners, Bob couldn't object that Kim Sullivan hadn't gotten the emotional boost she needed. An advisory board would also augment the new teen makeup counter, giving it more importance despite its small size.

"B Altman looks forward to working with our winners in the coming months, and I invite them to have a victory dance with their fathers and other relatives. We'll then be served coffee and dessert. Please enjoy the evening!"

Dana was on the way back to her table when Patrick Denner stopped her on the edge of the dance floor.

"I think that the event coordinator for this contest deserves a dance as well," Patrick said, "and since Brett must have stepped out for the moment, I'd be privileged if you'd do me the honor."

"Always the gentleman," Dana said, taking Patrick's hand while wondering where her husband was. Why wasn't he present to share her moment of accomplishment?

On the dance floor, Patrick congratulated Dana for her success with the contest. "I'm sure Brett will be back shortly," he added. "I suspect he may be on the phone since the firm put so much on his plate this morning."

"He's always so incredibly busy," Dana said, thinking nothing of the remark. "Just as all of you are."

Patrick laughed. "You're very understanding, Dana. Going to San Francisco goes far beyond simply being busy."

"San Francisco?" Dana said. "A business trip?"

"I'm afraid so. A six-month business trip, to be exact. You mean he hasn't told you yet?"

"Not all the particulars," Dana said, not knowing how to answer. She felt numb but finished the dance, trying to muddle through the awkward situation.

As Dana returned to the table, Brett walked into the ballroom and seated himself at the same time that Bea and Helen stood.

"Helen and I are going to the powder room," Bea stated. "Helen isn't feeling well." Bea looked over her shoulder at

Dana, giving her a knowing look. The news about catering to the youth market had obviously caught Helen off guard.

Brett sat and took a sip of scotch, looking at the dancers. He was smiling but had a faraway look in his eyes.

"Would you like me to help you pack for San Francisco?" Dana asked him.

He gave no response. Obviously focused on other matters, he had not heard the question.

Dana tapped him on the shoulder. "Do you have anything to tell me?"

"Wonderful job tonight, honey! You've done it again."

"Who won the contest?" Dana asked.

Brett paused before motioning to the dance floor. "Why, the winners, of course."

"When were you planning on telling me about going to San Francisco?" she asked.

"Oh, you know about that? You must have talked to Patrick."

"Yes. He was kind enough to dance with me after I made the announcement that all five girls were the winners."

"Gosh, sorry, honey. I had to make a business call. Five winners? That must have been something."

"Brett, you have a lot of explaining to do. Shouldn't I be the first to know that—"

Kim rushed to Dana's side. "Dana, could you come over and meet my parents?"

"We'll continue this later," Dana whispered. "I'm very upset with you."

Brett finished his scotch and started another. He had expected some initial resistance, and he'd gotten it. As always, he'd use his legal mind to lay out the merits of his case when he explained the situation to Dana. Even if Janice had never joined the firm, he would still have to litigate the case in San Francisco. Dana would come around.

• • •

At their table, Kim's parents were overflowing with appreciation for the interest that Dana had taken in Kim, noting how enthusiastic and motivated their daughter had recently become. The contest had been just what Kim needed, and in the last two days, she'd grown especially optimistic.

"We're still going to ask Kim to take the AP placement exam in chemistry," Dr. Sullivan said, "but we've also agreed to consider her request to study art history."

"Yes," her mother added. "Kim's father and I agree that it's only fair to keep both doors open right now since our daughter is still a sophomore. And now that she'll have duties at the store, she's going to be very busy. Her decision on a career is one of the biggest she'll make, and the three of us realize that it should be done with more deliberation."

"I'm very happy for all of you," Dana stated. "Kim is a terrific young lady, and I know she has great things in her future regardless of what she chooses."

Kim hugged Dana, and as she did so, she whispered "Thank you for everything" in her mentor's ear.

"Come by my office anytime," Dana said. "You'll be at the store quite a bit from now on, so let's keep in touch and have lunch sometime."

"That would be great!"

"By the way, how is Lisa taking the news?"

"Like Lisa. I think she feels she should have been the only winner, and she's acting like it, too."

Dana and Kim both laughed. "She'll be okay. You five will be a great asset to the store."

Dana was happy that she would be able to stay in touch with all the girls, especially Kim. Kim still had hard times ahead, plus Dana had grown very fond of her. Now that the contest was over, she didn't have to worry about the issue of favoritism.

• • •

The evening was drawing to a close. When Dana returned to the B Altman table, she decided to skip dessert and prepared to leave with Brett. They needed to have a serious discussion back at their apartment.

"Where is Andrew?" Dana asked.

"It looks like both Andrew and Helen aren't feeling very well," Bob said. "Andrew came back while you made the announcement but then left right after you went to Kim's table, and neither has returned. Andrew seemed troubled."

"I hope his father is okay," Dana said.

Brett remained silent. He knew, of course, that Andrew and Jack had engaged in a lover's quarrel, but he would hold that piece of information very close to the vest.

Brett was privy to a lot of secrets, and he liked it that way. It made him feel powerful.

Chapter Thirty-Seven

Dana went straight to the bedroom upon returning home while Brett took Wills out for a final walk. She had not uttered a single word on the way home, nor had Brett pressed her to open up and talk about her feelings about his impending trip. It was better, he knew, to explain the entire situation when he had her undivided attention. Juries were always stationary and positioned strategically, and tonight he would, for all intents and purposes, be delivering a closing argument.

When he climbed the stairs to the bedroom, he saw Dana sitting on the chaise lounge, her face showing no emotion whatsoever. She was motionless, still wearing her gown.

"When are you leaving?" she asked with no expression in her voice.

"Tomorrow morning."

"Tomorrow!" The response had instantly kindled Dana's anger.

"Just for three or four days. I have to find an apartment and check out the temporary office space Richard has leased in the firm's name."

"Why didn't you call and tell me the news about San Francisco this morning?" Dana asked. "This is not something minor, like passing up buying a Christmas tree. You should have discussed this with me as soon as you found out."

Brett sat on the edge of the bed, across from the chaise lounge. He leaned forward and looked at the floor, hands clasped. "It's something I have to do, so there would have been no discussion as to whether or not I would take the assignment. I've been litigating the case, and the task falls to me. It's that simple."

Dana raised her voice higher, her intense frustration growing. "Don't try to sidestep the issue, Brett. You know exactly what I'm talking about. This is about communicating with your wife."

"As far as informing you earlier, I didn't want to spoil your big evening. Listen, this separation is going to be difficult for both of us. You think I *want* to be away from you for six months?"

"I don't know what *you* want anymore, but what *I* want is an explanation of what to expect for the next six months. This affects my life, too. Are you going to be away for six months straight? For a few days each week? A couple of weeks a month? Will you be home on weekends? I'm not a child, Brett. I could have had a discussion about your news this morning and still handled my responsibilities at work. I don't appreciate learning about *my* life from your associate at work. I would think you would have wanted to share this with me the minute you heard about it. Is everything in our lives on hold until this case is finished?"

"Now just a minute," Brett said indignantly. "First things first. I tried to make sure that the ball this evening wouldn't be spoiled for you, and I'm paying a heavy price for trying to be thoughtful. I had no idea that Patrick would give you the news. I intended to tell you as soon as we got home. As for flying back to New York, I anticipate doing so at least one or two weekends every month, but that's just a guess at this point."

Dana rolled her eyes but said nothing.

"Second, you should at least know why the case needs to be tried in San Francisco," Brett continued. He related the judge's ruling based on where the construction files were currently located and how the decision to use asbestos in the building in lower Manhattan had been made in San Francisco. He also explained that he needed to have a subpoena issued requiring the California contractor to make available the appropriate documents so that he would be able to properly prepare the case when he arrived for his longer stay. These details had no impact on Dana.

Brett pressed on. "What if B Altman made you a buyer, Dana, and they told you to spend three months in Europe to acquire a new line? Are you telling me that you wouldn't accept the assignment?"

"I would talk to you about it first!"

"Yes, because you would have the choice of turning down such a promotion. I don't have that luxury. The judge made an unexpected decision, and Richard wants me on the coast."

"Brett, I clearly understand that. I have *never* put my needs—or our needs, for that matter—before your work. Isn't that true?"

"Yes," Brett said, "and I have always appreciated that."

Dana stood and looked at Brett, her face flush with resentment. "Well, you may be appreciative, but you have a lousy way of showing it. Your blatant indifference to me and our marriage is becoming unbearable."

Brett got up and stopped Dana from going into her dressing room. "Dana, listen to me. We're in the home stretch. We've both worked hard to get to this point, and we'll get through these rough spots somehow. I admit that I'm distracted and irritable sometimes. I can't stand them holding the partnership over my head, leaving me to feel that one false move and I'm gone. I'll be better when it's announced. You'll see."

"I know," Dana said, exhausted from the argument. "What's another six months, huh? Is the firm sending anyone with you?"

"Patrick will be flying out occasionally. He's also dispatching a couple of paralegals to help with research and to file motions. Richard knows this is an inconvenience, but everyone else is tied up with cases here in the city. I've been working on a case for the Landmarks Preservation Commission, but Janice will have to handle that on her own from now on. It's not difficult. As for the asbestos case, it's not something she could manage. She's a junior litigator, and there's too much at stake to put such a complicated case in her hands."

Brett had taken a risk by mentioning Janice's name, but he thought it was good strategy. It apparently had a positive effect on Dana.

Dana sat on the bed, her head buried in her hands.

"You can always come with me if you choose," Brett suggested. He already knew how Dana would respond.

"No," she said, shaking her head. "I have a full slate of events at the store, plus Bob told me that I'd have to write the mission statement for the Teen Advisory Board and schedule their duties. It was, after all, my brainchild. I also want to keep my eye on the new teen makeup counter to see if it can be expanded at some point in the future. And then there's my work with Diana Vreeland at the Costume Institute, which I'm really looking forward to. No, I couldn't get away."

Brett raised his eyebrows and tilted his head, the hint of a smile crossing his face.

"Yes, I take your meaning," she said. "I have my duties, and you have yours."

Brett put his arms around Dana and kissed her on the lips.

"I love you," Dana said, holding him close. "And thank you for not distracting me from my duties at the ball with the news. I realize that you meant well."

"I love you, too," he said. "Believe me when I tell you that everything I'm doing is for us in the long run. Everything."

They kissed again.

Later, when Dana was asleep, Brett got two suitcases from the back of his closet and put them in the hall by the door. He had packed earlier that afternoon, before Dana returned home from work. He was ready for his first trip with Janice to San Francisco.

Chapter Thirty-Eight

Dana awoke on Saturday morning feeling energized. Her work at the store during the past week had been exemplary, and the Sugar Plum Ball had been an incredible success. Her creative juices, however, were still flowing. As she dressed, she had yet another epiphany regarding the contest winners.

Dana had already arranged with Bob to have the girls model junior fashions around the store every other Saturday. But it was Christmas, the most natural season for gift-giving, and there was no sense in losing valuable time—not a single day. If she could reach the girls by phone, she might be able to get them onto the selling floor that afternoon to begin their modeling duties. Over coffee, Dana called the newly-created Teen Advisory Board and asked them to meet her at the store at ten o'clock. Some of the girls had already made weekend plans, but all were eager to get started as soon as possible.

Brett had showered and was ready to leave for Kennedy International to catch a nine o'clock flight. He would grab a bite to eat at the airport before boarding.

"By the way," Brett said as he put on his overcoat in the downstairs hall, "do you think there's a position for Patti with the Altman Foundation? Richard told me she had a top job with the Houston Endowment, and John Cirone told Patti that you might be able to pave the way."

"I heard one of the grant managers was leaving. I suppose I could try to get her a preliminary meeting with Bob, although he doesn't have the final say-so, but it wouldn't hurt."

"Grant manager? That would be perfect! I'm sure she'd also enjoy working with you at the store. Why don't you take her to lunch at the Colony Club next week and help her get into the swing of things here in New York a bit faster. I can see you two becoming good friends."

"I'll see what I can do." Dana stood and put her arms around Brett's neck. "I know it's just for a few days, but I miss you already. Call me tonight?"

"Of course I will."

Outside, the doorman haled a taxi, and Dana gave Brett a kiss as the cabbie put his luggage in the trunk. Brett turned and waved as he slipped into the backseat.

Dana watched the cab merge into the stream of morning traffic on Park Avenue. She was resigned to Brett's assignment, and she would use his time away to focus her creative energies on the new youth campaigns at the store. She went back upstairs and got ready for work. She was excited that she would be able to implement the duties of the Advisory Board so soon.

• • •

Brett looked through the passenger window of the cab. Since seeing Jack and Andrew in the cocktail area at the Waldorf the night before, he'd been thinking of ways to make sure Jack toed his line. Landing Hartlen Response would almost certainly ensure partnership, and he wasn't going to let anything jeopardize his chances. This morning, he'd recalled that Patti had worked for the Houston Endowment. Opening a door for her with the Altman Foundation would send a clear message to Jack that he was playing hardball. If Jack ever got cold feet about the consortium, Brett would remind him that he could tell Dana at any time about the affair, and Andrew and Jack would be history. So would Jack's marriage.

Brett found himself smiling all the way to the airport. He literally had every situation under tight control. He knew Janice would be proud of the clever, albeit devious, way that he was handling matters.

She was already waiting for him when he entered the main terminal.

Chapter Thirty-Nine

Earlier in the month, Jack and Ralph Hartlen had rented office space for Hartlen Response in the Chrysler Building on 42nd Street and Lexington Avenue. The two men took an elevator to the company's suite to inspect progress on its renovation. Carpets had been laid, and most of the office furniture had been delivered over the past two weeks. The telephone company was still wiring the offices, and interior decorators roamed the hallways as assistants hung pictures and brought in plants.

"What about staffing?" Ralph asked his son. "How far along are you?"

"Some of our key people in mid-level management are relocating from Houston, but not many. The assistant personnel director arrived a month ago and has been interviewing for various positions—everything from engineers to public relations to secretaries—and I'm confident that we'll be up and running by the second week in January."

Ralph nodded, obviously pleased. "You've done a great job as always, son. I never have to worry with Hartlen Response in your capable hands."

"Actually, I'd like to speak with you about something important," Jack said while trying to hide his nervousness. "Let's find a quiet spot and talk for a few moments."

Jack's office had been completely furnished and decorated, so he sat on the edge of his desk, one foot on the floor, while his father sat in a client's chair a few feet away.

"What's on your mind, son?" Ralph asked. "You look concerned."

Jack folded his arms and exhaled. He hoped and prayed that he could override his father's decision about waiting for a patent to be issued on their response technology.

"Dad, I've been thinking that if we're going to open the New York office on schedule, then we need to be ready for a spill from day one. That means positioning our equipment in strategic staging areas, such as the Gulf Coast, the Eastern Seaboard, and in the Caribbean. The machinery will therefore be at least partly visible no matter how much we try to shield it from rival companies. Unless we push back the expansion of Hartlen Response, we need the protection afforded by the consortium proposal of Richard and Brett. I don't think we have the luxury of waiting months or years for a patent to be issued. Some of the oil tankers now in service are twenty-five to thirty years old, and our research teams tell me that the hull integrity of these vessels isn't very good. In fact, the draft of some fully-loaded ships is dangerously low while navigating over shallow water and shoals, and that's asking for trouble. If we're going to be the leaders in this field, we need to move fast. I think Richard and Brett can give us both profit and protection."

Ralph remained silent for several seconds. "Are you convinced in your own mind that this is the best avenue? No doubts? No pressure from Davis, Konen and Wright?"

"Absolutely," Jack said, using his best poker face. "And no pressure. We've invested twenty million dollars in our response technology, and we need to be proactive to make sure that we get credit for using it first. If other companies sign a non-compete that binds them for several years, we'll be perfectly positioned. We'll see huge returns on our investment."

Ralph nodded philosophically. "Jack, I put you in charge of this company for a reason, and you've taken the initiative in opening this office, not to mention in guiding the development of our equipment at every stage. And the tanker issue worries me a great deal. As head of the company, it's your call. I'll stand by whatever you decide."

"I'll contact Brett and set up a meeting with him and Richard. Hopefully, we can get this done in the next week or so."

Jack breathed a sigh of relief as his father got to his feet. Brett had caught the luckiest of breaks the night before and now held the leverage over Jack's personal and corporate life. He wondered how far Brett might press him on other matters in order to hold his advantage. He didn't trust him, and yet he was about to put his company in the hands of a blackmailer.

• • •

When Jack returned to his suite at the Sherry-Netherland, he saw that Patti, dressed in a business suit, was on her way out.

"I thought we might do some Christmas shopping today," Jack told her. "In the mood?" He made every attempt to act upbeat and enthusiastic.

"Sorry, Jack, but I'm on my way to B Altman. Dana McGarry called early this morning and told me that there's an opening for a grant manager with the Altman Foundation. I'll get to know Dana and her friends that much faster. Everyone's been so helpful and friendly. It's not the big cold city I imagined."

Jack said nothing. She would be working in the same building as Andrew—might even come into contact with him on a regular basis. He'd been correct in his estimation of the opportunistic Mr. McGarry: he was a bastard.

"Jack?" Patti said. "Anything wrong? You looked blank for a moment."

"Not a thing," Jack said, giving his wife a peck on the cheek. "Good luck with the interview. I'm sure you'll get the job."

"I have the experience," Patti said, "but I'm only meeting with the store's vice president and general manager. The decision will ultimately be made by the vice president of the foundation. This is just round one."

"I've got a good feeling about it," Jack said. "A really good feeling."

Jack knew, of course, that Patti would get the job. It was a *fait accompli*.

Chapter Forty

Dana could feel the pulse of the store and the holiday shoppers as clearly as she had eight days earlier, when she, Andrew, and Mark had stood on Fifth Avenue to admire the window display. In a real sense, she had come into her own over the past week, and she loved her job more than ever. As Kim might have said, it was part of her big picture.

The five girls of the Teen Advisory Board were already waiting at Dana's office when she arrived a few minutes before ten. They spoke in excited whispers, and even the competitive irritability of Lisa Gelber had disappeared. It was obvious to Dana that they regarded themselves as a team. It was a good omen inasmuch as it validated her decision to create the board in the first place.

"You're going to be modeling throughout the store today," Dana explained. "It's close to Christmas, and the floors are going to be crowded. What you have to remember at all times is that you're ambassadors of B Altman. Answer all questions from customers, and not just about what you're wearing. If they want to know where a department is or where the restrooms are located, don't just answer them, but be their escorts. If they ask you something you can't answer, direct them to the nearest sales counter so a full-time employee can help them. It's going to be a long afternoon, and I want you to keep a winning smile on your faces at all times. In fact, regard our customers as guests and make them feel good about shopping here. Can you do that?"

"It sounds exciting!" Kate said. "Yes!"

The other girls, eyes wide, echoed the same sentiment, looking at each other with anticipation.

"We don't have time to select outfits or make alterations," Dana explained, "so I checked on my way in and saw pastel Fair Isle sweaters in the Junior Department. They're colorful and will draw attention for people who aren't quite sure what the teen on their list is looking for. They're the perfect holiday gift."

Dana directed the girls to follow her assistant, who would take them to the stockroom and get each girl the right-sized sweater and then to Charles of the Ritz for a touch of makeup. "Meet me on the main floor at the staircase when you're finished, and I'll assign each of you to various departments. Ready?"

The girls left and Dana went down to the main floor, where she was approached by Helen.

"Did I just see your contestants walking into the store a few minutes ago?" Helen asked.

"Yes. They're going to be modeling sweaters this afternoon. Bob thought Saturday modeling would be a good idea, and I wanted to take advantage of the holidays. And remember—they're no longer contestants. They're the Teen Advisory Board now."

Helen's voice remained steady, but it was obvious that she was displeased. "Am I going to be consulted about *anything* that affects my position as junior buyer?" she asked curtly. "Or is everything decided by you and Bob these days?"

"Of course I want your input!" Dana responded, trying to sound as sympathetic as possible. "That's why the girls will be reporting to you monthly."

"I thought I made my position perfectly clear last week," Helen shot back. "I'm simply not interested. In fact, I think I'll have a talk with Bob right now. Since you're on the selling floor, maybe I have a chance of getting in to see him more quickly this time."

Helen turned abruptly and left.

Dana was past being intimidated by Helen, although she hoped she would be able to work with the junior buyer in a constructive manner. Helen had been Dana's friend for many years, and she had taught her many valuable lessons about working at B Altman. Without the expertise of Helen Kavanagh, the Junior Department wouldn't have become the success that it was, and Dana sincerely wished to work with a colleague possessing such insight.

When the girls arrived, Dana saw immediately that the Fair Isle sweaters had been the right choice. The girls looked great.

"Robin, I want you to model on the fifth floor, focusing on the Trim-the-Tree Shop and the Book Shop," Dana said. "Kim, I'm assigning you to Charleston Garden, but it won't get busy until about twelve-thirty, so start by covering the Sporting Goods section, the Toy Fair, and the World of Games, also on eight. Lisa, the main floor is yours. Try to catch people's eye as soon as they walk in. Kate, I'd like you to cover the fourth floor, especially the Waterford and Wedgwood Galleries and the Silver Shop. They'll be buzzing with gift buyers. And we can't forget the Children's Department on two. Mari, will you model there, please? Also, don't forget to stop into the Charles of the Ritz salon."

Dana proudly watched as the girls spread out through the store. Just a few days ago, Kim Sullivan was slated to be the sole winner of the contest. Because of Dana's ingenuity, the other four girls, who might otherwise be feeling more than a little despondent in the aftermath of the Sugar Plum Ball, were walking around with pride and self-esteem. And what they were doing was going to be great for the store as well. Dana had no doubt that they would be an integral part in attracting the growing youth market, and the beauty of it was that she would not have to utter the word "Biba" even once.

Dana had seen what was needed and gone after it. She now realized, probably as a result of her talks with Kim, that this was an important and necessary part of the narrative of her life.

Chapter Forty-One

Brett and Janice walked down the jetway to the concourse leading to terminal two at San Francisco International Airport. Brett felt elated to hold Janice's hand in public. It represented enormous freedom compared to the secrecy that had forced him to furtively glance over his shoulder when going to Janice's apartment in Greenwich Village during the past several days. For Brett, this new sense of liberty also reinforced Janice's belief that he had become horribly set in his ways. While he had always felt quite comfortable with the well-ordered routines of his life in New York City, he realized more and more each day that he had always suppressed a certain restlessness in his spirit. Thoughts of how he would approach the months and years ahead no longer tried to push their way into his thinking. He was far too happy now to spend time considering the repercussions of his actions. He would, as did Janice, live in the moment. The future would take care of itself.

He checked at the information desk in the terminal to see if Thomas Parks had arrived from Seattle. Parks was Brett's client, the owner of the insurance building in lower Manhattan. Brett and Richard had scheduled a brief, on-the-fly meeting with their client at the airport before Parks caught a connecting flight to Los Angeles. Parks needed to sign several papers authorizing actions to be taken by Davis, Konen and Wright, including the right to have his employees deposed in a new jurisdiction. Richard had also urged the meeting since he believed it was good policy to press the flesh, as the old saying went, with one of the firm's biggest clients. The quantum legal assessment made by the firm indicated that this new phase of the case had a high percentage of being successfully litigated, but there were never any guarantees in the courtroom. Clients needed reassurance before incurring additional—and very large—legal fees. Parks had the opportunity to drop the suit against the contractor when the judge ordered a change in jurisdiction, but he decided to press on despite the cost. Part of Brett's duty was to keep his client apprised of their ongoing strategy and hopeful of the outcome.

Parks' plane had not arrived due to bad weather in the Seattle area—the almost constant rains of the northwest—and Brett and Janice were informed that his flight was experiencing a two-hour delay.

"I guess we're stuck here for a few hours," Brett said. "I'm famished. Want to grab a bite to eat?"

"Absolutely," Janice answered. "The stewardess said that our in-flight meal was beef Wellington, but it tasted like cardboard. I couldn't eat it."

"I know a place in terminal one. Good local cuisine. Why don't we go in and relax? I've asked the information booth to page us when Parks' flight arrives."

Janice kissed Brett on the lips. "Relaxation. I want you to get used to that concept, which means far more than your precious honey buns. I'm your new morning treat from now on."

"I like the sound of that very much."

The two kissed again before heading to the restaurant.

Chapter Forty-Two

Dana's brother had to look twice to make sure he was seeing clearly, but he was. He sat down in one of the plastic seats in terminal one of San Francisco International Airport, his mind reeling. What should he do? Who should he tell?

Matthew had left his parents' home at Macy Channel on Saturday morning to board a nonstop eleven o'clock flight to San Francisco in order to catch a connecting flight to Hawaii. With three hours to kill before he left for the islands, he sat and read for a while, wandered through the terminals to do some shopping, and then decided to have lunch. He hated airline food, and his appetite was still on New York time. He settled on a gourmet deli specializing in Napa Valley cuisine and walked to the restaurant's entrance. That's when he stopped dead in his tracks before moving away from the door. Brett and Janice were sitting in a dimly-lit booth against the far wall of the restaurant. His first thought was to walk in and tell Brett hi—"What a coincidence! Are you two on a business trip?"—but he quickly checked the impulse when he saw Brett slip to Janice's side in the curved leather booth, raise a glass of wine, and kiss her on the lips.

He had retreated to the seat in the terminal to collect his thoughts. Several times he started to get up in order to walk to a bank of pay telephones on the far side of the terminal, but each time he sat down again. How could he break the news to his sister? Would she think it was some crazy joke? No. Dana knew Matthew's humor wasn't so coarse, but he would still sound incredulous. "Hi, Dana, and guess what? Your husband is making time with that floozy from your party." He considered calling his mother for advice on exactly what to say, but he felt that it might be a dangerous move. He knew that his mother had a hands-on personality, and whatever was transpiring in the restaurant constituted a highly personal matter between Dana and her husband. What Dana chose to disclose to the rest of the family was her business and no one else's.

Thoughts sprang into Matthew's mind like lightning flashes. Was Brett tipsy and simply flirting with Janice? Matthew himself had fallen prey to her beguiling charms just a few days earlier. His assumption that Brett was having an affair might be totally off the mark even though there could be no justification for his giving Janice an overtly romantic kiss. A kiss and an affair were two different things. The more he thought about it, the more he convinced himself to tell no one, not even Dana. He ran the fingers of his right hand through his hair, unable to exorcise the image of Janice and Brett from his mind.

That's when he remembered Janice's call to him Friday morning, and immediately everything fell into place. She told Matthew that she'd been given a lot of last-minute work by the firm and that she would be busy for quite some time. Neither Brett nor Janice had mentioned anything about a business trip to the West Coast—nor had Dana or their parents, for that matter—and that was strange in itself. The trip had obviously come up at the last minute. Matthew was convinced that Janice had genuinely planned on spending time with him, and she could have easily rescheduled her trip to Hawaii or their drive up to New England. But she hadn't, and there could be only one reason why. She'd never really been interested in him in the first place. Her sights were set elsewhere, and she had merely been using Matthew as a decoy—a "beard" in the parlance of affairs, someone to throw one's spouse off the trail.

Matthew was tempted to walk in and confront Brett, not with anger, but with the simple knowledge that he was aware of what was going on. Matthew quickly realized that Brett, a shrewd lawyer, would try to explain away the situation.

Matthew felt intense anger rise in his chest, and he knew that he would have to tell his sister. But he would get some insurance just in case Brett or Janice attempted to either deny what he was seeing—"You must have been looking at the wrong table, Matthew"—or offer up some implausible explanation. Matthew reached into his leather carry-on bag and pulled out his 35mm Nikon, loaded it, and attached a zoom lens. He got up and walked to the side of the restaurant, which was separated from the terminal by a trellis half-wall, on top of which sat tall, lush ferns. Brett and Janice were still there. Good. He would obtain indisputable proof with a few careful shutter clicks. He adjusted the camera's setting for the dim light, turned the f-stop ring to bring the lens into focus, and began to shoot, the ferns offering him ample cover. The couple kissed each other every minute or two, and the waiter had brought them a new bottle of wine. Matthew captured every detail on film—every kiss and laugh. There could be no doubt: his brother-in-law was having an affair.

When he had shot two rolls of film, Matthew went to the airport's U.S. Post Office.

"How soon can I get this back to New York?" Matthew asked the postal worker at the counter. "Yorktown Heights."

The man rubbed his chin. "It'll get to New York tomorrow by Air Mail, but it won't be delivered."

"Why not?"

"No Sunday delivery, son."

The look of frustration on Matthew's face was plain.

"But the mail is sorted and sent to substations twenty-four hours a day, seven days a week," the clerk said reassuringly. "It will get to its destination by Monday. Tuesday if there's bad weather."

"That's fine," Matthew said in a dispirited voice. How could Brett do this to Dana?

The clerk gave Matthew a mailer, which he addressed to his friend Bobby Munsen. He inserted the film into the brown padded envelope and paid for the postage.

"Thanks," Matthew said.

The clerk nodded and tossed the package into a large canvas sack behind him.

Matthew walked calmly and methodically away from the small postal substation. He knew what he had to do. He went to a pay telephone and called his friend Bobby, a photography buff with his own darkroom.

"Bobby, this is Matthew. Say, I'm in San Francisco. On my way back to school, but I just sent you a package containing two rolls of film. Could you develop them when they arrive on Monday or Tuesday and then take the pictures straight to my sister, Dana McGarry, at 77 Park Avenue? You can leave them in a sealed envelope with the doorman in the lobby."

"Sure," Bobby said. "No problem. Sounds pretty important."

"It is. And there's one more thing. Don't mention what's in the photos to anyone, okay?"

"Consider it done," Bobby said. "And hey, catch a wave for me out there in paradise."

"Got it. And thanks. I owe you one."

Matthew hung up and put two more nickels into the telephone. He was about to make the most difficult call of his life.

"B Altman," said a female voice on the other end of the line. "How may I direct your call?"

"Connect me with Dana McGarry, please."

"One moment please."

A minute passed, after which the operator came back on the line. "I'm sorry, but Ms. McGarry has left for the day."

Matthew sighed. "Thanks."

He'd forgotten about the time difference. It was mid-afternoon in California, which meant that Dana had already left work back in New York.

The airport public address system announced Matthew's flight for Hawaii. He glanced at his wat ch and hurriedly dropped more coins into the phone's narrow metal slots. He dialed Dana's home number, but there was no answer.

He put the receiver back on its cradle and started walking to the concourse where his gate was located. A second announcement over the PA called out his flight number, and time was running out. Matthew felt despondent. How was he going to carry this information on a long flight over the Pacific? He felt awful for Dana, but he needed to get the news off his chest. Suddenly, he stopped and reversed his steps, heading back to the telephone. He thought he knew where Dana was.

He would make one more phone call.

Chapter Forty-Three

Dana picked up the telephone in the library on the third ring. "Hello?"

When the long distance operator informed Dana that she had a person-to-person call from Matthew Martignetti, she accepted it immediately.

"It's me—Matthew. I've been trying to call you."

"I was out walking Wills."

"That's what I figured. I don't have long, sis, since my connecting flight is about to leave, but there's something I need to tell you."

"What's wrong, Matthew? Are you alright?" Dana could clearly tell from her brother's voice that he was troubled.

"I'm fine, but the thing is—" He paused. "The thing is that I just saw Brett and Janice in a restaurant here at the airport."

Dana sat down in the English club chair next to the phone. Brett had made no mention of Janice going to the coast. In fact, he had specifically said that Richard was sending two paralegals with him—no one else. Despite a sinking feeling in her stomach, she supposed that Richard might have dispatched Janice at the last minute. But she knew there was more to the story or Matthew wouldn't sound so upset.

"Are you still there?" Matthew asked.

"Yes. Go on."

"They were in a booth, Dana, and they were kissing." Matthew's voice was low and subdued.

Dana shut her eyes tightly, feeling dizzy. "Are you sure it was them? Were you close enough?"

"I saw them across the restaurant at first, but I'm positive it was Brett and Janice. A few minutes later I took some pictures using a zoom lens. They seemed to be very . . . intimate. I've sent the film to a friend of mine in Yorktown Heights. He has a darkroom and will deliver the developed photographs to you in a sealed envelope in another day or two. I'd rather not describe the scene. It's all on film. I'm so sorry, Dana. I don't know what to say."

"There *is* nothing to say," Dana said, holding back her tears. "I know how hard this was for you, but I'm glad you told me. I've had my suspicions, but that's all I'll say for now."

"Do you want me to fly back to New York?" Matthew asked. "I can change my ticket if I move fast."

"No, Matthew. I know you'd do anything for me, but I want you to finish the semester."

The third and final boarding call for Matthew's flight echoed through the terminal.

"I'll be praying for you, Dana. And don't be alone. Maybe you should call Andrew."

"Don't worry, Matthew. I'll be okay."

Matthew hung up and hurried to his gate, tears forming in the corner of his eyes.

• • •

Dana stared ahead, feeling numb. She didn't know how long the affair had been going on, but Brett had reeled her in with all of his excuses and talk of a country home and a family. He'd done so, she realized, to appease her and, in the process, to allay any suspicions she might have. Her mind was assaulted with recollections from the past week: learning of his trips with Janice to Mrs. John L. Strong and Saks; his odd behavior when her parents came over for dinner; his sudden absence from the ballroom the night before and the glassy stare on his face when he returned to the table. It all made sense now, even Janice's flirtation with Matthew. It had been nothing more than smoke and mirrors.

And then the tears came as Dana moved to the couch and rolled into a ball, a pain deep within her gut. The sense of betrayal she felt was overwhelming. She had been patient with Brett through the years as he had gained a stellar reputation with Davis, Konen and Wright, including his determination to make partner. She had not begrudged him success even though he had not always been emotionally or physically present to her. She was a professional woman with a rewarding job, and she didn't need Brett hovering over her every second of the day. He had grown distant recently, and still she hadn't made any demands on him. This was her reward for her patience and understanding.

She cried for an hour, and then anger surfaced. She pounded her fists into the cushions of the couch over and over again until she was out of breath and her strength was depleted. She had been treated cruelly, and the normally even-tempered Dana McGarry clenched her fists repeatedly until she finally breathed evenly and sat up straight. She knew what she had to do. Regardless of how long the affair had been going on—a day or a week or a year—she could no longer tolerate Brett's behavior, could not look past his lies and neglect and manipulation, nor was the lifestyle she would be leaving behind a cause for her to entertain second thoughts. She was a survivor, and she could make it on her own.

She would need to tell her parents, but that call would have to wait for another time. She was not emotionally ready to listen to her parents' reassurances and recommendations, however well-meaning they might be. She made another call instead.

• • •

Andrew was sitting next to Dana within the hour, his arms wrapped tightly around her. He let her cry more, her eyes already swollen. He would like to have said a great many things, all clichés: it was for the best; Brett didn't deserve her; it was a chance to start a new life. But Andrew knew better. Dana needed his presence, not his words.

At last Dana spoke. "I'm going to consult a lawyer this week," she said, "and then I'm going to look for an apartment. I want papers filed before the end of the year."

"I'll be with you every step of the way," Andrew said. "If you need a shoulder to lean on, that is. Maybe you should take the week off."

"I'll take your shoulder," Dana said, "but I'm going in to work next week. It's what I need right now. And I don't want anyone at the store to know about this for the time being. I couldn't handle all the sad looks and condolences. I'll tell everybody when I think the time is right. For now, I just want to do my job. B Altman is going to be my therapy for quite some time."

Andrew nodded. "I think you're probably right. Just remember I'm here for you any time, day or night."

Dana kissed Andrew on the cheek. "I know," she said. "That's why you're sitting here now."

• • •

The telephone rang an hour after Andrew left. Dana knew instinctively that it was Brett, the dutiful husband who was checking in to say that he had arrived in San Francisco safely. She thought of just letting it ring, but he would persist in calling, tonight and in the days ahead, until she answered. Indeed, if he couldn't reach her, he would almost certainly call her parents, and she couldn't have them worrying about her whereabouts.

Inhaling deeply, Dana steeled herself. She would not confront Brett yet. She would use his absence in the next few days to start processing the changes that would manifest in her life and also to take the preliminary steps to legally separate from Brett. She knew that if she told him she was aware of his affair, she would receive the obligatory lines used by all cheating husbands: "It's not what you think, honey! I can explain. This is all just a big misunderstanding."

"Hello," she said.

"It's me. Just wanted to say that I'm in San Francisco safe and sound. And, of course, to say I love you. Everything go okay at the store today?"

"Fine," Dana said, summoning every ounce of strength she had. "The Teen Advisory Board came in and did a great job modeling this afternoon."

"You sound like you have a cold," Brett said.

"Yeah, it started suddenly this afternoon. Been sniffling all evening."

"Make sure to drink lots of fluids," Brett counseled. "Hot tea and honey and get some rest. You've had a heck of a week."

"That's what I'm planning on. Don't worry about me. Just take care of business in San Francisco."

Dana's own words stung as she uttered them. Brett would indeed take care of business, and not just the firm's.

"Okay, honey. I'll say goodnight so you can go to bed. I love you."

Dana knew that she had to end the call on the right note or Brett would know immediately that she'd discovered his secret.

She closed her eyes and forced the words from her mouth: "I love you, too. Good night."

Dana hung up and looked at the pictures in the library, pictures of her life with Brett for the past eight years. That life was over now.

Dana had sensed that big changes in her life were in the offing when she'd walked home from B Altman the day after Thanksgiving. She'd been right.

Chapter Forty-Four

For Dana, Monday was a busy day. She had to work on the mission statement for the Teen Advisory Board and oversee a dozen other events related to the holiday season with Christmas Day growing closer. She steeled herself from the moment she entered B Altman to make sure that her mind was focused and her manner pleasant. It was Bea who remarked that she seemed quieter than usual—"Is everything okay, kiddo?"—but Dana reassured her that she was preoccupied with duties for the Advisory Board and drawing up its schedule. Her thoughts turned many times throughout the day to the news Matthew had given her on Saturday, and each time she recalled his words spoken from the pay phone in San Francisco, she felt a new pain in her heart, a feeling of disbelief at her husband's betrayal. And yet she managed to get through the day without anyone noticing her inner turmoil since store employees were in full holiday mode, barely able to keep up with their own duties. Helen was especially busy and called Dana into her office in the late morning.

"Have you heard the news?" Helen asked, her face beaming.

"News?" Dana said.

"I thought you of all people would know," Helen said. "The Fair Isle sweaters sold out on Saturday. The sales staff had to transfer sweaters from White Plains and Manhasset to fill the orders. That's quite a job your teens did. In fact, I'm planning a luncheon for you and your junior staff next Saturday."

"That's a wonderful idea, Helen. The girls should hear of their success from you, and it's a nice way for you to get to know them. They're brimming with ideas and enthusiasm! I'm here to help, too. Let me know if there's anything else I can do."

"Oh, there will be *plenty* to do!" Helen said as she got up from her desk. "I have to run to the sales floor now, but we need to start talking about the look for that teen makeup counter when the holiday rush is over."

Dana's colleagues were coming together as a team—indeed, as a family—and Dana knew that she would need that closeness and support very soon.

Helen flew out the door, charged with energy, as Dana smiled to herself. It was a bittersweet moment. She knew that her career at B Altman would keep her sufficiently busy in the months ahead, and yet she had hoped she would be able to go home at the end of every day and share her triumphs with Brett. The latter was never going to happen.

Brett had called again Sunday night, but Dana told him that everything was fine and she was heading out for dinner with Andrew. The reality was that she had no dinner plans with Andrew, but the excuse had enabled Dana to avoid a long phone call. She didn't think she could listen to Brett's voice for more than a minute or two. Brett seemed unconcerned since Dana and Andrew often went out for dinner when Brett was kept late in court or at the office.

His call Monday night was lengthier. He related to Dana that Richard had set up a meeting with a realtor earlier that day and that he had found an apartment in the affluent Corona Heights district that he felt would be perfect. He also enumerated a long list of motions he'd filed at the San Francisco Court

House's civil division. He obviously was detailing his duties for Dana's benefit.

"And how is that cold of yours?" Brett asked.

"Much better," Dana replied. "I must have caught it in time."

"That's great, honey. By the way, I'll be home Wednesday night. I arrive in New York late morning, but Richard wants to see me in the afternoon. I should be home for dinner. I can't wait to see you."

Dana answered with an obligatory "You, too," with the call mercifully ending after the quick exchange of "I love you."

Dana was on the verge of picking up the phone to call her parents—the news wouldn't keep forever—but she decided against it. She would tell her mother and father about the divorce after she'd seen a lawyer and secured an apartment. If she didn't wait, her parents would almost certainly recommend scores of names and locations that she should check out. And then there was, of course, all the personal advice she'd receive. That was fine—she knew her parents were concerned for her welfare—but she would be able to better handle a conversation with them once she had taken the initial steps on her own. She would tell them later in the week since she intended to act quickly.

Dana picked up the second call on Monday evening immediately since she knew it would be Andrew checking up on her.

"I've got some good news," Andrew said, "not that any news right now is what might be termed good. Max tells me that Rosamond has a friend named Julien Armand, who owns a carriage house that he'd like to lease quickly since he's returning to Paris for a special assignment at Sotheby's."

"Where is it?" Dana asked. "I made a few calls today, but everything I found is in sixties buildings. I can't do that."

"Sniffen Court. Thirty-sixth Street between Third Avenue and Lexington."

"Sniffen Court! You're kidding! I purposely walk pass the gated mews and gape every time I'm grocery shopping on Third Avenue. The alley is paved with flagstones and flanked by townhomes."

"Exactly. They were brick stables and carriage houses built around 1863 and converted to homes in the 1920s. It has a private courtyard, and the style is Romanesque Revival. It's on the National Register of Historic Places. Do you want to look at it tomorrow afternoon?"

"Of course! Right after lunch. I only wish I could find a good lawyer in the next day or so, but it might take time to get an appointment. Brett just told me he's coming back Wednesday night, and I'll have less back and forth with him if he knows I'm serious about a divorce and that he has no chance for redemption with me."

"That's the other good news. I ran into Mark today, and immediately thought he would be the perfect guy to provide a reference for a good lawyer. I told him that a friend just received upsetting news and wanted to start divorce proceedings as soon as possible, although I didn't mention you by name. He said he knew one of the best divorce lawyers in Midtown, and if he made a call you could probably get in tomorrow morning."

Dana didn't have to think twice. "Please, get the lawyer's name, Andrew. You can tell Mark it's for me, but ask him not to tell anyone."

"Consider it done," Andrew said. "I'll call you first thing in the morning with the address and exact time."

"You're the best, Andrew. Where would I be without you?"

"You'd handle things just fine. You proved last week that you can do anything you set your mind to, but I'm glad to help. I just wish you didn't have to go through all this, and certainly not during the holidays."

"I feel so foolish," Dana said. "Last week at the Christmas tree farm, I told you I might be starting a family. This week I decide to get divorced. How could I be so naïve?"

"No need to feel foolish on my account," Andrew said. "As you know, I have my own set of domestic problems, which I won't bore you with, but it's like a soap opera. I suppose we all have a little drama in our lives. It's nothing to apologize for."

"You know all the right things to say, Mr. Ricci," Dana said. "I'll be waiting for your call tomorrow morning. And thanks."

"De nada, as the saying goes. Good night."

Dana had been fighting off tears at odd moments during the past two evenings, but being proactive was helping her cope. Work had been a good tonic, and by the end of tomorrow she hoped she would have taken two of the biggest steps involved in the divorce process. And that was the trick of it all: to keep moving and face forward. Her life was in the future.

• • •

Dana looked at the painted chest in the foyer, a manila envelope sitting next to a small lamp and a silver tray for mail. The return address simply said Yorktown Heights, so she knew that it contained the photos developed by Matthew's friend. It had been waiting for her in the lobby when she arrived home from work.

She slowly picked up the envelope and stared at it. She knew Matthew's report had been truthful and accurate, but he'd felt it necessary to document the awful scenes. She decided that she would look at the pictures once and then never again unless it became legally necessary. She was on the verge of changing her entire life based on what her brother had seen, and as painful as the images might be, they represented closure and would help her remain calm and resolute when Brett offered his excuses. She would give them to her lawyer in the interest of fully explaining her reasons for seeking a divorce, but would retain the negatives. If she were going to meet with a lawyer the following morning, she needed to have seen the photos at least once.

She undid the clasp and pulled the glossy color photographs from the brown sheath. She looked at the two dozen pictures in less than a minute and replaced them in the envelope, her face expressionless. There was no need to torture herself with the images. She replaced the envelope on the table and went upstairs. There was some housekeeping of a personal nature that needed to be done in the bedroom.

Chapter Forty-Five

Alan Rudnick, attorney, was not the typical legal shark Dana had envisioned, but Andrew had assured her when he called her at six-thirty Tuesday morning that Mark's friend was who she wanted to represent her. She now sat in his office, feeling quite comfortable in his presence. He was a slender man in his mid-forties and had thinning blond hair and pale blue eyes. He wore small rimless spectacles and looked at the photos Dana had brought him as quickly as she herself had the night before. She had told him her story, and he'd made a few notes on his legal pad, but otherwise his focus was on Dana.

"I don't want to use the pictures unless I have to," Dana stated. "I simply want Brett to sign papers granting us a legal separation before he begins his assignment in San Francisco."

Rudnick nodded slowly. "We'll file for irreconcilable differences rather than adultery, but is your husband likely to do things as amicably as you anticipate?"

"One of his greatest ambitions in life . . ." Dana began before pausing. She couldn't help but think that one of his ambitions included the very thing that brought her to Rudnick's office. "His greatest ambition is to make partner at Davis, Konen and Wright. He won't want a protracted, high-profile divorce jeopardizing his standing with the firm. And then there's the issue of naming Janice as co-respondent. She's a member of his firm."

"And you're certain that there's no hope for a reconciliation. Forgive me, but it's a question I always have to ask."

"None whatsoever."

Rudnick picked up a silver pen and made additional notes on his legal pad. "Are you going to seek alimony?" he asked quietly. "You've indicated that you're moving out of your present home, so I strongly recommend that Brett contribute to your support since his income exceeds your own and he'll be keeping the apartment."

"Yes. I believe it's appropriate, and given that he will soon make partner, I don't think that will be a problem either."

"Do you have a new residence picked out yet?" asked Rudnick.

"I'm looking at one this afternoon. I want to move as soon as possible. There are too many memories where I am now."

"That's quite understandable, and it's usually the case. From a more practical standpoint, however, someone needs to vacate the current premises for any motion of this sort to move forward."

Rudnick leaned back and rested his elbows on the arms of his chair, fingertips together. "I anticipate that this will be fairly straightforward given Brett's professional concerns, although that can never be taken as a given. I recommend that the initial agreement also stipulate that he pay all of your legal fees plus any filing costs. Even in an uncontested divorce, legal fees can be very expensive. Later, when it's time to partition community property, I think you should ask for a very generous settlement. He can afford it, but we're not at that stage yet. It's just something to think about right now."

"Oh, I intend to," Dana said.

She was relieved that the "shark" was quiet yet confident.

"I'll hold on to these," Rudnick said as he gathered the photos and put them back in the envelope. "It's good insurance. Give him one of my cards and tell him to contact me when he gets back from the coast. Such a request usually has a sobering influence on the other spouse. It will demonstrate that you mean business. Does he, in your estimation, pose any threat to you when you make your wishes known? It's another question I have to ask."

"No. He'll try to talk his way out of it, but that's about all."

"They all do, Mrs. McGarry. Try to keep the conversation short and to the point. Ask him to spend the night at a hotel or with a friend."

Dana nodded.

"That's all I'll need for now," Rudnick said, standing and walking around the side of his desk and extending his hand. "Please call if you have any questions, day or night. My answering service will notify me if you run into any trouble. I'm sorry that you need my help, but you'll get through this. I'm here if you need me."

Dana shook Rudnick's hand and left. Sitting in the lawyer's office had been surreal. The life she and Brett had so carefully planned had dissolved in a matter of minutes. She'd never anticipated taking such action, but she knew she was doing the right thing. She left Rudnick's building and headed for B Altman.

• • •

Dana arrived at her office and had time to work on additional events the store was staging for the holiday season before she met Andrew at Sniffen Court after lunch. Although the carriage house was small, Dana immediately fell in love with its charm. Armand's living room had a wall twelve feet wide with original lead-paned windows rising to the full height of the twenty-foot ceiling. The windows afforded a view of some of the other brick carriage houses that would be covered with ivy in the spring. While there was no formal dining room, the kitchen opened to an eating area with a banquette and a stone fireplace.

On the second floor, an open landing lined with bookshelves and leading to the master bedroom overlooked the living room below. A sitting area off the master bedroom gave a view of the small landscaped roof deck. An additional bedroom was on the main floor, and there were two more fireplaces: in the living room and the master bedroom.

"Max told me that Julien originally planned to lease it completely furnished, but he's willing to put many of his items in storage. I told Max that you would probably want to bring your antiques and oriental carpets."

"It's perfect," Dana said as she walked to the wall of windows in the living room and gazed absently at the flagstones in the alley outside the front door.

"Penny for your thoughts?" Andrew said.

"Tell Max that I'll take the house," Dana said. "It's just that life was normal when Brett left a few days ago. How could things have turned around so quickly?"

Andrew heaved a sigh and approached Dana, standing by her side. "I've known you for a long time, Dana. Brett allowed the marriage to drift during the past several years, and when people do that, it's asking for trouble. To be honest, I'm surprised he didn't stray earlier."

"But I believed he loved me," Dana said, brushing away a tear.

"I'm sure he does," Andrew countered, "but relationships need to be nurtured, and while I know he's busy, he's just not able to give you what you need. If he could find time for Janice, he could have found time for you. He made his decision, and now you've made yours." Andrew paused for a moment to allow his words to sink in. "If you don't mind my saying so, I think you're making the right one."

Dana turned and hugged her longtime friend. "Yes, I am. And you're right. This has been coming on for years. It's time to move on."

"You said Brett gets back tomorrow?"

"Yes. Late evening."

Dana and Andrew walked back to the store, neither saying a word. Dana had wanted to see a lawyer and find an apartment, and she'd done both. She now realized that the third and most important step needed to be taken when Brett walked through the door on Wednesday night. She would have to tell him that their eight-year marriage was over. It wasn't going to be easy.

Chapter Forty-Six

Wednesday at B Altman passed uneventfully for Dana. She went through the motions, but her mind was constantly rehearsing the words she would use when Brett arrived home that evening. How did one broach such a matter? How did you tell a husband that he was going to be excised from a marriage forever with almost surgical precision? By the afternoon, however, Dana realized that the most direct way was the best. It would have been a different matter if she had decided she didn't want to wait for Brett to give her more attention, or that he was simply an irritant she could no longer bear. In such a case, her announcement would come out of the blue, but he had made her decision easy. He was having an affair, and the matter was black and white as far as Dana was concerned. She left work an hour early since she wanted to be home before Brett arrived. His eyebrows were going to be raised by what he found in the apartment.

At exactly seven o'clock, Brett arrived on the twelfth floor of 77 Park Avenue and opened the door, which was where the bedrooms and library were located. As usual, Wills barked and greeted his master enthusiastically.

"Dana? Are you home?"

There was no reply.

"Honey? Where are you? I've got some big news."

He found her seated in the library, but she stood as soon as he entered the room.

"Are you going out of town?" he asked. "There's luggage by the door."

"I know," Dana answered. "I put it there, but I'm not going out of town."

Brett could tell something was wrong by his wife's calm and measured cadence. She seemed very distant. "Then what's going on?"

Dana didn't hesitate. "I know about you and Janice, Brett." The words hung in the air for several seconds before Dana received a reply.

Brett frowned as he searched for the proper response. "When did you become the suspicious wife? Do I have to go through this every time I go out of town?"

"We won't be going through this ever again. Matthew saw you and Janice at a restaurant in the airport in San Francisco."

"Is *that* what this is about? Yes, Janice was with me. Richard asked her to go at the last minute. He feels that it's too big a case for a single attorney, even with the help of paralegals." He laughed, as if the matter was cleared up. "I made an eight o'clock reservation at Cheshire Cheese, unless you'd like to go somewhere else," he said nonchalantly as he went through mail piled on the desk.

Dana walked towards Brett and pulled the mail from his hands. "Look at me! Matthew took pictures of the two of you kissing repeatedly."

"Okay. Janice got a little tipsy and started flirting a bit. For God's sake, Matthew, of all people, should know the way she likes to tease. Too bad I didn't have a camera when she was all over him at our party. Let me see those pictures."

"The pictures are with my lawyer."

For the first time since arriving home, Brett was taken aback. "You have a lawyer?"

"Yes. I have a divorce lawyer. There is no marriage without trust, and I can *never* trust you again. It's really quite simple."

"Now wait a minute, Dana. Let's put the brakes on here. You've been plotting this while sweet-talking me every night, pretending everything's okay. You're blowing up our marriage without giving me a chance to explain. I don't even recognize you."

Dana's eyes were cold and she didn't respond.

"Janice is a silly and impetuous woman. I've admitted as much, haven't I? We may have had a few too many drinks, but it's not like there's something between us. She doesn't mean anything to me."

Dana backed away, angry. Brett was indeed using all of the tired clichés that she expected to hear.

"Richard just told me that the firm is going to extend partnership to me, Dana! That's why he wanted me to stop by the office this afternoon. I wanted to surprise you at dinner. Will you please burn those damn pictures so we can get on with our lives? Forget about Janice. Now that I'll be a partner, I'll find a way to get her dismissed from the firm."

"I don't want this life anymore, and this is not about Janice, Brett. Believe me. It's about me. I don't expect a perfect marriage, but I do deserve a kind and loving husband, and that will never be you. Your partnership status will not change the way that I feel. I found a charming carriage house and I'll be moving before Christmas."

"A carriage house! You have a lawyer *and* a carriage house?"

Brett could not believe what he was hearing. He hadn't seen Matthew in San Francisco, although he was aware that his brother-in-law was a photography buff. Was it really possible that his calculated plans and deceptions had been uncovered by such an outrageous trick of fortune?

"Dana, let's try to get through Christmas. I don't have to be in San Francisco until January fifteenth. We have time to make things right. I'll go to counseling if you like. I know I can make it up to you. I don't like to see you this way. I'm sorry."

Dana shook her head and folded her arms. "It's over, Brett. I want you to leave tonight. You can stay at a hotel, which is why I packed some of your clothes. I'm not going to stand here for hours and listen to your pathetic excuses."

Dana picked up Rudnick's business card from the desk and handed it to Brett. "My lawyer is expecting your call tomorrow. I want papers for a legal separation signed before you leave for San Francisco in January."

"You're the one who's ending this," Brett said, pointing his finger at Dana. "This isn't my decision." He was now visibly shaken.

"Don't try to turn the tables, Brett. You were caught, and now you're just trying to win your case. You don't even know what you're saying. This is your fault, and you'll have to live with the consequences."

"No!" he said loudly. "We're going to—" Brett stopped in mid-sentence. He slowly lowered his outstretched arm, defeated. He could see that Dana was deadly serious and that he wasn't going to talk his way out of his indiscretion, not even with courtroom rhetoric.

"I'm going to stay in the guest bedroom tonight," he said quietly. "I'll be gone in the morning."

Brett turned and shuffled out of the library while Dana went to the master bedroom and closed the door. She'd mourned the end of their marriage and was now composed. She knew there would be more tears in the weeks ahead, but tonight she was calm and resolute. It had been a difficult conversation, but now it was over, with Brett accepting her decision faster than anticipated. His predictable reactions had confirmed that Dana was right, not that she needed such validation any longer.

She expected to hear a knock on the door—Brett trying to plead his case one last time—but thankfully there was none. Dana fell asleep almost immediately.

• • •

The following morning, Brett saw Dana standing at the living room window. She turned as she heard him approach, and they embraced. "I do love you, Dana," Brett said.

"I believe that, but you obviously need something more. And so do I."

They both shed brief tears before Brett dropped his arms and turned around.

"I'll call your attorney when I get to the office," he said as he walked to the front door, not looking back.

"Thank you."

And then he was gone.

Dana turned to the window. She would never sleep under the same roof with Brett again. The legal formalities still had to run their course, but the marriage was now dead, her life with Brett finished. Down on the street, people were rushing to work, taking their places in the world as they did every day.

Dana would join them momentarily. She would be alone, but that was acceptable for now. The alternative was intolerable.

Chapter Forty-Seven

Two days had passed since Brett had been informed his marriage was over. He called Jack Hartlen and told him that Patti would shortly be telling him of the divorce. Jack was, in no uncertain terms, not to mention the divorce to anyone. Jack understood the unspoken consequences if he did not comply. Richard would be told, of course, but Brett needed time to explain the separation in a manner that would reflect sympathy towards him rather than criticism or suspicion.

It was Saturday afternoon, and Brett sat on the living room couch in Janice's Greenwich Village apartment. He sipped from a tumbler of scotch and stared ahead vacantly. Janice's apartment was tastefully decorated, but it didn't approach the standards to which he'd grown accustomed—Dana's standards, if the truth be told. He was sorry that he'd hurt Dana—and just as sorry that he'd gotten caught. He was a methodical, well-organized man, and his steel-trap mind, which served him so well as a lawyer, had failed him in his personal life. Short of Dana's hiring a private investigator to monitor his movements, which is something she would never have done, being on the West Coast with Janice had been a fortuitous turn of events that should have virtually ensured his affair would remain clandestine. And sooner or later the affair would have ended, as almost all do. He would have been able to claim no harm, no foul and return to his life, knowing inwardly that he was not growing old before his time, as Janice had claimed. His wild oats would have been sown and no one would have been the wiser.

Janice, of course, was delighted and felt no guilt or remorse. Her estimation of Dana and her upper-class lifestyle, with its wine journals and neighborhood meetings to remove prostitutes from her microcosmic world, had not changed. She detested Dana and everything she stood for. As for Brett, she had tempted him, but he was a grown man, responsible for his actions. As far as she was concerned, she had liberated him from the tyranny of a staid and proper life that he'd conducted at the cost of suppressing his visceral impulse to indulge his desires and throw caution to the wind. She could read people as accurately as Patti Hartlen, and she had always seen into Brett's mind in a way that she doubted Dana could. Bumping into Patti at Saks might indeed have raised the suspicions of the astute Mrs. Hartlen, but Janice doubted that it would have brought Brett's world to an end. Janice, however, had known how to exploit the situation to her advantage. Brett's immediate fear of being caught and her ability to seduce him so quickly was, to her way of thinking, further evidence of how conflicted he was, of how much he wanted to give free rein to his restlessness.

"Is the proposition that we now have an opportunity to be together without so much secrecy so horrible?" Janice asked, sitting next to Brett. "You look positively glum."

"No, of course not. It's just that this isn't the way things were supposed to play out. Nobody was supposed to get hurt."

"Don't be so naïve," Janice said. "You're a lawyer, for God's sake. Our profession involves winning and losing every day, and when people lose, they get hurt. But when a case is decided, both parties move on. Unless there's an appeal, that is, and you don't have that option with Dana."

Brett shrugged. "I suppose so."

"Have you been truly happy with Dana?" Janice queried.

"Yes, I've always been comfortable with Dana."

Janice shook her head and closed her eyes. "I asked if you'd been happy, not comfortable."

"Sometimes." He paused. "Well, most of the time, I guess." In his heart, he knew he loved Dana but hadn't done much to demonstrate it in the last three years. Their lives had been on cruise control. "It's still hard to end a marriage and a part of my life," Brett said in his own defense as he turned his head to face Janice.

Janice nodded. "I don't deny that. *All* change is hard. Despite what people think of me, I've been around the block and know a thing or two about life and relationships. But the only question that's important is whether you consider yourself a winner or a loser now that your case has been decided."

Brett knit his eyebrows. "What do you mean?"

"You've been extended a partnership, and I'm your lover. We can go anywhere and do anything. We're going to be in San Francisco together, and you can explore a new lifestyle if you have the courage to do so. You're a young man with no children, and you've been offered a kind of freedom that most men would kill for. Yes, you're getting divorced, but the sky's the limit, Mr. McGarry. So did you win or lose this week?"

"I get it," Brett said, smiling for the first time all day. "Is the glass half empty or half full?"

"Exactly. Now which is it?"

Brett leaned over and kissed Janice passionately on the lips. "Does that answer your question?"

"It's a beginning, but I'm not convinced," Janice replied as she put her arm around Brett's neck and drew him close.

"Why don't we finish the Q and A in your bedroom?" he said.

There was no more talk of divorce for the rest of the day.

Chapter Forty-Eight

Dana sat at her desk on Tuesday morning, December 17th. The Teen Advisory Board had again modeled clothing lines the previous Saturday, and the girls had displayed great poise and maturity as ambassadors for B Altman. Helen had not been able to stop talking about the youth market and the enormous sales potential that it held. At the luncheon she'd given the previous day for Dana and the contest winners, she'd been animated and enthusiastic and had taken time to get to know each of the girls.

It was a week before Christmas Eve, and the store was bustling with holiday activity. Bea had called Dana into her office half a dozen times in the past two hours, and Dana already knew by lunchtime that it was going to be a hectic afternoon. That was okay with Dana, who relished the opportunity to stay busy. Andrew had been checking with her several times a day over the past week to see how she was holding up, but Dana did not experience any holiday blues as predicted by Andrew, family, or friends. She felt free to pursue her life and realized that living with Brett had been constraining to a degree she hadn't perceived until she had decided to end her marriage. There were brief moments when she reflected on her eight years with Brett and felt a note of sadness, but such times were brief and transient.

Alan Rudnick had notified Dana on Monday that Brett had signed the papers and had not requested a single change in the documents. He had stoically put his signature to the dozen papers granting Dana a legal separation and left Rudnick's office.

Dana's parents did not seem surprised at their daughter's announcement. They arrived at the carriage house at Sniffen Court early Saturday morning, offering Dana minimal advice on how to proceed with her new life. In his usual comforting manner, Phil told Dana that they were always there for her and he was sure that everything would work out in the end. "You're only twenty-nine, and your whole life is ahead of you. God will take care of things. Just wait and see. It will be a good life." Virginia refrained from discussing Brett and only gave Dana a brief speech, the gist of which was a version of the "when life hands you lemons, make lemonade" philosophy of moving on. She and Dana worked quickly to get the house in order, and when Uncle John, Johnny, and Phoebe arrived at seven o'clock to take Dana and her parents to dinner, evergreen boughs draped the mantles and three fires were burning. Wills, adjusting to his new home, claimed a strategic spot in front of the wall of windows that had a clear view of a golden retriever's front door across the courtyard.

Patti Hartlen, who had secured a position with the Altman Foundation, stopped by Dana's office to say hi and that she would be starting in January. "I am so thankful that you recommended me for the position," she said. "And tell Brett thanks for everything. I hope you both have a Merry Christmas."

Dana just smiled and nodded. She felt certain from Patti's facial expression that she knew something had changed in Dana's life. Patti was a discerning woman, but whether she knew of the impending divorce was anyone's guess. Dana thought it likely that Patti would be fishing for information when January rolled around if she hadn't heard the news by then. She was a woman, in Dana's estimation, of insatiable curiosity.

Dana had lunch with Kim at Charleston Garden since the girl was on Christmas break.

"So how is everything?" Dana asked.

"Different," said Kim. "This is the first Christmas that my parents have been . . . well, you know. But I feel okay. Things worked out with the contest, and I've been thinking that maybe that's how life is in general. It's a bit unpredictable, but things seem to work out."

"You sound like my father," Dana said, "but I agree. It's the big picture that counts, right? Not just the facts and figures at any given time. We'll let the learned astronomer handle those kinds of details."

Kim laughed. "I like that. Say, would you like to go to the Met with me after the holidays? Maybe we could attend a lecture series?" Kim paused, as if her request was out of line. "But I know you're always really busy, so I understand if you can't."

"That would be fun," Dana replied. "I'd love to. In fact, let's plan to see *The Impressionist Epoch* right after the holidays. The show is closing soon. Apparently there hasn't been an Impressionist exhibit from this perspective. The focus is on the diversity of the artists' styles and their individuality rather than their common aesthetic. It's the broader view of Impressionism. Our theme surfaces again!"

After lunch, Kim hugged Dana, who returned to her office.

• • •

Dana continued her frenetic pace for most of the afternoon, but she paused for a few moments to reflect on her conversation with Kim. Brett was a man much like the learned astronomer she and Kim had discussed, a man given over to detail, a man who assessed life based on hour-to-hour accomplishments, always calculating the return on his investment of time. A quiet walk in the park or the countryside with his wife on a Saturday afternoon was obviously of little value to him. Whether he had always been that way or had become so over the years, she really wasn't sure. Maybe *she* had changed, and what was acceptable at twenty-five was inadequate now. Regardless, second-guessing was exhausting, and her job and personal life needed all her attention and energy.

Dana had to pick up one final article from her apartment, and Brett had assured her over the phone that he would be in court all day on Tuesday and that she was free to stop by and get anything she might need. Accordingly, Andrew procured one of the store's Ford Econoline vans and drove Dana to 77 Park Avenue at four o'clock.

"Wait here," Dana told Andrew, as he pulled over on East 38th Street, just off Park Avenue. "This will only take a few minutes. The superintendent is waiting for me upstairs."

Dana went to the apartment and met the super outside the front door. Inside, she led him to the library. "This may seem silly," Dana said, "since I asked you to carry this small tree up here just a couple of weeks ago, but I'm taking it with me." Dana motioned to the five-foot Concolor Christmas tree. It was the tree she had wanted all along, and it was the one she wanted to put in the living room of her new home at Sniffen Court.

"We'll miss you, Mrs. McGarry," the superintendent said.

"And I'll miss you," Dana said, handing the superintendent an envelope with his usual Christmas present enclosed—a card and a check. "Please take the tree down to the white Ford van waiting around the corner on 38th Street. I'll manage the bags of ornaments and the table skirt. I'm taking the passenger elevator. Tell my friend I'll only be a minute."

Dana rode the elevator to the lobby and put her apartment keys into a white envelope, sealed it, and gave it to the concierge. "Please make sure Mr. McGarry gets this," she said.

Mrs. Riley took the envelope, smiled, and wished Dana well.

Dana exited through the front door of the apartment building; she wanted to wish the door staff a Merry Christmas. They were happy to know that she was moving just three blocks away and made her promise to stop by when walking Wills.

The late afternoon sky was already starting to turn a dark blue, but the sun had not yet set. It was a cold, clear day, and Dana smiled as she walked along the sidewalk, headed for the B Altman van. She had no regrets about leaving the apartment for the last time. In fact, she had no regrets at all about her life. She would continue to be busy at work, and in the coming year, she would be working with Diana Vreeland at the Costume Institute. Her father's words echoed in her mind: *Just wait and see. It will be a very good life.*

And Dana realized that he was right. She intended to lead one very good life.

The End

About the Author

Lynn Steward is a successful business woman who spent many years in New York City's fashion industry in marketing and merchandising, including the development of the first women's department at a famous men's clothing store. Through extensive research, and an intimate knowledge of the period, Steward created the characters and stories for a series of five authentic and heartwarming novels about New York in the seventies. *A Very Good Life* is the first in the series of books featuring Dana McGarry.

Made in the USA
San Bernardino, CA
15 March 2014